ESCAPE PLAN

Copyright © 2016 Elizabeth Hein

All rights reserved.

ISBN: 0-9911185-7-X

ISBN-13: 978-0-9911185-7-1

WINTERFIELD PRESS

ESCAPE PLAN

ELIZABETH HEIN

For Kate and Emily

A mother's love is a fierce and powerful thing.

one

April 1976

Seth Haskell deserved killing - Stacia Tate Curran didn't doubt that for one second. Still, she didn't enjoy seeing it happen.

It was an enchanting spring evening. The shocking pink redbuds on the far side of Lake Tate extended their delicate limbs over the water in the warm breeze and reminded Stacia of her days as a ballerina. She picked up her binoculars and followed a line of pale ducklings as she recalled the rush of adrenaline she felt just before leaping on stage. Her reverie was broken when something disturbed the smooth surface of the lake and sent the ducklings scrambling after their mother. Stacia stepped back and retrained her focus on a boat making its way out of Tranquility Cove.

"Why is Seth home? Kitty said she isn't expecting him home until tomorrow night." The tiny dog at Stacia's feet looked up at his mistress and raised his eyebrows. Stacia lifted the binoculars to her face again and watched the Haskells drift toward the dam at the southern end of the lake. Kitty lifted a bottle of champagne as Seth turned away from the engine.

"How sweet, he must have come home a day early to celebrate with Becky." During their morning jog, Kitty had recounted how Becky had jumped around the kitchen waving her acceptance letter from Brown University. It was an impressive accomplishment. She was the only member of the class of '76 to get into an Ivy League school. Stacia watched the small boat rock as Kitty stood up and leaned over to hug Seth. Stacia hoped Becky's news would help them put Seth's infidelities behind them and focus on their children; that was until Kitty hoisted the champagne bottle and slammed it down on the back of her husband's skull. Blood spurted across Kitty's face as Seth slumped over the side of the boat.

Stacia moved to call her daddy's friend Sgt. Lafferty down at the police department; however, Kitty's actions in the next crucial seconds froze Stacia in place. Kitty reached for the emergency flare, but didn't pick it up. Instead, she paused, wiped the blood from her face and pulled off her sweatshirt. Stacia's heart dropped. It turned her stomach to watch Kitty wrap her bloody clothes around Seth's head, weigh him down with the anchor, then kicked the plug out. If she hadn't witnessed Kitty deliver the blow, Stacia could have continued to think of Kitty as her sweet, organized friend that made beautiful cupcakes and knew far too much about art. If Stacia hadn't seen it with her own eyes, she wouldn't have believed her friend was capable of pummeling her husband, then efficiently disposing of his body.

While Kitty watched the boat sink, Stacia decided no good could come from reporting the crime. Whether it was a murder or a moment of passion, Seth was dead and Kitty needed help. Becky and Bobby Haskell needed their mother, and, more importantly, a murder would reflect poorly on the neighborhood. Stacia couldn't have that. A scandal in Overlook wouldn't have been good for anyone, so Stacia did what needed to be done. She called Kitty's house and invited Becky and Bobby to spend the night at her house under the guise of an impromptu pizza party. Then, she turned on the floodlight above her patio as a beacon to guide Kitty back to shore, Once the sun had disappeared behind the coal plant at the lower dam, Stacia ran down the stairs to her dock with a pile of clothes for Kitty to put on, and kept her mouth shut.

★★★

Kitty appreciated Stacia helping her get back to shore, however, the person she needed most was Rose. Although her sister rankled at times, Rose was the one person Kitty could depend on when push came to shove, or more accurately, smash came to blub blub. All Kitty had to say when she called was, "Rosie," for Rose to reply, "How bad?"

"He's gone."

"He left you?"

"No...I...bottle...head...blood."

A few seconds of silence on the line were followed by the sound of a heavy bottomed glass thumping on the surface of Rose's chintzy coffee table. "Well, it's about time."

"Lake...boat...sunk." Kitty could barely spit out the words.

"Holy crap, Mary Katherine," Rose snorted. "Okay, think. Is there a lot of evidence to clean up? Do I need to bring anything?"

"I don't think so." Kitty slid down the kitchen wall and sat with her legs splayed in front of her. "I don't know."

"Where are the kids?"

"Umm...I don't know. They should be here."

"Sit tight. I'll be right there. We'll deal with them when I get there." Ten minutes later, Rose burst through the door like a general entering a war room. "His car's in the driveway. We have to get rid of that."

Kitty hadn't moved since calling Rose. The weight of what she had done anchored her to the floor. Rose took the buzzing telephone from Kitty's hand and hung it up. "Christ, you're shaking like a leaf. Let's get you out of those damp clothes and into a hot shower." Rose eased Kitty up the stairs and into the master bathroom. She leaned her sister against the shower stall and turned the water on. As steam filled the room and obliterated their reflections in the mirror, Rose peeled the sweat suit off Kitty as if she was a sleepy toddler.

"Whose clothes are these anyway? This isn't Becky's school sweatshirt."

"Stacia. Dock." Kitty's shoulders shook as she recalled the beacon that guided her back to shore. "She saw me."

Rose froze in the middle of pulling the sweatpants down Kitty's thighs. "Someone saw you? Are you sure?"

Kitty stepped out of the sweatpants and into the shower. She stood under the hot stream of water until she stopped shaking and her toes felt like part of her body again. When she slid the shower door open, Rose had a towel ready and dry clothes waiting for her.

"How am I going to explain what happened to the boat?" Kitty said as she let her sister towel her off.

Her voice sounded far away. Kitty wasn't sure if she had even spoken out loud until Rose replied. "You sunk it, right?"

"Uh huh, I kicked out the plug and it just sunk." Kitty couldn't focus on Rose. The tiny flowers on her staid wrap skirt seemed to move like insects swarming over her thighs. She vaguely felt the towel sliding down her back as she slumped forward on the vanity.

Rose yanked her upright and attacked her hair with a brush. "Look, you can freak out later. We need to deal with that car before someone notices it." Rose took Kitty's face in her hands and gently slapped her cheeks until she snapped out of her stupor.

Kitty pulled away from Rose. "Okay, okay, I'm okay." She looked at her reflection with wide eyes. "What am I going to do?"

"Well, while you were slowly going catatonic in the shower, I think I've come up with a plan." Rose folded and refolded the hand towel. "So we need to get rid of that car and explain why the boat is missing. Right?"

"He said his latest floozie is pregnant so he wouldn't allow Becky to go to Brown. She got in. She has to go. She has to."

"We'll talk about that later, okay?" Rose put the towel down and put her arm around Kitty's shoulders. "Now, does Seth ever take the boat anywhere other than out on the lake and back to your dock?"

"Slip," Kitty corrected her. "We have a slip. Stacia has a full dock."

Rose gave Kitty's shoulders a quick shake. "Concentrate, Mary Katherine. Does the boat ever leave the water?"

"Sure, when it needs to be serviced." Kitty fiddled with the hem of the Fleetwood Mac concert t-shirt Rose had pulled over her head. It belonged to Becky. "Sometimes he and Bobby go fishing on other lakes."

"But how does he move it? Is there a marina or something?"

"He uses the boat trailer," Kitty replied as if that was self-evident. She and Rose stared at each other for a moment before a smile spread across Kitty's pale face. "It's under the deck. All we'd have to do is lift the lattice and slide it out."

Rose brushed Kitty's hair behind her ear. "I think I've got it. What if we hitch the trailer to the back of the Volvo? It has one of those ball thingies on it, right?"

"Yeah."

"Then we drive the car and the trailer around to the far side of the lake, so if anyone goes looking for him, they'll think he took the boat out fishing and had an accident."

"They can't find his body." Kitty shuddered at the memory of blood trailing from Seth's head as he sunk to the bottom of the lake. "As soon as the police see the big dent in the back of his head, they'll know it wasn't an accident." Kitty turned and grabbed Rose's arms with both her hands. "Oh my god, I killed him. I flipped out and actually killed him."

Rose shook her sister off. "Yeah, yeah, yeah, you're a real badass." She nudged Kitty into the bedroom and pushed her down on the satin bedspread. She twisted a pair of Keds onto Kitty's feet. "But you do have a point. We don't want Seth found. And if he is, it needs to look like someone else killed him."

"Or an accident. An accident would be good." Kitty lay back and let her feet dangle off the edge of the bed. "We need to make it look like he went out on a different lake and disappeared." She flopped over onto her stomach. "Or faked his own death."

"Why would he do that?"

"I don't know," Kitty said. "I'm just thinking out loud."

"Okay, think. Where would go? Where should we leave the car?"

"Maybe somewhere near that Shelly's place in Charlotte. That way, when someone notices the car, the police will link the car to Shelly."

Rose went to the window and played with the blinds. "That's too iffy. We need to make it obvious to any idiot that he went out in his boat and drowned." She turned to Kitty. "Is drunk driving a problem with boats."

"Yeah, every year someone cracks up their boat on the Fourth of July because they've been sitting out in the sun drinking too many beers."

"Okay then, let's go," Rose said. "Let's get that car out of the driveway before your nosey neighbors notice it."

An hour later, Kitty parked the Volvo and boat trailer at the edge of a lake just a few miles from Charlotte. Before she climbed into Rose's car, she splashed a bottle of Seth's stinkiest whiskey on the floor mats, so whoever found the car would assume Seth was drunk when he took the boat out on the lake.

It was a good plan.

★★★

Stacia pulled herself out of Lake Tate and perched on a fallen tree. She peeled her wetsuit off her upper body and let the warm afternoon breeze dry her skin. Her legs would have to stay encased in neoprene. Once the suit was wet, it was too difficult to pull back on. In a few more weeks, the water would be warm enough to swim in just one of her colorful racing suits.

She took a moment to admire her lake. Spring in North Carolina was breathtaking. From the island in the center, the redbud and dogwood looked as though they were floating under the tall pines near the dam. If she looked back toward Overlook, the last of the azaleas blooming in her neighbors' yards looked like coral rick rack along the hem of a dark green dress. The neighborhood appeared happy, from a distance.

Stacia pulled her right arm across her chest and leaned into the stretch. Over her shoulder, she could see backhoes and cement trucks lumbering on the shore near the dam. A new subdivision was going in on the western end of the lake. For two decades, Overlook had been the only community on Lake Tate. When Tate Power & Electric built the hydro-electric plant that flooded the valley, a hardscrabble hilltop became a lush promontory into the lake. Stacia and her husband, Weldon, had transformed the land into a showcase of mid-century casual architecture. At the time, polite society looked askance at Stacia Tate marrying a black man, but her family's acceptance of Weldon along with his decorated military service and his sister's tragic death allowed them to tolerate him. The fact that the Curran family was one of the richest banking families in Durham and owned more land than the Tates didn't hurt either. Still, Weldon and Stacia chose to build Overlook near the technology park where most home buyers were originally from up north and less likely to care if the Tate Currans were an inter-racial couple. Now, this new Fox Chase sub-division threatened Overlook. It looked to be a hippie-dippie blend of brown wood-sided condominiums and cheap pre-fab ranches that were only one tiny step up from a double-wide. Who knew what kind of people would move into an anarchic place like that? Swingers? Druggies? The childless?

Stacia switched arms to stretch the other side of her body and shifted her gaze away from Fox Chase. She had other, more immediate things to worry about. Even after the exertion of her mile-long swim out to the island, her brain still raced through all the ways Kitty could get caught and Stacia could be implicated. She'd hoped they could talk during their morning jog, but when it came time to call Kitty and arrange to meet, Stacia couldn't pick up the phone. She didn't know what to say. Had Kitty killed Seth in a moment of passion? She had punched him in the nose when she found out he was sleeping with her tennis partner, but she was still drinking at that point. Or had it been a cold-blooded murder? Stacia didn't really want to know.

She wanted to talk to Von. She slipped her arms back in her wetsuit and zipped it up. As she kicked out into the deeper water, a familiar voice echoed inside her head. *At least she killed him near the lower dam. The current will keep his body from surfacing near Overlook.* Stacia smiled to herself as she started to swim back toward home. The voice of her long-dead best friend and sister-in-law was always in her head whenever she was physically or emotionally exhausted. Stacia hung on to Von's memory almost as tightly as she hung on to her guilt for surviving the car accident that had killed Von and ten of her classmates.

"Did I do the right thing helping Kitty?"

Hard to say. It'll be hard to look her in the eye after seeing her wrap that anchor around his corpse.

"I keep thinking about how he's down there near where the old town used to be. What if the boat sunk on the old school or the church? I hate to think of him decomposing where people once worshiped."

It's been decades since your grandfather flooded the valley to form Lake Tate. I'm sure the buildings have disintegrated by now. Still, you're right not to involve the police. The last thing you and Weldon need is police cars swarming around Overlook when there are newer neighborhoods popping up on the other side of the lake.

With any luck his bloated corpse will turn up near Fox Chase. Then they'd have proximity to dead bodies and a coal plant.

two

Monday morning, Becky and Bobby went back to school and left Kitty alone with what she had done. The silence in the house felt like a reproach. The strain of keeping up a facade of normality for the kids all weekend had left her exhausted, yet she knew who that woman was - Happy Mommy. Now that Seth was dead, she didn't know who she was. She wasn't Kitty Haskell - wife of a successful businessman, efficient PTA mom, and congenial hostess anymore. Alone, she was a husband killer, a felon, a liar. She didn't like that woman. That woman was unpredictable, passionate, dangerous.

She wandered through the house and paused in the parlor. When they bought the house in 1958, they'd assumed they would entertain, but they'd rarely had guests worthy of such a formal room. Seth's friends preferred to swill beer in front of the television or speed around the lake in their boats. They wouldn't be doing that anymore. No more Seth. No more boat.

She didn't invite the Lookers, Stacia's clique of fashionable Overlook moms, to sit around sipping tea on the low-slung settee either. She hosted the annual Christmas cookie swap and that was enough. Her doorbell rarely rang, yet her house was perpetually ready for inspection. She assumed her neighbors had similarly well-appointed but unused rooms in their houses, although she couldn't swear to it. For all she knew, their front rooms were empty or filled with packing boxes years after they moved in. The Lookers met poolside or in the clubhouse where their public faces could be seen and their private lives could remain hidden.

Kitty kicked off her shoes and sat on the shell-pink velvet settee.

It looked the same as the day it was delivered in 1962. The blue silk drapes were the only part of the room that showed their age. Like her, they were beginning to fade along the leading edges. She leaned back and examined the room. It needed art, but Seth had refused to let her hang any paintings. He didn't allow any references to Kitty's life as a museum curator before she became his wife. The phone rang in the kitchen. Kitty left her shoes in the middle of the foyer and went to answer it. It was her house now; she could leave her shoes anywhere she wanted.

She hoped it was Rose on the line; but it was Suzie, Seth's secretary. "I hate to bother you, Mrs. Haskell, but could I speak to Seth?"

Kitty took a deep breath and tried to sound as pathetic as possible. The plan required her to act worried at this point. "He's not here. I missed him when he flew back from Ohio to pick up his boat. Where did you all send him this week? South Carolina?"

"Excuse me?" Kitty heard the muffled sounds of conversation on Suzie's end. After a few moments, Suzie said, "Seth isn't scheduled to do any traveling this week and he wasn't on a work trip last week neither. I thought y'all were on vacation."

Kitty's stomach dropped. That was unexpected news. When she and Rose had devised their plan to explain Seth's disappearance, they had assumed Seth had been on a work related trip and that Golf Systems had known his travel plans. She wasn't sure what to do next. Should she tell them Seth had lied about being on vacation with his family? Should she imply he was interviewing for another job, or would that further confuse things? Or, should she simply play dumb?

"Well, I don't know what to say. I haven't seen him in over a week. I thought you knew where he was."

"Wow," Suzie said. Kitty could almost hear the woman thinking through the phone. Suzie spoke to someone in the office. "Should I tell her?"

"Is there something else, Suzie?"

"It's just that," she said. "Well, it's been over a week since Seth has been in the office, and well, this woman has been calling all morning looking for him."

Kitty could guess who the woman was, the infamous Shelly. She was Seth's pregnant mistress that was going to replace Kitty in Seth's life. Shelly was also the reason Seth had been willing to short-circuit his daughter's future.

"Who is she? Couldn't one of the other fellas help her?"

"I don't think she's calling about Golf Systems business. I think it was a personal matter."

"Oh," Kitty said. "I guess you'll just have to take a message then."

"Do you want me to keep her number?"

"Of course, dear," Kitty said. "I'd hate for you to misplace important names and phone numbers while Seth is away."

If anyone ever suspected that Seth didn't die of his own stupidity, Kitty wanted there to be some form of paper trail to lead the police to Seth's mistress. Frankly, she didn't much care if the police found Shelly or some other unfortunate soul that had fallen for his empty charms, as long the trail didn't lead back to her.

"Thank you, Suzie. I'll call you if I hear anything from Seth."

"Me too, Kitty."

Kitty looked at the handset before hanging it up. Something had shifted between her and Suzie during their conversation. Suzie hadn't ever called Kitty by her first name before. Kitty disconnected the long spiral of cord from the bottom of the avocado green phone and watched it uncoil itself before dropping it on the ground.

At a loss for what to do next, she wandered toward the liquor cabinet. She picked up a slender bottle of clear, tasteless oblivion. After her weeks of binge drinking when Seth had given her gonorrhea the previous year, he had quietly restocked the liquor cabinet with her favorite brands of vodka. Their mutual desire to not talk about things like her drinking and his infidelity had been a hallmark of their marriage. Kitty scanned the cabinet under the bar for tonic water, then slammed the door shut.

No, I can't do this. I learned my lesson last year. It was hard enough to manage my drinking when I was just trying to forget Seth was cheating on me. I'd never sober up if I drank to forget that I'm a murderer.

She placed the vodka back on the bar and brushed her fingertips across the shoulders of Seth's bottles of Jack Daniels and Johnny Walker.

I should get rid of all this stuff before I end up drinking it. Get it out of my house.

17

My house?

She turned and looked at Seth's spot on the couch. *When can I start really acting like it's my house? I can't change things yet. I need to act like I expect him back any day now.*

What a colossal drag that's going to be.

★★★

An hour later, Kitty was sprawled across Seth's favorite teak lounge chair on the deck. She scraped the bottom of the half gallon tub of chocolate ice cream with a serving spoon. If she couldn't drown her guilt in vodka, she would deploy the heavy artillery; ice cream and the biggest spoon in the drawer. No dainty long handled ice tea spoon could get the sugary panacea in her mouth fast enough. She dropped the tub on the deck and rolled over on her side to look at the lake through the railing. The family's golden retriever, lounging beneath her chair, lifted her head and licked a drop of ice cream from Kitty's cheek. "Thanks, Daisy, I love you too." Kitty rubbed her distended belly through her skirt. "Ugh, I can barely move. Why'd you let me eat all that ice cream? Now I'll need to run an extra five miles to work off all those calories."

A flash of bright pink out in the lake caught her eye. Stacia Tate Curran was swimming out to the island in the center of Lake Tate. Before Stacia had witnessed Kitty kill Seth, she would have asked Kitty to join her. They were supposed to be training for a triathlon. Now that Seth's body was moldering under its water, Kitty doubted she would ever swim in the lake again.

Kitty felt lucky to have Stacia on her side. If Stacia hadn't had the presence of mind to light a beacon to help her swim to shore and leave that pile of clothes for her on the dock, Kitty may have drowned that night. Stacia had given Kitty the opportunity to get home unseen, and cleared the way for Kitty and Rose to come up with a plan. Essentially, Stacia had helped Kitty get away with murder.

Kitty's stomach churned. *She saw what I did that night. What if she changes her mind about helping me? What if she tells the police, or the other Lookers? What will they think? I'd become a pariah.* The prospect of being a social outcast made Kitty reconsider going inside and getting a glass of vodka to ease her nerves. *Just one glass. No one would have to know. Just to get me through today. What would it hurt?*

Kitty's heart began to race and her breath came in short bursts. She had taken a step toward the house when the ice cream rose in her throat and poured across the deck. She quickly ran to the spigot, hosed down the deck, and rinsed out her mouth. Heaven forbid anyone find out she had done anything as base as vomit outside the privacy of her own bathroom.

Spent, she leaned on the railing and looked out over the water. Stacia was almost to the island. Kitty could barely see the flash of her bright suit in the shadows cast by the loblolly pines. She looked away as Daisy jumped up and let out a sharp bark. A deeper bark came from the raised walking trail that skirted the shore. A greying Irish setter lumbered up the path and greeted Daisy like an old friend. A moment later, Molly Blevins emerged from the underbrush, dressed in her usual outfit of paint-splattered cutoffs and a peasant blouse. Where the Lookers dressed to impress, Molly went out of her way to look like an aging hippie. She taught a painting class at the Arts Center and poked fun of the conventional Lookers. Molly's offbeat attitude had been one of the things that Kitty liked about her. "Sorry to barge in unannounced like this. Dana must have smelled Daisy up here."

"Always glad to see you," Kitty replied as she toed the empty ice cream container under the chaise.

Molly patted Daisy for a moment. "Guess what the check-out girl at the Food Lion gave me this morning, one of those new two dollar bills. Looked like play money to me."

"It's part of the Bicentennial celebration," Kitty said. "They've also made a new silver dollar and a bunch of stamps."

Molly looked away from the dogs and glanced at Kitty's damp blouse. "Kitty? What's going on?"

Kitty ran the back of her hand over her mouth. She wasn't really prepared to start telling people that Seth was gone, but how else could she explain her behavior? Molly and Kitty had known each other for years. They had been room-mothers together since their sons were in first-grade, so Molly knew that Kitty liked to smother her troubles in sweets. If Kitty was honest with herself, Molly most likely knew she also liked to drown her sorrows in vodka. But, they didn't talk about things like that.

Kitty couldn't stand there and pretend nothing was wrong. The gossip that Seth was gone was going to get out soon enough. Best to control the message, as Stacia would say. "Oh, Molly," she said. "It's Seth. I think he's left me."

"Goodness gracious, that's awful." Molly rushed across the deck. "What did he say?"

"Nothing actually. He just never came back from his business trip last week." Kitty inhaled deeply and reached out to steady herself on the railing. "His secretary just called looking for him. No one seems to have heard from him in days." She didn't need to fake feeling weak. Between the rush of sugar in her bloodstream and actually saying out loud that Seth was gone, she felt genuinely unsteady on her feet. "I thought he was on a business trip all last week, but his secretary thought he was on vacation. I don't know what to tell the kids."

Molly gestured to the empty ice cream container. "So this is the way you're handling it? "

"I'm upset!" Kitty was genuinely surprised by Molly's reaction. She considered Molly a friend. She had been so sympathetic the previous fall when Kitty had found out that Seth was sleeping with Marni Kaur, Kitty's long-time tennis partner and fellow PTA mom. She had even confided in Kitty about her own husband's affairs and made her feel less alone.

"How long has he been gone?"

"Ten days, maybe eleven." Kitty wiped at the ice cream spots on her blouse.

"Did he take his clothes? Close his bank account?"

"He took his boat."

"That's nothing." Molly turned to look out over the lake, yet Kitty still saw her roll her eyes. "One time, Tom was gone almost a month." Molly's marriage had been rotten for years. Like Seth, her husband didn't bother to hide his indiscretions. Unlike Kitty, Molly refused to confront her husband. She planned to wait until their son, Ethan, was grown, then conveniently move to Florida to care for her ailing mother. She and Tom would never divorce.

"If you keep this up, you'll get fat. Then Seth really will leave you." Molly ran her palm over her round belly. "You know he likes you fit and trim."

"Molly!"

"I'm sorry, Kitty, but I can't believe you're really all that surprised he left. I mean, like…that whole thing with Marni last year. Don't get me wrong. I'm glad that all blew over, but…you weren't exactly making things pleasant for Seth at home, now were you?"

"Well, I——" Kitty didn't know what to say. If Molly preferred to stay in the leaky dinghy that was her marriage, who was Kitty to imply her laissez-faire attitude toward Tom's infidelity was anything less than appropriate. Kitty had rocked the boat and it hadn't turned out well at all. She wiped her face with the damp corner of her blouse and took a step closer to Molly. "Are you saying it's my fault he left?"

Molly flinched when she realized Kitty was standing directly behind her. "I'm not saying you did anything wrong. I'm just surprised that you're so surprised." She nudged Kitty with her elbow. "Come on, let's go inside and have a cocktail. You know that always makes you feel better."

Kitty was tempted. A couple vodka tonics would have made her feel much better, at least for a few hours, but vodka couldn't solve her problems anymore than the ice cream had. Seth would still be dead, and she would still be a murderer.

"I don't know, the kids'll be home soon."

"Why isn't your pal Stacia over here holding your hand. She seems to stick her nose in everybody's business." Molly picked up the end of her dog's leash and moved toward the steps. "She'll make a meal of this when she finds out."

Kitty stiffened. Stacia was the one person who had actually stepped up to help Kitty. When she found out that Seth was sleeping with Marni, she had run Marni out of town and when Kitty finally got rid of Seth, she helped her get away with murder. It was amusing to poke fun at the Lookers with Molly; however, Molly would never have put herself at risk for Kitty like Stacia had.

Kitty pulled the empty ice cream container from under the lounge chair and slid open the door. "I'm sorry, I'm feeling a bit sick. I'll have to take a rain check on that drink. Give my best to Tom." With that, she stepped inside and locked the sliding glass door behind her.

three

Rose's Gremlin was parked in front of the house when Kitty and Bobby came home from baseball practice. As Bobby climbed out in his stocking feet to push the heavy garage door open, Kitty thought how nice it would be to let Becky park inside the garage instead of leaving her car out in the North Carolina heat and humidity. *I'll tell them their father is gone tonight. Then we can stop pretending he's coming back and make the house our own.*

Once the old Volvo had been found beside Lake Wylie, Kitty planned to sell it. She didn't need two cars and she'd never particularly liked the Volvo. It reminded her of how much she had compromised for Seth. He bought the staid station wagon because a proper mother of two drove a safe reliable car, rather than a car she enjoyed driving.

Kitty pulled her brand new 1976 Mercedes 450SL, the only good thing to have come out of Seth's affair with her tennis partner, into the garage and paused to let Bobby pull the heavy door down behind the car. The warm smell of roasting carrots and something cheesy wafted through the open kitchen door. Rose stood at the counter with her back to Kitty. She wore Seth's leather barbecue apron and was stabbing something with a paring knife. "What are you doing?" Kitty asked.

Rose turned toward her sister, knife still in her fist. "I found these fabulous steaks in your deep freeze," she said with a wide smile. "I'm stuffing them with garlic cloves."

"You don't know how to cook."

"I can read, dummy. You've only got about two hundred cookbooks. It wasn't hard to find a recipe for scalloped potatoes to go with the steaks."

Bobby emerged from the laundry room in a thin blue robe. His baseball uniform lay on the floor in a muddy mound. "Can I watch TV before dinner?"

"No, go take a shower. You smell like a billy goat. Later on, come down and set the table in the dining room."

"Why are we eating in the dining room?" He slouched his way through the kitchen, all arms and legs. "We only have to eat in there when Dad's here."

"Aunt Rose is here and is making us a wonderful meal, so we're going to eat in the dining room." Kitty pushed a sweaty curl away from Bobby's forehead. "And I think we need to have a family meeting tonight."

Bobby scowled and thumped up the stairs. Kitty heard him grumble, "This is bogus. We should totally wait for him to show up before we have a family meeting." She waited to hear the shower start before turning to Rose, still wielding a knife over the pieces of raw flesh in front of her. "How did you get in the house?"

"Becky let me in. She's on the phone upstairs." Rose adjusted the apron on her hips. "I thought you might need some company tonight." Rose stabbed the steak again. "You know, to keep you on track."

Kitty wrinkled her nose at her sister. She loved Rose, but she invariably annoyed her. "But why are you cooking? You knew I'd be home in a few minutes." She stepped into the laundry room and tossed Bobby's muddy uniform into the washing machine. "Scalloped potatoes? On a Wednesday? We were going to have fondue."

"You and your rules," Rose said loud enough for Kitty to hear her in the laundry room. "Even Mother wasn't that rigid about what to eat on a week night and what to save for Sunday."

Kitty returned to the kitchen with a small stack of clean dish towels. "Mother didn't care about food. She had a repertoire of four recipes, all of which involved a pot of boiling water." Rose raised her eyebrows, but didn't argue the truth of Kitty's statement. "She only cared if the table looked pretty. Remember the time I picked a fistful of Queen Anne's lace and had the audacity of wanting to put them on the kitchen table?"

Rose smiled to herself as she shoved a garlic clove into a slit in the meat. "I'd forgotten about that. It was a bit kooky to yell at you for wanting to put wildflowers on the table. I guess it didn't seem so nutty when we were living it."

Kitty stepped over to the wall oven and peeked inside. "So what are we having again?"

"After I found these thick steaks, I looked up recipes on how to cook them. The book suggested the scalloped potatoes and carrots as sides. It sounded like a good idea at the time."

Kitty closed the oven door and smiled at her sister. "It was a fine idea, Rose. I was just a bit thrown." She ran some hot water into the dishpan and dropped in the glut of bowls Rose had accumulated. "I guess I've become a bit rigid about my meal plans. What with the kids' sports practices, and my schedule, and Seth's schedule——"

"Won't have to worry about that anymore," Rose muttered.

"I've lost my spontaneity. I used to love poring through all those cookbooks and trying out new recipes. I can't remember the last time I did that."

Rose dropped the steaks onto a plate. "When do you want to eat? The recipe says to grill these for ten minutes."

"I'd give them at least fifteen," Kitty replied. She wiped up the blood and garlic skin Rose had left on the counter with a clean towel. "Let's give the potatoes time to cook. I'll let Bobby off the hook and set the table myself." She pulled four plates out of the plate rack and set them on the counter. "Actually, it's good you made a special meal. I want to tell the kids that Seth is gone."

"Yes," Rose said. "You need to start telling people. Stick to our plan."

"Speaking of which," Kitty whispered, "his secretary called earlier looking for him."

Rose put a finger to her lips and tilted her head to the ceiling. She signaled for Kitty to go into the dining room. "And?"

"He wasn't even on a business trip last week. They thought he was on vacation."

Rose opened the wide bottom drawer of the breakfront and pensively flipped through the starched, neatly labeled tablecloths before selecting an orange cloth with brown flowers. She unfurled it over the table. "So how does that change anything?"

"I don't know. What was he doing? Where was he all that time?"

Kitty straightened the cloth on the table. "His secretary did say that Shelly woman keeps calling."

Poor thing. She'll never know what a favor I've done her. She should just get on with her life and forget all about good ol' Seth.

Rose's eyes lit up. "Perfect. Then when they find the car, his secretary will remember that she called from a Charlotte number."

Kitty leaned across the table. "What if no one ever finds the car? Then what?"

"I thought you parked it illegally. Didn't you look for the 'No Parking' signs?"

"It was dark and I was concentrating on not being seen." Kitty went back into the kitchen and returned with a handful of silverware. Her heart raced from simply thinking about that night. "What if we were seen, Rose?"

"You weren't," Rose replied. "It's a good plan. It'll work. Just be patient." She went back to the kitchen and left her sister alone with the dishes and her thoughts. Kitty arranged the plates and silverware in neat settings with napkins folded into tiny linen crowns. At least she could keep that little part of her life neat and controlled.

Pull yourself together. Do what Rose says, and everything will be okay. They'll find the car any day now and then we can move on. Do what you have to do. Think of the children.

By the time she'd finished, Becky and Bobby were bickering on the stairs and Rose was on the deck wielding Seth's preposterously long barbecue tools. In the leather apron and gauntlet-style oven mitts, as if she was fighting dragons rather than grilling steaks. Kitty pulled the bubbling casserole of potatoes out of the oven. It was more brown around the edges than it should have been, but still edible. She took it into the dining room and placed it on a cork trivet in the center of the table. "Bobby, bring the dish of carrots when you come. Aunt Rose is bringing in the steaks now."

"Why do we have to eat in here? I wanted to watch TV."

"I told you. We need to have a family meeting," Kitty said.

The smell of Love's Baby Soft accompanied Becky into the room. "Did you just say family meeting? That's totally lame, Mom." She slumped into her chair. "Where's Dad? Did he call?"

Kitty straightened her steak knife so it lined up with her water glass.

"That's what I wanted to talk to the two of you about." Rose stepped into the room soundlessly and sat down. Bobby speared a steak onto his plate.

"Really? Steak?" Becky put her palms on the table and moved to get up. "Mom, I can't sit here and watch you people eat an innocent cow."

"Sit down, young lady!" Becky dropped back into her seat and folded her hands in her lap. Kitty so rarely raised her voice, her children obeyed when she did.

Kitty took a sip of water and collected her thoughts for a moment. "Rebecca. Robert. I'm worried about your father. If you recall, your father was expected home last Friday." She took a deep breath and swallowed hard. She looked at Bobby apologetically. "I was annoyed that he never showed up to spend time with you this weekend, but I wasn't that upset. I assumed he met someone in the airport and went on a junket out to Pebble Beach or something."

"He's flaked like that before," Becky said.

"Right, I expected to get a call yesterday saying that he'd sold lots of equipment and would be home last night. I was a little worried when I didn't hear from him, but you know your dad, he's not always that great about calling to say he'll be late." She took another sip of water. Her tongue felt like sandpaper. She caught Rose's eye across the table. Rose nodded that she was doing fine. "Then, this morning, his secretary called. She hasn't heard from him either. He wasn't at work all last week."

Becky and Bobby exchanged anxious looks. Kitty wondered if they already knew about Shelly and suspected their father was with her in Charlotte. She felt her face flush. That would explain why neither one of them has asked about their father's whereabouts in almost a week. I can't believe this. I was, yet again, the last to know.

Bobby scooped some potatoes onto his plate. "Do you think he'll come back this week?"

"Maybe, I thought he might be sleeping off a wild weekend somewhere but, as the day went on today, that seemed less and less likely. Then, I noticed that the boat is gone."

Becky flipped her hair over her shoulder, a portrait of teenaged indignation. "Bummer! He took the boat?"

27

Kitty pressed her hand against her belly. It sickened her that Becky seemed to care about the loss of the boat more than her father. "The boat and the trailer. I hate to say this kids, but I don't think he's coming back any time soon."

Becky and Bobby both nodded thoughtfully, yet their eyes were dry. They didn't seem upset; they seemed relieved. Bobby took a bite of his steak and chomped away while Becky asked Rose to pass the potatoes. Kitty suddenly felt overwhelmingly tired. For days, she had been worrying that the children would be devastated that Seth was gone, but now that she'd told them, they seemed unfazed. She stood up from the table. "I think I'm going to go upstairs and lie down. I'm feeling a bit upset."

"Okay, Mom. I'll come check on you in a bit," Becky said. As she climbed the stairs to go to her room, Kitty again was struck by the poor job she was doing as a mother. She should be checking on her children, not the other way around.

★★★

An hour later, long after the clattering of dishes and the groan of the dishwasher had subsided, Becky slipped into the bedroom and sat on the corner of Kitty's bed. "You mellowing out, Mom?"

"I'm okay, sweetie," Kitty whispered. "I'm just a bit unhinged by all this."

"So you think he's left us?"

Kitty reached out and took Becky's hand. "If he's left, he's left me, not you." She rubbed her daughter's hand between hers. It was difficult to tell Becky's fingers from her own; their hands looked so similar. "Your father loves you very much."

Becky pulled away with a scoff. "He has a funny way of showing it."

"What do you mean?"

"He's doing this just to screw up my going to Brown."

"No, honey," Kitty said, sitting up and putting her arm around Becky's shoulders. "Your father will be so proud of you when he hears the news about Brown."

"You think that if you want, but I know he's going to find a way to keep me from going."

Becky's words made all the emotions that had boiled up within

28

Kitty that night out on the lake - rage, indignation, disbelief, regret and hope - come back up to a simmer. She remembered why she killed Seth; to give Becky a chance to be an independent woman. "I would never let that happen, sweetie. I may not be the best mother in the world, but I won't let anyone get in the way of your dreams."

"Thanks, Mom." Becky leaned over Kitty and gave her a hug. When had she gotten so strong? "Don't worry. We'll be fine, Mom. You're a smart cookie. You'll figure something out." She sat back and patted Kitty's hip. "What is it that Gloria Steinem says? 'A woman needs a man like a fish needs a bicycle.' Come on, it's 1976. Declare your independence."

four

Kitty awoke on Tuesday morning feeling hopeful. The plan would work. Someone was bound to find the Volvo soon. Seth would be declared dead. Kitty would collect his life insurance. She and her children would be fine.

She planned to spend most of the day at the Arts Council, yet decided it would be good karma to stop by Debbie Manning's house on the way. Debbie had completed her latest round of chemotherapy treatments and deserved a visit. Kitty thought about bringing a casserole, then decided against it. She didn't know how Debbie was feeling; it would be horrible to bring something she couldn't stomach. She put a batch of her carrot cake muffins in the oven before making the kids' lunches. Everyone liked carrot cake.

When Kitty got to the Mannings' house just after nine, a young woman answered the door. From her white uniform, Kitty assumed she was a visiting nurse or helper of some sort. "Hello," Kitty said. "I'm a friend of Mrs. Manning. Is she at home?"

The young woman scrutinized Kitty for a moment before stepping out of the doorway to let her in. "Have you been ill in the last seventy-two hours?"

"No, I'm healthy as a horse."

The young woman took the plate of muffins from Kitty's hands and walked toward the kitchen. "She's in the family room. Please wash up in the powder room before you go in." Kitty stepped into the small windowless bathroom under the stairs and scrubbed her hands and wrists with plenty of Zest soap.

Debbie was dozing in a burnt orange Barca-Lounger in the sunny family room. Her dark hair had grown back and was styled in a gamine style around her slim face. If Kitty hadn't known that Debbie had lost weight due to the leukemia, she'd have envied how slim she'd become. The Today Show blared from the television cabinet. As she walked over to the console and turned the knob, Kitty wondered if Jane Pauley was going to make it as an anchor. She hoped so.

Debbie jerked awake when the sound went off. "Kitty," she said, sitting up in the recliner. "What a lovely surprise."

"Sorry it's taken me so long to drop by. I've been meaning to come by for weeks."

Debbie pulled the light blanket up over her shoulders, even though the sunny room was warm. "If you'd put it off much longer, you could have saved the trip."

"Come now, you shouldn't talk like that."

"Why not?" Debbie's cocker spaniel scampered in from the kitchen and hurled herself up onto Debbie's lap. "I'm dying Kitty. I'm going to talk whatever way I want."

Kitty sat down on the gold flowered sofa beside Debbie's recliner and busied her hands with arranging the pile of magazines littering the coffee table. It had been Debbie's habit of saying whatever popped into her mind that had pushed Kitty and Seth's marriage into a downward spiral. Once Debbie told Kitty that Seth was sleeping with her tennis partner, Kitty couldn't ignore the STD Seth had given her. She couldn't pretend that the gonorrhea was just another harmless infection. Kitty wasn't sure if Debbie had hurt or helped her by blurting out the news. If Kitty had never been told about the affair, she could have drowned her suspicions in vodka and forgotten the infection as soon as she finished her course of antibiotics; and Seth might still be alive. Kitty straightened the TIME magazines so the issue with Dustin Hoffman and Robert Redford in "All the President's Men" was on top. She thought it was good that handsome men had been cast to tell such an ugly story.

"Stop fussing, Kitty. The magazines are fine. So, how are things now that you're single?"

Kitty felt her neck and ears flush. "I don't know what you mean."

"Poor Kitty, always the last to know. Seth told Dan that he was going to ask you to move out last week."

Kitty swallowed hard. *How dare he tell his golfing buddies before me. Okay, keep it together. Think! If he told Dan, he probably told a bunch of the other guys, and they will have told their wives.*

Okay, that's good, right? People think Seth's left me. That's the plan. It's not how we planned it to happen, but it works. Just roll with it. She leaned forward on the couch. "Debbie, tell me the truth. Have you told anyone else about this? Did Dan?"

"No, I learned my lesson with that whole Marni business. I haven't told anyone anything." Debbie took a sip from a half-empty cup of tea on the side table. "Then again, no big loss."

Kitty bit the inside of her mouth to keep from guffawing. *I can't believe she just said that to me. For all she knows, I could be devastated. Then again, any idiot would know I wouldn't be. That's pretty sad when you think about it. He's gone and no one gives a damn.*

Kitty moved to get up. "Can I make you a fresh cup of tea?"

"No, stay. Bonita will get me some later when it's time for my pills." Debbie replaced the tea cup on the saucer and went back to petting the dog on her lap. "I'm sorry if I offended you. I keep putting my foot in my mouth around you."

"Don't worry about it. I appreciate your honesty. I'm just not used to it."

"I just don't see any point in playing stupid games anymore."

"How so? Has someone said something to hurt you?"

"Not at all, none of the Lookers have said anything at all. They haven't called. They haven't visited. It's like I'm already dead."

Kitty felt drops of guilty sweat beading up on her forehead. She could have visited more often. "Doesn't Stacia come by?"

"She is an angel straight from heaven, that Stacia. She would kill me if I told you all the things she's done for me over the last few months."

Kitty leaned over to pick up a stray magazine. She couldn't risk Debbie seeing the effect of her words on her face. When she felt in control of her emotions, Kitty replied, "Stacia is a true friend in a crisis."

Debbie ran her hands over the dog's ears. "That's why I'm so worried about her."

"Excuse me?"

"Haven't you noticed how nervous she's been the last few days?

She was shaking like a leaf when she was here last night. Something's wrong. Do you think she could be popping pills?"

"Stacia? Taking drugs?" Kitty looked away as if considering the idea. "I don't think so, Debbie. Stacia is just not the type to take uppers."

"I wouldn't be so sure about that. Where does she get all that energy then?"

Kitty decided to change the subject. "So, how are you, really?"

"I feel fine, weak, but fine. The doctors tell me I'll continue to feel fine, until I don't anymore."

Kitty felt a heaviness in her chest. Poor Debbie. She's never going to see her little girl grow up. Seeing Becky and Bobby grow up to live their own lives is the most important thing to me right now. I don't know if I could deal with everything Debbie is dealing with.

I guess you just muddle through, though. At least she's got Stacia helping her.

"Is there anything I can do to help?"

Debbie played with the dog's ear then looked back up at Kitty. "You can live your life out loud. Stop putting up with people like Seth and just keep on truckin'. Be happy. Don't put things off. I planned to do things later, and now there's not going to be a later."

Clipped footsteps approached across the kitchen linoleum. "Miss Debbie, it's time for your pills and your nap." The young woman that had greeted Kitty at the door carried a tray into the family room and put it down on a side table. It contained a small cup of assorted pills, a fresh cup of tea, and a glass of water.

Kitty rose from the couch. "I should go." She was tempted to kiss her on the head like a child, but thought better of it. She didn't want to come across as patronizing. She ended up patting Debbie on the shoulder. "You hang in there, okay? I'll see if I can get some of the other girls to drop by. Would you like that?"

Debbie's eyelids were already drooping as she let her head loll against the side of the recliner. "That would be great."

★★★

After her morning swim, Stacia sat on the patio to let her hair dry. She was worried about the algae growth in the lake this early in the season. She made a note to talk to her brother to get Tate Power's people out there to check the water quality, then returned to the collection of maps and charts spread across the table in front of her. Baillie gnawed on the end of his bone with the same level of concentration with which Stacia pored over the documents. They made no sense. Stacia suspected that the army of consultants the school board had hired, had intentionally made the proposed redistricting plan confusing. They wanted people to give up before they parsed the details of the plan. If they didn't read beyond the big print on the first pages of the proposal, it sounded fabulous. Who wouldn't want the children in the Magnuson Public Schools to get an equal education?

The people of Magnuson hadn't paid close attention to the legal battle that had raged on for years in Charlotte. Stacia, on the other hand, had closely followed the Swann case. As the mother of biracial children, she was sensitive to how bigoted Magnuson could be. As the wife of the owner of Curran Construction, she understood how school system problems could affect the property values in Overlook. And, as a Tate, she didn't want the city her grandfather built tarred with the same brush of racial tension that had marred Greensboro.

She ran her fingers across Baillie's soft fur as she tried to decipher an attendance zone map. The people of Magnuson County wouldn't fully understand what the school board was doing to their schools until it was too late to demand changes. Stacia feared that when the people in the exclusive Oaks area realized that children from the housing projects were going to be bussed into their neighborhood schools, they'd pull their children out of the public schools and enroll them in Magnuson Country Day School. She slipped her reading glasses (a recent addition to her wardrobe) off her nose and gathered the papers into a rough pile. "We'll have to figure all this out another time, Baillie. I told Debbie Manning that I'd drop by this afternoon." As if she understood Stacia's words, the dog jumped off her lap and trotted to the patio door.

Stacia went inside and returned with a foil wrapped dish. Before opening the gate that led to the Overlook walking trails, she paused for a moment to gaze out over the lake. It was thankfully devoid of police boats. "That's a good sign, Baillie. At least Seth's body hasn't popped up yet."

She noticed Lester Hendricks' boat moored a few hundred yards off shore. Judging from how tightly the anchor line held the boat and how little it moved side to side, Stacia guessed the lower dam was open.

Lake Tate may have appeared placid, but the water was moving swiftly below the surface.

★★★

As soon as she stepped off the path leading from the walking trails to Debbie's street, Stacia knew something was wrong. Debbie's car had been pulled out of the attached garage and unceremoniously left in the middle of the cul-de-sac. The garage door was up and the door to the kitchen was wide open.

Oh, no. I thought Debbie was starting to feel better now that the chemotherapy was over. She seemed fine when I saw her last night. Was she putting on a happy face for me? Did I miss something in her voice? Has this whole thing with Kitty distracted me from my other responsibilities?

As soon as she started up the driveway, Blaire Morton came out of the house next door and waved. "I'll be right back, honey. Miss Stacia is here," she yelled over her shoulder as she bounded across the lawns. "Isn't it awful?"

Stacia didn't respond. She hoped Blaire would give her a clue as to what had happened, without Stacia having to ask any questions. Usually, Blaire wouldn't stop talking until Stacia told her to be quiet, so it shouldn't have been too hard. "The ambulance left a couple of hours ago."

Ambulance? Why didn't anyone call me about an ambulance in Overlook?

"I would have pulled Debbie's car back into the garage. I know you don't like it when people park in the street, but it didn't seem right to go in the house to look for the keys."

Really, Blaire? Do you really think I care about proper parking procedure right now? She could be dead! "Thank you, Blaire. I'll take care of it."

"Did Dan say how Debbie's doing when he called you?"

Stacia let Blaire assume that Debbie's husband had called her for help. That way she could keep Blaire out of the loop as long as possible.

"Just the basics. They'll know more later."

"Do you think I should keep Amy?" Blaire asked.

Stacia looked over Blaire's shoulder. Debbie's daughter stood on Blaire's front steps watching them. Stacia waved. Amy didn't wave back.

"Did Debbie ask you to keep her before they took her away in the ambulance?"

"No. I just thought it was a good idea to go pick her up from school." Blaire rubbed her lips together as if holding back a smile. "Poor Amy. She started crying as soon as she saw me in the front office."

Stacia could imagine. Blaire Morton, with her big hair and her giant teeth, would be the last person she would want to pull her out of school, even under the best of circumstances.

"You knew I've been driving Amy back and forth to school every day, right? I go get Amy at two thirty, even though my Mark has baseball until five."

"I'm sure that's a huge burden off Debbie's mind to know Amy has transportation."

"So should I keep her?"

"I'll take her with me. Why don't you go back inside and help Amy gather up her things? I'll be over in a few minutes."

Stacia made her way inside. The house was a mess. It looked like the paramedics had tipped over everything in their path when they had taken Debbie out. She must have been sitting in her recliner when they arrived. The coffee table had been unceremoniously pulled across the living room, the TV was still tuned to Debbie's favorite soap operas, and her favorite pale blue blanket lay in a heap on the floor.

Stacia's heart felt like a lead weight in her chest. She sat down at the kitchen table and put her head in her hands for a moment. She knew she should be thinking about Debbie and her family, but Stacia was remembering Von. Unlike the night Stacia, Von, and a car full of other girls slammed into a tree, someone had been on hand to call an ambulance for Debbie. When Stacia was thrown from the car that fateful night, she had crawled to the nearest house with a shattered leg, but she couldn't get there in time to help Von and the other girls. Von died and Stacia had spent the last thirty years trying to make up for that.

She took a deep breath and stood up. She would find a way to help Debbie. That was who she was. A helper.

Stacia turned off the television, put the furniture back in place, and tidied up a bit. Amy and Dan didn't need to see the room like that. Beside the recliner, half a cup of tea and one of Kitty's muffins had been upended on the shag carpet. Stacia knew it was one of Kitty's creations because no one else would go through the effort of decorating a carrot cake muffin with perfectly curled carrot shavings atop a fluffy cream cheese frosting.

She carried the plate and tea cup to the kitchen sink. One of her casserole pans sat on the drain board along with a couple of mugs.

I hope my tuna noodle casserole doesn't end up being Debbie's last meal. It's not that good.

She opened the refrigerator to put away the casserole she brought. It was empty except for Kitty's Tupperware container of muffins. Kitty and Stacia seemed to be the only Lookers that had been visiting Debbie. She slammed the refrigerator closed. *Those women are like a bunch of little kids. Do I actually have to tell them to help each other out? They all knew Debbie was sick.*

★★★

All day, while she sifted through the piles of applications to be featured in the tiny Art Center gallery, Kitty kept thinking about Debbie. She was ashamed of how the Lookers had abandoned her. Debbie had lived in Overlook almost as long as Kitty. She was one of the founding members of the Overlook book club, played bridge with a bunch of the gals at the clubhouse every week, and was a staple in their yearly tennis round robin. She deserved to be treated better.

She tossed an application with Polaroids of watercolor landscapes paper-clipped to the front of it into the NO pile, and reached for the telephone extension on the conference room wall. She dialed Betty Oliphant's number. Kitty heard Betty's hyperactive little boy in the background before she heard Betty say hello.

"Hey, Betty," Kitty said. "You have a second?"

"Just one. Georgie is on one of his tears this afternoon."

Kitty rolled her eyes. Georgie Oliphant seemed to always be in motion. Between Georgie's exhausting behavior and her daughter supposedly running off the year before, it was no wonder Betty was rumored to be addicted to Mother's Little Helper. No one was that calm without chemical assistance.

"I'll be brief. I was wondering if you could swing by sometime this week and visit Debbie Manning over on Tranquility?"

"Haven't you heard?" Betty shushed Georgie. "An ambulance took her away around lunchtime."

"An ambulance? But I just saw her this morning." *Oh no, did I put something I shouldn't have in those muffins? Are carrots dangerous for people who are so sick?*

"Stacia took Amy to her house until they know more."

"Stacia was there?" That made Kitty feel a bit better. Stacia would help. She would handle the situation. "Look, Betty, I've got to go. Thanks for telling me about Debbie."

She hung up the phone and scooped all the applications into an empty file box. They could be dealt with another day. Kitty needed to get to the hospital. She hoped she wasn't too late.

★★★

Kitty had never been to the new Ellery Hospital. The hospital complex was ten times the size of the old brick building where she had given birth to Bobby. Stacia said the hospital brought a higher class of people to Magnuson. Doctors bought expensive houses and pushed up housing prices. Kitty parked along the street and hiked back to the building. She refused to pay to park in the monstrous cement parking garage, a dangerous place for a woman alone. She had to think of herself that way now. She was alone.

Once she had navigated the maze of information desks and hallways, Kitty finally found Debbie's room. Stacia was sitting cross legged on the foot of the bed. The tubes running from her arm and the oxygen tube looped across her face made Debbie as small as a child. Kitty struggled to believe this was the same woman that used to return her tennis serves with such vigor. She lightly knocked on the open door. Both Debbie and Stacia turned and smiled.

"Hey, I heard you were here. Is this a good time to visit?"

"It's now or never, Kitty," Debbie said. "I might not be here tomorrow."

"Don't say that," Kitty said. She stopped when Stacia shot her a steely glance. She nodded and understood. The time for platitudes had passed. It was time to say goodbye. She bit the inside of her lip and willed herself not to cry. That would not serve either of them.

"Are you comfortable? Can I get you anything?"

Debbie scooted up a bit in the bed. Stacia gracefully jumped off the bed and rearranged the pillows behind Debbie's back. She picked up the cup from the side table and gave it a shake. "Could you run down to the nurse's station and get some more ice chips? They aren't letting her eat or drink anything but she can suck on as much ice as she can stand."

Kitty rushed forward and took the cup from Stacia's hand. She nodded, but couldn't confidently say anything without starting to cry. She went out into the hallway and leaned against the wall for a moment to collect herself. Stacia came out after her and motioned for her to step down the hall. "Thanks for coming."

"How is she?"

Stacia ran her fingers though her hair. She looked exhausted and older than Kitty had ever seen her, even after her most punishing long distance swims. "Not good. They got her stabilized and are pumping her full of morphine, but there's only so much the doctors can do for her."

"Where's Dan?"

"He was here with her all afternoon. Bonita—"

"Is that the nurse I met?"

"—called him right after she called for the ambulance. I sent him and Amy home to change their clothes and eat something." Stacia rubbed the palms of her hands over her face.

"What can I do to help? Should I call around and see whether some of the other girls can come visit?"

Stacia shook her head. "Just you being here is help enough. Debbie told me you dropped by earlier."

"I should have gone more often. I've been so wrapped up in my own problems that I've neglected my friends."

Stacia bit her lip and leaned her head back against the wall. "You're not the only one," she whispered.

five

It took a long week for Debbie Manning's body to finally give up. She died with her husband and daughter at her side. During Debbie's final days, Stacia and Kitty took shifts making sure Dan was eating and little Amy stayed occupied all while dancing around the awkward truth of what Stacia had seen that night out on the lake. Concentrating on helping the Mannings allowed them to get back into the rhythm of their friendship. When they saw each other, they talked about Debbie, or their training schedule for the triathlon they'd planned to try, or the agenda for the final PTA meeting. Neither one of them uttered Seth's name or made any reference to his absence until Dan mentioned him to Stacia.

Debbie was in a drug-induced slumber when Dan entered her hospital room one evening. "Thanks for sitting with her while I took Amy back to the house." He sat down beside his wife and took her pale hand in his own.

"Is your sister-in-law okay staying the night with her?"

"They're both exhausted. I think she'll give Amy something to eat, then put her right to bed. You and Weldon have been so helpful. I've been so focused on Debbie, I didn't think to call her sister. Thank Weldon for flying her in from Wisconsin. I'll repay him somehow."

Stacia leaned back in the rocking chair the nurses had brought in and stared out the window. The sun had set and the waning moon hung just above the tree line. She thought about her conversation with her husband the night before. They'd both agreed that Debbie's family should get the opportunity to say goodbye. Weldon would have given anything to have been able to say goodbye to his little sister, Von, when she died. Weldon wanted to give Debbie's family that moment.

"Don't worry about it. We just wanted her to have a chance to be here."

"I'm such a mess," Dan said. "I might not have called her until it was too late."

"You just concentrate on Debbie. Kitty, Weldon, and I will pick up the slack."

"I can't thank you all enough. Kitty has completely filled our refrigerator with food over the last couple of days. That was so nice of her, especially now."

Stacia abruptly stopped the motion of the rocker. "Excuse me?"

"Didn't you hear about Seth?" The blood froze in Stacia's veins for a second. "He's divorcing her."

Stacia struggled to keep her face expressionless as she straightened the sheet over Debbie's legs on her side of the bed. "Wherever did you hear that?"

"I ran into Seth on the golf course. He said Kitty and the kids hated him, and he wanted to start over again with some new girl."

"He told you he wants to take a Mulligan?" Stacia snorted. She deftly tucked a bit of sheet under the edge of the mattress. "I wouldn't believe everything you hear, Dan. Seth may have found a new girl, but he wasn't man enough to ask Kitty for a divorce. He just split like the coward he is."

Dan raised his eyebrows and shook his head. "So where does that leave Kitty and the kids?"

Stacia hadn't really thought about that. Where did that leave Kitty? How were she and the children going to get by financially, now that Kitty had killed Seth? "I'm not sure exactly. Maybe Seth will resurface and take responsibility for his actions. If not, Kitty's smart. She'll figure something out. She always does."

★★★

The next morning, Stacia called Kitty first thing and left a message with Bobby to have his mother meet her at the pool. She'd spent a sleepless night thinking about her conversation with Dan. What was Kitty going to do now that Seth was gone? Stacia couldn't do much to help Debbie at this point, but she could still help Kitty and her children.

Stacia let herself into the locked pool area and dropped her things on the closest chair. Her body felt heavy. She wondered if it was from more than a simple lack of sleep. She hadn't felt herself since the night she saw Kitty and Seth go out in his boat. Every noise sounded like a siren. Her hands had begun to shake and she had fallen back into chain-smoking. Weldon had frowned at her buying a carton of cigarettes the day before, but he hadn't said anything. He would assume that spending so much time in Debbie's hospital room reminded Stacia of the month's she spent recovering from the car accident and his sister's death. Weldon had worked through his own grief by helping Stacia relearn to walk and come to terms with the fact that her ballet career was over. Giving up the dream she and Von had shared of becoming prima ballerinas was like losing her friend all over again.

The breeze had a cool edge to it that ruffled the irises planted along the fence as Stacia fished her goggles out of her bag and snapped them over her eyes. As soon as she dove into the pool, she felt better. The water was cool and soft against her skin as she swam a few easy laps. Swimming was her yoga. Training for long-distance races allowed her to stay competitive without straining her artificial knee. In the water, she also didn't need to think. Muscle memory told her arms and legs what to do. She unconsciously knew where the walls were and could clear her mind of all the noise of daily life and talk to Von.

The shadows were shorter on the pool deck and the breeze had lost its edge by the time Stacia heard the clang of the gate. Kitty waved as she slipped out of her shoes. "Sorry it took me so long to get here. I dropped by to see how Debbie's sister is doing. She's a bit of a talker."

Stacia pulled herself out of the pool and perched on the edge. "She must be a wreck. It probably helps to talk."

Kitty nodded as she peeled off her simple dress. She wore a yellow and green racing suit underneath. Since she started training with Stacia, Kitty had adopted Stacia's habit of wearing bright suits. Stacia pulled her goggles off and twirled them around her forefinger.

"Look, Kitty, I've been thinking." Kitty's body visibly tensed. "Relax," Stacia said. "I'm not going to call the police or anything. I just want to talk to you about the triathlon."

Kitty collapsed onto a deck chair and put a hand on her chest. "Phew, I thought I was going to have a heart attack there for a second." She wiped her forehead with the back of her hand and took a deep breath. "What about the race?"

"I don't think we should do it."

Kitty furrowed her brow. "Because of Seth?"

"Yes and no." Stacia tossed her goggles in the air to avoid making eye contact with Kitty. "I don't think I can be ready by race day and you don't have the time to help me train—"

"But—"

"No, you don't. What are you going to do for money? Eventually, Golf Systems will catch on and stop paying Seth, and he can't have accrued more than a week or two of vacation pay."

Kitty bit her lip and looked out over the lake. "There's his life insurance. That could hold us for a little while. And I could get a better job. More hours. More responsibility." She looked back to Stacia. "I've already got a couple of consulting projects. I could get more."

"What makes you think you'll be able to get his life insurance? If anyone finds his body, you'll go to jail for the rest of your life."

"Rose and—" Kitty put her hand to her lips. "I don't think I should tell you." Kitty's face turned an unhealthy shade of red. She pulled her goggles out of her bag and stretched the cord between her fingers. "Look, I appreciate everything you've done for me, I really do. So I don't want to put you at any more risk than I already have. Like they say on TV, the less you know the better."

"What do you mean by that? What have you done?"

Kitty looked up with a calculating gleam in her eye that reminded Stacia that her sweet friend was also a brutal killer. "Rose and I did a few things later that night to make people think Seth had an accident. Somewhere else. Far away from Overlook. Far away from us."

"Your sister knows? Why did you burden anyone else with this thing?" Stacia slid off the edge of the pool. She needed to put some space between her and Kitty. "Still, it could take months, a year even, to get the life insurance. You're going to have to lean on your friends at least for a little while." She thought about Debbie and how the Lookers had abandoned her in her time of need. "We're going to have to get the Lookers on your side. Who else knows that Seth is gone?"

Kitty jumped in the shallow end of the pool. She splashed water on her arms and face. "I have a feeling a lot of people already know. Debbie told me that Seth told Dan that he was going to divorce me."

"Dan said the same thing to me."

"Really?" Kitty rubbed pool water out of her eyes. "I think I should use that to my advantage. If people have already heard that Seth was getting ready to ask me for a divorce, it won't seem so strange if I say he chickened out and simply left me. Molly Blevins didn't seem surprised at all when I told her."

Stacia slipped her goggles over her head again. "Why'd you tell Molly, of all people?"

"She showed up at the house. I couldn't very well pretend nothing was wrong." Kitty related the highlights of her conversation with Molly while leaving out the ice cream and vomiting.

"Typical." Stacia ran her tongue over her teeth like there was a bad taste in her mouth. "Molly's always pulling that high and mighty act."

Kitty pensively adjusted the strap of her bathing suit. "She's not usually like that with me."

"That's because you're always agreeing with her." Stacia flicked Kitty's hand away from the strap and untwisted it for her. "When you're both on the same side, she's a crunchy granola peacenik. It's only when she's in the wrong that she becomes a real drag."

Kitty grabbed a kickboard and pushed off into the deep end. "Are you talking about the dog fence thing? I explained that to you. Their dog is way too old to be chained up."

"It's in the bylaws." Stacia rolled her eyes. "No chicken wire or chain link fences, and no fences in the front yard."

"Is that why you don't like each other?"

"Rules are there for reason," Stacia said. She dove through the water and surfaced near the far end of the pool. She slowly kicked her way back to Kitty. "But that's not why I dislike her. It actually goes back to when the boys were in preschool."

"Were they even living here when the boys were in preschool? I didn't meet Molly until the boys were in kindergarten."

"They moved in that July. She met Deirdre here at the pool and they got talking about how our boys were all going to Little Acorns that fall."

"But Molly's Ethan didn't go to Little Acorns," Kitty replied.

"They weren't members of the church, and he wasn't on the waiting list." Stacia stretched her arms across her chest. Her back felt tighter

45

than usual. "Now, if they had joined the church right away and given a sizable donation to the preschool, I might could have gotten them to bump a non-member out. But Molly didn't ask for my help." Stacia's nose twitched like someone had pooped in the pool.

Kitty's eyes widened. "She didn't go to Bitsy Magnuson-Evans, did she?"

"She did," Stacia said. "When Molly found out that Bitsy controlled the preschool's board, she called her and demanded in her eewey gooey everyone-gets-a-trophy way of hers, that Bitsy let Ethan in."

"That was unfortunate." Kitty barely knew Bitsy Magnuson-Evans but she knew that demanding anything from Bitsy was tantamount to social suicide. As much as Stacia ruled over Overlook in northern Magnuson, Bitsy ruled The Oaks area downtown. The two women were polite rivals.

"Did you even try to get Ethan in at that point?"

Stacia pulled her legs up in preparation to push off the wall. "I didn't bother. The damage had been done. Bitsy would rather die than let someone like Molly push her around."

★★★

By late April, baseball season was winding down and the teams were vying for spots in the championship. The competition was fierce, both on the field and in the bleachers. Lake Tate Junior High's team had not lost a game all season, much to the chagrin of the teams from southern Magnuson County.

Low clouds threatened to burst over Oak Avenue Comprehensive's field as Kitty pulled her Mercedes into a spot at the back of the lot. She pulled one of Seth's promotional golf umbrellas from the trunk and joined the crowd of spectators making their way up the low hill behind the bleachers. She fell in step with a red-faced man in his shirt sleeves. He heaved himself to the top of the rise and shook his head. "Can you believe we have to play this Tate team?"

Kitty looked around her for the target of the man's grumbling. "Are you talking to me?"

"It's not fair. They're naturally better athletes than our children." The man spat tobacco juice on the ground. Kitty hopped to the right to avoid getting spittle on her green suede loafers. She liked those shoes. "I don't like my Beau playing against the blacks."

46

"Oh my, that is…upsetting," Kitty replied through clenched teeth. She fought the urge to ram the pointed end of her golf umbrella through the man's fat belly.

The crowd rounded the bleachers allowing Kitty to get away from the man. She had never been so proud to march around the field to the visitors' side. For once, she was glad Stacia was not there. She would hate to have Stacia hear what that awful man had just said. For all her bravado, Kitty knew the man's bigotry would have unnerved Stacia. The world could be a hateful place and she feared for Lana and Marcus's safety.

Kitty slowed her pace as she thought about where Stacia was that afternoon. Debbie Manning had died early that morning and Stacia was helping Debbie's sister pick out flowers for the service. None of the other Lookers had even sent over a casserole.

Kitty spotted Overlook's biggest gossipmonger, Blaire Morton, sitting high up in the bleachers and set her sights on her. Kitty had a mission and Blaire was going to unwittingly help her achieve it. The flock of other Overlook moms hadn't gathered yet to start pecking at each other, so this was the best time to speak to Blaire one-on-one. Kitty studied Blaire while she jostled her way up the bleachers. She looked worn. Blaire still wore her yellow hair in a Jackie Kennedy puff, where many of the other moms had changed to a Farrah flip or practical Dorothy Hamill cut. Kitty's clean cut bob was always in style. Blaire looked lumpy and dull in pedal pushers and a structured blouse beside the other spectators wearing bell bottom jeans and peasant blouses. Kitty wondered if Morton Motors was doing so poorly that Blaire couldn't afford to buy the current fashions, or if she had merely given up.

The crowd in front of Kitty dissipated as she sprinted up the last few sections of bleachers to sit next to Blaire. "Hey, great seats. You been here long?"

"I brought the snacks for after the game, so I got here early."

"Speaking of snacks," Kitty said. She wanted to ease into their conversation by reminding Blaire of the Marni and Seth scandal from the fall. "The PTA is going to need a new Hospitality chair now that my Bobby will be moving up to the high school and Marni, well, moved away. You have another year at Tate Junior High. Could you do it?"

"Me? No, I can't do it." Blaire ran her hand over her shellacked hair. "I don't think I'm even going to have time to do PTA anymore." Kitty waited. She knew Blaire wanted her to ask why and wasn't going to take the bait. "Didn't you hear?"

"I've had a lot on my mind," Kitty sniffed. "With Debbie being sick and—"

"No, not that. I'm going back to work full-time."

"Really?" Kitty hadn't expected that. Things at Morton Motors must be worse than she thought.

Her stomach did a nervous flip as she mentally switched gears to set up her move. "What a coincidence. It looks like I'll be going back to work full-time too."

Blaire's eyes sparkled under her garish blue eyeshadow. "Well, I...I did hear something."

Yeah, I bet you did!

A squadron of umbrellas simultaneously unfurled on the other side of the field in response to the low clouds spitting at them. Kitty opened her enormous umbrella above Blaire's head and leaned in. "It's Seth." She covered her mouth with her fingers and arranged her face to look as pathetic as possible. "He never came home from his latest business trip, and now I can't reach him anywhere."

"How awful." A smug smile threatened at the edges of Blaire's coral lips.

"I'm terribly worried. What if he's lying in a ditch somewhere?"

Blaire's over-plucked brows shot up. "Dead?"

Kitty had practiced how to respond if someone went down this line of discussion until it was as automatic as her backhand. She tried to sound breathy, like Marilyn Monroe, rather than weepy. "Well, I can't think of any other reason for him not to come home."

Blaire stifled a laugh under a cough. "Excuse me, Kitty. I seem to have a tickle in my throat. I'm going to run over to the concession stand and get a drink. I'll be right back." Blaire jumped up and ran down the steps to the grass. She didn't even pretend to go to the concession stand. She intercepted a clot of the Lookers near the entrance and pulled them aside. Kitty could see her color rise and her upper arms flapping as she gestured wildly.

And the point goes to Kitty Haskell. Blaire will tell everyone in Magnuson that

Escape Plan

Seth has either left me or is dead by the third inning. Kitty stood up to walked slowly back to her car. My work here is done. No need to stick around for the pitying looks.

six

reparing finger sandwiches and cupcakes for Debbie's funeral was oddly cathartic. As Kitty filled frilled paper liners with her signature devil's food batter, she thought about how much Debbie would be missed by her husband and daughter, but by the time the cupcakes were cooling on the counter, she was mourning how little she would be missed by the Lookers. They would feign remorse for not spending more time with her during her last months, then change the subject. Kitty picked at a cupcake that broke when she removed it from the muffin tin and pondered how much she would be missed if she was gone. She'd like to think that the Lookers cared for her, but knew they were more interested in her as gossip fodder than as a person. In all honesty, the Lookers didn't know her anymore than they knew Debbie. Kitty was an excellent tennis player, a marvelous cook, and a luckless wife. By the time she'd finished decorating the petite mounds of devil's food with tasteful swirls of white buttercream, she lamented the loss of her sense of community more than Debbie's death.

Kitty was dispassionately cutting the crusts off a tray of cucumber sandwiches when the phone rang. She licked a bit of cream cheese off her forefinger and reached for the phone. "Kitty Cat?" a deep voice said. "It's Rick Reynolds from Golf Systems. How's everything going?"

Kitty wiped her hands on her apron. *What does he want?* She swallowed hard and tried to conjure a lump in her throat in order to act the abandoned, dumb wife again.

"Not so great, Rick."

"Right." Rick exhaled heavily. Kitty could tell he was uncomfortable calling her. He had only called her Kitty Cat the few times she had asked awkward questions about Seth's whereabouts.

Kitty concentrated on making her voice sound weak. "What's up? Have you heard from Seth?"

"No, none of us here have heard from him at all."

"He hasn't called the office?"

"Yeah, about his office. His secretary …you remember Suzie, right?"

"Oh course I remember Suzie. She's been incredibly helpful the last couple of weeks." Kitty folded a cucumber sandwich into a doily and tucked it in next to its neighbor on the silver platter. She checked the clock above the stove. The funeral would be starting in an hour and she wanted to swing the platters by the house before she went to the church. "Look, Rick, I've got to run. I appreciate you calling. It means a lot to me that you're concerned."

"Sure, that's it. I'm concerned." Rick cleared his throat. "Actually, what I was calling about is, well, it's a courtesy call really. I thought someone should call and… Do you remember old man Naylor's kid, Sam?"

Kitty did not remember Mr. Naylor's children. She barely remembered Seth's boss, other than that he was a frat buddy of Seth's father and liked to grab her bottom at the annual picnic. "Well, we're giving Seth's accounts to Sam Naylor."

She pulled the phone cord away from the wall with a quick yank. "I see." She paused to sniff loudly and collect her thoughts. "Actually, I don't understand. Do you mean you're firing Seth."

"Well…I, uh…not firing as much as reassigning his accounts."

Wow, that was quick. Seth's body has barely started to decompose and they've replaced him with the boss's kid. I guess what goes around, comes around.

Kitty dropped the frantic wife tone from her voice and got right to it. "So why are you really calling, Rick? Do you want me to come get his stuff or something?"

"That would be great, Kitty Cat. If it wouldn't be too much of a bother."

"No, I understand. The wheels of business don't stop for people's personal problems. I'll come by this afternoon."

"That's a good girl." Kitty wanted to reach through the telephone and gouge Rick's eyes out with the cheesy golf club pin he always wore on his ties. Instead, she covered the tray of finger sandwiches with wax paper and went upstairs to put on a black dress.

★★★

Later that day, Kitty tossed her black dress on her bed and stood in front of her closet in her bra and panties. She wasn't sure what she should wear to clean out Seth's office. On one hand, there might be some actual cleaning involved. On the other, this was probably the last time she would ever see Seth's co-workers. She wanted to make a good last impression. After much deliberation, Kitty wore a simple lime green eyelet sheath and a pair of navy blue Keds. The dress was youthful enough to ward off comments like "Poor Kitty, her husband left her," yet demure enough for an abandoned woman. After standing around dodging pitying looks at Debbie's funeral, she was looking forward to working out some of her restlessness by lifting a few boxes.

Kitty had been in the Golf Systems parking lot many times over the last ten years to switch cars with Seth whenever he needed his car serviced, but she hadn't been inside since she had initially decorated Seth's office in 1965. The Golf Systems headquarters had been poorly designed with a southern facing glass foyer. In mid-May, the air conditioning was already loudly losing ground in its battle against the strong North Carolina sunshine. By July, the foyer would be unbearable. "Good afternoon," she said to the red-faced security guard. "Kitty Haskell for Suzie Bryant."

The security guard raised an eyebrow, but didn't otherwise react. Kitty wondered if he learned stoicism in the military, or if he was an avid poker player. "I'll call up to Suzie. I bet she's expecting you."

I bet they all want to get a look at the woman Seth Haskell ran out on. If they only knew. She felt a sudden flush run up her neck. *Well, not really. They can just keep thinking he left me.*

Kitty glanced at the display of famous golfers mugging for the camera with their Golf Systems clubs, and sat down in a square plaid chair. *What is it with the orange and brown plaids lately? Why do people think that men need plaid chairs? With all this direct sunlight these things are going to fade within a year. Their decorator should be shot.*

She heard the security guard talking into the phone. Kitty couldn't hear everything he said but she did catch a few words like "doesn't know" and "walk her back." Moments later, a woman Kitty recognized as Seth's secretary appeared. The last decade had not been kind to Suzie. The cute ingénue Seth had hired straight out of secretarial school had turned into a beach ball with a Dorothy Hamill haircut. Suzie waddled over. "Mrs. Haskell, so nice to see you." Her smile was forced and her eyes looked everywhere but at Kitty's face as she led her out of the reception area. Suzie paused just inside the door to the executive offices. "That woman keeps calling and I keep taking the messages. That's what you want me to do, right?"

"Sure," Kitty replied. "Seth might need to speak to her when he gets back."

Suzie touched Kitty's arm sympathetically and turned away to hide the pitying look on her face. Kitty fought back a smile. The plan was working perfectly.

"I'm not sure if I should have done this," Suzie whispered, "But, I called her back, and asked her if she'd heard from Seth. If it makes you feel any better, that tramp hasn't heard from him either."

"Thank you, Suzie. That's sweet of you. To tell you the truth, I don't know how to feel at this point. I'm angry, sure, but I just want him to come home." She inched further down the hallway. It was too difficult to play the sad little missus for more than a few seconds at a time.

Little had changed since she had last been there. Seth had been an up and coming executive when Golf Systems had built the headquarters in 1965 and had been given one of the coveted corner offices. He had always been proud of that achievement, even if he hadn't deserved the honor. The ivory linen drapes still looked crisp and authoritative eleven years after she had hung them. The restrained blue couch and chairs were still there; however, the line of golf related statuary she'd spent weeks scouring antique shops for, were gone.

A Lynda Carter look-a-like in a tailored black pants suit sat behind the desk talking on the phone. *This Naylor guy lets his secretary sit at his desk and use the phone? I doubt Seth ever let Suzie do that. Or maybe he did. I knew so little about his work life.*

Suzie came up behind her. "I'm real sorry about all this. I did the best I could, but once the ball gets rolling, things move real quick around here."

"I understand. If this new guy, Sam, wants his secretary to start moving his stuff into Seth's office before I could come to get his things, so be it."

Suzie tilted her head with a wry smile. "I'm still the secretary for the VP of Sales, Kitty." She pointed to the brunette. "That's Samantha Naylor."

Kitty looked again at the woman behind the desk. "Old man Naylor has a daughter? But she's so young. How can they make her a VP?"

"She has an MBA and some very interesting ideas about how to move the company forward." Suzie pointed to a short stack of brown file boxes near the window. "I packed everything up for you when Sam took over. You probably don't want most of it, but I thought I'd let you decide what to keep. When Sam gets off her call, I'll introduce you."

Kitty continued to watch Sam Naylor talk on the phone. She was exactly what Kitty wanted her Becky to become, a confident well-educated woman who was succeeding in a male-dominated world. At one point, Sam looked up and saw Kitty standing in the hall. A flash of recognition passed over her unlined brow. She quickly ended her call and stood up.

"You must be Seth's wife. I recognize you from the pictures he had on the desk." Sam extended her hand. Kitty couldn't remember the last time she'd shaken hands with another woman. The Lookers rarely made physical contact.

Kitty stepped toward the pile of boxes near the wide windows overlooking a nine-hole golf course. "I'm sorry it's taken me so long to come in." Kitty paused for effect. "It just seems so final, coming to get his things and all."

To her credit, Sam blushed. "Of course, I can't imagine how hard this must be for you and your children. I would be devastated if my husband left."

"You're married?"

Sam picked up a heavily carved wooden frame from the desk and showed it to Kitty. "My husband and our little boy."

The photo was of a handsome young man with full beard and a toddler sitting on a boulder. *Your husband lets you work these kind of hours when you have a toddler? Listen to me. She doesn't need his permission.*

Sam put the frame back in its spot at the corner of her desk and scooped up a file folder. "Well, I have to get to a meeting. I'll leave you alone to go through the boxes in peace. If you need anything, Suzie is right outside the door."

Kitty waited until Sam was gone before opening the top box in the pile. It was mostly clothing Seth kept in the office in case he spilled food on himself during the day. Kitty didn't want anything in there. The second box contained the golfing statues. Kitty definitely did not want to take those home with her.

Suzie appeared in the doorway behind her. "I remember when you bought those. I didn't know if you'd want them."

Kitty sat back on her heels. "Not really. I can't see me using them anywhere in the house." She looked over her shoulder at Suzie. "Do you want them? Can they be used somewhere else in the building?"

"I'll take care of it." Kitty wondered if Suzie wanted to keep the statues or if she planned to sell them. If so, she had certainly earned any profit she made from them.

"Could I bother you for a garbage bag? Some of these things aren't worth keeping."

Suzie took the box of statues and moved to the door. "I'll be right back."

When she was alone again, Kitty opened the last of the boxes. This one contained what Kitty considered Seth's personal items. She lifted out a silver-framed formal portrait of her and the children. It was supposed to be their family portrait for the Pinnacle Pointe church directory, but Seth had called an hour before the sitting and said he wasn't going to make it. She had gone ahead with the sitting and ended up throwing out all but this eight-by-ten print. She studied the photograph. She looked so young and happy with her two little cuties sitting on her lap in their coordinating blue sweaters. Kitty remembered the day differently. Becky's cheeks looked rosy in the portrait because she was coming down with a virus. The next morning, she had woken up vomiting. All three of them had spent the rest of the week in bed.

Kitty laid the portrait in the empty box along with three seemingly unused Cross pen sets and a World's Greatest Dad coffee cup. When Suzie returned with a garbage bag, Kitty dumped the clothes in along with everything else from Seth's desk. Kitty pushed herself up to her feet.

"Wait, Mrs. Haskell," Suzie said. "Before you close up the box, I have a few more things for you." She opened a drawer and pulled out a bulging manila envelope. She slipped it in the box. "Seth had some of his bills sent here. I'll forward things to your house but you might want to contact the companies and change the address."

Why would he have bills sent here?

"Of course, Suzie. Thank you." She stooped to pick up the box.

"Can you stick around for another few minutes?" Suzie asked. "I know Rick wants to speak to you."

Kitty shifted the box in her arms. "I need to get home."

"I'll buzz him right now."

Seconds later, heavy footsteps came down the hallway and around the corner. Kitty arranged her face to seem pathetic yet resolute before she turned around. "Rick, thank you for coming down to say goodbye."

"I wanted to catch you before you left." He looked surprised to see only the single box in Kitty's arms. "I hate to ask you this, but what do you want to do about the car?"

Kitty shrugged her pocketbook more securely over her shoulder and took a step toward the entrance. "What do you mean?"

"The Mercedes. I saw you drove it here." Rick pushed his glasses up his nose. "Do you want to take over the lease or do you want to give me back the keys?"

Kitty's stomach dropped. "I don't own that car?"

"It's a company car, Kitty."

Seth passed off his company car as a gift? The white convertible had been a gift of contrition after Seth had given Kitty gonorrhea.

"Oh!" *I wish I could bring him back to life so I could kill him all over again.*

Rick looked down at the slip of paper in his hand then back to Kitty. "The loan still has twenty-eight months on it at $300."

"A month?" Kitty made less than $100 per month from her part-time job at the Arts Center. She felt her face growing hot, and tried to take a deep breath. She put the box down on Suzie's desk and fished her keyring out of her purse. She detached her house key and dropped it back in her purse. "Do I have to sign any paperwork or can you just give the car to someone else?"

"I can take care of any paperwork."

"Could you excuse me for a second, Rick?" She reached across the desk, picked up the phone, and dialed her home number.

Suzie looked at her with pity in her eyes. "You okay, Mrs. Haskell?"

"Of course I am," Kitty replied curtly as she punched the buttons on the console. "Why wouldn't I be? I simply need to ask my daughter for a ride." Thankfully, Becky was home and picked up the phone on the second ring. Kitty didn't relish the idea of loitering until she could reach someone to drive over there.

"Hey, sweetie. I need you to jump in the Bug and meet me at the coffee shop on the corner of Industrial and Coventry." Becky must have heard the edge in her mother's voice and didn't protest. "Oh and by the way, you won't need to pay your own car insurance anymore because I'll be driving the Bug from now on."

Kitty hung up and flashed Rick a clenched tooth smile before hoisting the box to her hip like an unwieldy toddler. "Perhaps you could let me get my things out of the Mercedes before you repossess it?"

"Aww, come on," Rick said. "I can't just let you keep the car."

Kitty walked down the hallway aware that every man on the floor was watching her walk out with Rick Reynolds gamboling beside her like a puppy.

In the parking lot, she thrust the file box into his hands. "Could you hold this while I get my things out of the car?" She opened the passenger side door and slid across the smooth leather to retrieve her sunglasses from the dashboard. It felt petty to toss the small pile of loose change in her pocket book, but she didn't know, she might need that quarter and few nickels soon. She leaned into the backseat and reached for the plastic tub Bobby kept his cleats in. *The hell with it. Bobby can get mud on the carpeting from now on.* She popped the trunk and climbed out again. The sunglasses got unceremoniously dumped into the box in Rick's arms.

"I'm really sorry about this, Kitty. Can I do anything for you?"

"I'll be fine." *Why am I being such a witch right now? It wasn't Rick's or Golf Systems' fault that Seth had passed off his latest company car as a seemingly grand gesture.* She felt more the fool for believing he was making amends for his bad behavior.

She opened the tiny trunk. Other than her collapsible camp chair, there wasn't anything there she wanted. Golf Systems could keep their logo-covered golf umbrella. She looped the chair's strap over her head and across her back before plopping her purse in the file box and yanking it out of Rick's arms. She handed him the heavy fob with the shiny three point star on it. "Well, I can't say it's been a pleasure."

"Come on. I'd be happy to drive you home."

"Not necessary." Kitty spun on her heel. "See you around, Rick." As she walked past the line of luxury cars in the executive parking lot she hummed, 'Oh Lord, won't you buy me a Mercedes Benz...'

seven

The Magnuson City school board met on the first Thursday of the month at eleven. Just as Stacia and the Lookers did with their PTA board meetings, the school board chose to schedule their meetings at the least convenient time for the general public and announced them deep in section F of the newspaper. Most Magnuson residents weren't aware the public could attend.

Stacia knew.

She made it her business to be on a first name basis with each of the school board members and to know something about their families. Joe Neilly's wife lost a foot to diabetes a few years back and refused to the leave their house on Oak Hollow. Jason Feingold's son had recently passed the bar and joined his practice, and Garrett Reed's wife had quietly left him the year before. Stacia had played tennis against Muffin Reed in the all-city championship, and was not surprised to hear she had taken off for California with the Oak Hollow tennis pro. It required hours of tedious conversation during church coffee hour to glean the nuggets of useful information on the important people of Magnuson, but Stacia felt it was worth it. Connection was influence.

At 11:15, Stacia pulled into the small visitor parking lot beside City Hall. She liked to make her entrance after the school board had gone through the tedious tasks of opening pleasantries and reviewing the minutes from the last meeting. She quickly reviewed her notes on the proposed redistricting plan before climbing down from the cab of her Jeep. She wanted to appear to be speaking from the heart when she gave the school board her thoughts on the plan, rather than notes.

The late morning sun reflecting off the art deco brass doors forced

Stacia to keep her giant white sunglasses on until she was inside the dim lobby. City Hall was cool after the growing humidity. Stacia pulled the edges of her bright pink lace cardigan more securely over her bare shoulders. Out of deference to the staid board, she wore a simple navy sheath with only some pink and white ribbon as embellishment. It's sedate color made the ten-inch scar running down her leg all the more prominent.

"Good morning, Roxanne," she said to the receptionist. "How's your sister doing these days?" Stacia made a point to always ask after Roxanne's youngest sister, Joy, who had been born with Down's Syndrome. Their mother had refused to send her away to an institution and had been much reviled by the proper ladies of Pinnacle Pointe Presbyterian until Stacia and her cousin, Quentin, spoke up on her behalf. In the intervening years, the congregation had come to love Joy and celebrate her achievements.

"She's real good, Miss Stacia. My mama really appreciated you putting in a good word with the manager over at Belk's. She feels so grown up getting on the bus and going off to work every morning."

Stacia signed her name in the visitor log with a flourish. "I just hope it's not too hot for her working in a warehouse." She glanced up at the daily schedule of meetings and hearings posted in plastic moveable letters behind the reception desk. The school board meeting was not listed. "Is the school board meeting in their usual room?"

Roxanne twisted in her chair. "It's not up there? I saw the board members come in a while ago." She spun in her chair and pushed a series of buttons on the massive switchboard console to her right. "I'll call up to Gail in Mr. Feingold's office and find out where they're at."

Stacia stepped away from the reception desk while Roxanne made the call and looked around the lobby. Magnuson City Hall represented Magnuson well. Her grandfather and Mr. Magnuson had bullied the city planners into hiring the same architect that had designed the Empire State building in New York and the Hill Building over in Durham. The art deco architecture may have seemed dated next to the sleek new steel and concrete buildings that had sprouted up around it during the last few decades, however Stacia hoped future generations would come to appreciate the arched figures etched into the marble walls and stylized sconces that looked like water flowing over stone.

Even if one out of a hundred citizens recognized the reference to the hydroelectric industry that built their city, the building was a success.

Stacia paused in front of a display of children's artwork near the elevator bay. It was an honor for a child to have their work displayed at City Hall, but the children would want their drawings back before the end of the school year. She made a mental note to speak to Kitty about using the space over the summer to advertise one of her Art Center projects.

"Miss Stacia," Roxanne said. Stacia turned back to her with a questioning smile. Roxanne sounded almost apologetic as she said, "The school board is meeting with some consultants in one of the conference rooms today."

Stacia pushed the up button next to the gilt elevator doors. "Which one?" The doors whooshed open before Roxanne responded. Stacia held the door with her arm. "Roxanne?"

"I'm sorry, Miss Stacia. The meeting isn't open to the public."

Stacia pulled her arm back and let the doors glide shut. "Not open to the public? But—" Stacia cut her words short. It would be inappropriate to finish her thought out loud. "My goodness, silly me. I must have read the article in the newspaper wrong." She pulled her sunglasses off the top of her head and propped them on her nose. "Oh well, I'll just have to give Jason Feingold a call to give him my two cents. Say hey to your mama for me."

Stacia walked out to her Jeep and flung her cardigan and bag across the front seat.

Those no good cowards. If they think they can quietly bulldoze their ridiculous redistricting plan through by keeping it behind closed doors until it's too late for anyone to do anything about it, they've got another think coming. They can't just bring in a bunch of smooth-talking New York consultants and change things without consulting the people of Magnuson. They have to have public hearings.

Don't they?

The Jeep's clutch complained as she quickly reversed out of her parking space. She liked to think the school board would consult the prominent families of Magnuson before making such big changes, but she wasn't so sure anymore. Times were changing. She welcomed the fact that there was more and more racial equality in Magnuson and that women were beginning to make some headway, yet she feared she was falling behind. The old ways of exacting change became less and less effective every year. The Tate family name held less sway now that so many new people were streaming into Magnuson and didn't know the history of how the city had been built.

Stacia didn't go directly home. Weldon and his brother were working from the house that day and she didn't want to admit that she hadn't been able to speak to the board. Instead, she swung into the offices of Tate Real Estate to hash out the situation with her cousin, Quentin. They usually saw eye to eye on how the Tates should represent themselves in their city.

She left her Jeep in front of the door and stormed into Tate Real Estate. A young agent popped up from her desk and intercepted Stacia on her way to Quentin's office. "Can I help you?"

Stacia maneuvered around her and pushed open the door to Quentin's wood-paneled office. She reared back to the agent. She was unfamiliar to Stacia. Quentin's real estate associates seem to come and go like mayflies. "Where's Quentin?"

"He's out with a client, ma'am. Is there something I can help you with?" The agent tried to steer Stacia back into the reception area. "We have some fabulous new listings. If you'll come back to the desk, I can show you a gorgeous house in Overlook that just went on the market."

Stacia walked further into the office and dropped her bag on the desk. "Excuse me?"

"I'm sorry," the young woman said. She glanced around for one of the other agents to come to her assistance. "Are you looking to sell your house, Mrs.—?"

"Don't you know who I am?" Stacia picked up the silver frame from the corner of the desk and shoved it in the young agent's face. It was a picture of her and Quentin arm-in-arm at the Overlook Christmas party. Quentin liked to be photographed with his petite cousin to make him look taller in comparison. "I'm Stacia Tate Curran."

The young agent took a step back. "I'm so sorry. I didn't know Quentin had a sister."

Stacia wasn't in the mood to explain that they were cousins, not siblings and didn't correct the young woman. "When will he be back?"

"Not for a few hours. He's out with a couple down from Minnesota.

They're only here for a few days, so they're seeing, like, twenty houses. Do you want to wait?"

"Sure," Stacia replied as she closed the door on the agent. She wished Quentin was there, but she would accept cooling off for an hour or two in his office. She sat down at the desk and put her head down on the linen blotter.

No one seems to know who I am anymore. There was a time when I couldn't get away from people who knew my mama and daddy poking their nose into my business. People used to be interested in what the Tates and the Magnusons were doing. Hell, the year Bitsy and I were debs, they did a two page spread on the party in the Magnuson Register.

Hmmm, the Register.

Stacia raised her head and looked around the office. Behind her, on an antique Stickley table, sat Quentin's Smith-Corona. She threaded a piece of paper into the machine and started typing. If the school board wasn't going to listen to what she had to say about their redistricting plans, the newspaper would. Over the next several hours, Stacia pecked out her thoughts, first in a vitriolic deluge of words, followed by several less angst-filled drafts. By the time Quentin returned, she had four concise paragraphs of well-reasoned arguments for why the proposed redistricting plan would not serve the children of Magnuson, and calling for public hearings.

"Hey, Cousin," Quentin said as he entered his office and peeled off his seersucker sports coat. "What brings you by today?" His blue eyes, so like her own, twinkled. "Do you need pledges for that race you and Kitty are doing?"

"We're not doing that race, after all. We both have too much on our plates right now."

He put his briefcase on the desk. "I heard something about that? How's Kitty holding up?"

"She'll be fine. She has a plan." Stacia crumpled up the first drafts of her letter to the editor and tossed them in the waste paper basket. "How was your day?"

"I think I have that house on Redbud sold to a couple from Minnesota."

"I hope they go into escrow before they realize what that new redistricting plan is going to do to the schools around here. Did you read the article about it in last week's paper?" Stacia shoved the editorial across the desk for Quentin to read.

He read it once, moved to the globe near the window, and opened it to reveal a drinks cart. "You can't put your name on this, Ladybug."

"You don't agree with what I said?"

"I didn't say that." He poured two glasses of whiskey, then sat down across from her. "You make some good points."

"And?"

"You need to stay out of it. Don't get involved."

Stacia blinked at her cousin. She couldn't believe what she was hearing. "Don't write the editorial?"

"I mean don't say anything at all." He took a long sip from his drink. "Magnuson is not ready for forced integration, Ladybug. People are going to revolt when they figure out that the school board plans to distribute the black kids from downtown throughout the city and move the white kids from the southern sections to downtown."

"Exactly! Bussing isn't the solution to our problems. We need to make the downtown schools as good as the schools out here, not just mix the kids up like bingo balls, and hope to get a winner. People won't stand for it. They'll put their kids into private schools before they see them bussed downtown."

"That's what I just said." Quentin swirled his glass before taking a gulp of whiskey. "They won't understand." He lifted his wire-rimmed glasses off his nose and rubbed his eyes. He seemed war weary. "I'm already getting questions from clients about what 'type' of children go to the schools around here. Northerners may be more polite about it, but they're just as racist as the folks around here. There's going to be a lot of mud-slinging before this is done. Don't get your hands dirty."

Stacia sat back in her chair and stared at her cousin. The ice in her drink cracked and fell into the amber liquid. "I have to say something. It's our responsibility."

"Then send in your editorial under a fake name." Quentin got up and started unpacking his briefcase. "It's a good editorial. You make excellent points. People will read it." He walked around the desk and put his hand on her shoulder. "You just can't use the Tate name. The fine ladies of Pinnacle Point Presbyterian would cast you out like a leper. Think about what that would do to your father."

eight

Kitty knew she had an appointment with a young sculptor to discuss his application to display several pieces in the exhibit space she had recently carved out of the Arts Center's expansive lobby; she couldn't remember when the appointment was. Her memory was not what it used to be. At one point, she'd been able to rattle off who painted what canvas when and where for an entire museum wing. Now, she frequently forgot people's names minutes after she met them. She relied on her tooled leather Filofax to remember things for her. She frantically flipped through its pages. It was imperative she make this new interactive display space a success because it could relaunch her career as an exhibits coordinator after eighteen years of being a full-time mother. Perhaps if she identified some fresh new talent, she could ride their coattails to a better position at a bigger museum.

She clearly recalled writing the sculptor's name and number down when he had called the week before; she simply couldn't remember on which piece of paper. She upended her pocketbook on the kitchen table and sorted through the flotsam and jetsam of her life. Among the tubes of lipstick and wadded up tissues, she found the dry cleaning slip with Heath Bigelow's phone number on it. They were meeting at ten that morning.

Kitty rolled her eyes and transferred his information to her Filofax. *Heath Bigelow. What a stupid name. His real name is probably Bill or Jimmy. He probably thinks Heath makes him sound cool. What a loser.* She crumpled the piece of paper and held it over the waste paper basket before she realized what was in her hand - a dry cleaning slip for a week's worth of Seth's dress shirts. *Should I pick up those shirts? It's not like Seth's ever going to need them. Then again, if I'm supposed to expect him to come back, should I pick them up?*

She ran the slip across the edge of the counter until it was smooth again. She would retrieve the shirts, then take them to the shelter. He had nice clothes; someone should wear them.

★★★

Her meeting with Heath Bigelow went as she'd foreseen - his sculptures were unnecessarily confrontational for a municipal arts center. Children passed through the Arts Center lobby on their way to music lessons and watercolor classes. Kitty couldn't put lewd depictions of women in the new gallery space, especially derivative lewd depictions. Even though she had only a teaspoon of power over twenty-square-feet of a public building, she would wield that power in any way she saw fit, and it wasn't going to be in service of a patronizing young man named Heath.

After the meeting, she went to the dry cleaners, then drove downtown to the An Open Hand Ministries. Signs along the driveway directed people to the right for residential relief or to the left for nutritional relief. Kitty laughed to herself at the fancy names given to a warm bed and free meal.

The square solid building, its large windows propped open with planks of wood, reminded Kitty of Roger Williams Elementary, where she and Rose had gone to school. The homeless shelter was one of the old school buildings the city had decided were not worth bringing up to code and had sold on the cheap in the Sixties. The crumbling old foundations couldn't support the weight of elevator shafts and retrofitting the old buildings with air conditioning vents was impractical. It was cheaper to simply build new schools in the suburban parts of the city. In what had once been a bus lot, Kitty pulled up to the curb and pulled the shirts from the backseat of the Volkswagen. She walked up the broad stone steps and yanked on the door marked 'OFFICE.' It wouldn't budge. She tried the other three doors across the front of the building before noticing a handwritten sign Scotch-taped to the inside of the mesh reinforced window. The office was only open for a few hours in the afternoon. Kitty leaned her head against the glass. "Now what do I do?"

A little boy with big brown eyes and a bowl cut that made him look like he had walked out of a Mayan temple painting appeared beside her. "Hey lady, you looking for Father Mike?"

"Is that who I give donations to?"

"I guess so."

"Where can I find him right now?"

"I'll take you." The little boy took her hand and dragged her back down the steps.

Kitty worried about leaving her car unattended in front of the building, but there was no getting away from the little boy's viselike grip on her hand. "Shouldn't you be in school?"

"My dad is trying to get the school to let me in."

"They have to let you go to school. It's the law. All you need is proof of residence." She paused and looked at the boy again. He looked well fed and his clothes were clean, but they were worn and several sizes too large. The boy's sneakers were held together with duct tape. Kitty wondered how this boy came to be at a men's homeless shelter.

She pulled away from the boy as he dragged her around the corner of the building. "Where are you taking me?"

The little boy pulled her along faster than she could walk in her espadrille wedges. "The chapel."

"There's a chapel? This used to be a public school."

He ran through a set of double doors into what had once been the school's gymnasium. The basketball hoops still hung from the ceiling at one end of the room. At the other end, a movable screen had a crucifix attached to the center panel. The boy ran around the side of the screen. "Padre, esta mujer está buscándote." Kitty slowed her pace when she saw the priest stood off to one side talking to a handful of men. Mass had just ended. The chalice and communion plate were still on a rolling alter, waiting to be loaded back in their battered suitcase.

"Excuse me, Father. I didn't realize you were saying Mass."

The priest smiled and waved to Kitty, but didn't move to come speak to her. Instead he gestured to the rangy young man stacking folding chairs onto a rolling rack. With a short dark beard that made his face appear paler and thinner than it actually was, he reminded Kitty of an El Greco portrait.

Kitty moved toward the young man and held out the dry cleaning bag. "I, umm, I brought some clothes for your people."

The young man brushed his hands against the thighs of his faded jeans and took the bag from her. "Groovy!"

A jolt shot through Kitty's body as they made eye contact. There was a unique depth in the young man's green eyes.

"Men's or women's clothes?"

"Men's. They're in excellent condition." Kitty felt her cheeks color as the young man's gaze ran over her jade green jumpsuit. She knew she should leave; she'd done what she came to do, but couldn't seem to move her feet toward the door.

"Do you need a receipt for your taxes?" The young man gestured to the few remaining chairs near the rack. "I'm Aaron, by the way. Can I offer you a cup of rotten coffee?"

"That would be nice." Kitty sat down and held her purse in her lap with both hands as she watched Aaron fetch two paper cups of coffee from the urn on the other side of the room. Father Mike was still talking to a small group of men near the rolling screen. When Aaron returned, she said, "I hope I didn't upset Father Mike by barging in like that."

"It's fine. It's casual." Aaron took a sip from his cup and gestured to the bag of dress shirts hanging over the back of another chair. "Death or divorce?"

Kitty pressed her lips together. She was beginning to lose touch of what the truth was. The plan required her to lie to the Lookers, but this man was a complete stranger. He knew nothing about her yet. "Neither, actually. My husband seems to have disappeared off the face of the Earth. He was on his way home from a business trip one day and just never showed up." Kitty sat down. "He's a bit of a tomcat so I'm assuming he's run off with another woman."

Shut up, Kitty! Why are you telling him any of this? Just leave the shirts and go.

"Why would anyone leave a pretty lady like you for a minute longer than necessary?"

"He managed."

"Children?"

"Two."

"And you are?"

"Kitty. Well, Mary Katherine."

"Mary Katherine is a much better name than Kitty."

Kitty smiled. "That's what my sister Rose says."

"Is she as pretty as you are?"

"No," Kitty replied. She felt her ears turn red and bit the inside of her lip.

"So, what do you do with your time, Mary Katherine?"

"I curate art exhibits part-time, but mostly I'm just a housewife."

"There's nothing just about raising kids," Aaron said. "Would I have seen any of your exhibits?"

"There was a folk art quilt exhibit and I did a benefit last year at the Arts Center to raise money for art programs at the women's prison."

Aaron looked at Kitty as if seeing the art expert beneath the suburban mom. "The sweaters thing? It was awesome the way you put the women's pictures next to each of the sweaters. Really deep."

"Thank you." She felt herself blush in a whole different way. "It turned out well."

The sun moved out from behind a cloud and illuminated a large stained-glass cross which cast a pool of green and blue across the marred gym floor. Kitty jumped up. "Oh my goodness!" She stepped closer to get a better look at the cross hanging in front of the high gymnasium windows. What she initially thought were large glass roundels making up the bulk of the cross, turned out to be the bottoms of wine bottles. The rest of the cross was broken pieces of glass cleverly placed around the round pieces to create the effect of water flowing through stones.

"I call it Liquid Grace," Aaron said over Kitty's shoulder.

"It's amazing." Kitty couldn't pull her eyes away from the glass. "How did you get someone to donate such a piece to the shelter?"

"It wasn't a donation. It was commissioned."

Kitty spun around to see if Aaron was joking. "Really?" She looked across the room at the group of men playing basketball. "Who's the artist? I'd love to meet him." Aaron's green eyes twinkled above a wide grin. "You?"

"I've been here for two years now on a community-enrichment grant."

"Where's your studio?"

"I work here as well, so I use the old art room in basement."

A plan began to hatch in Kitty's mind. "Do you have more pieces I could see? Are they all like this?"

"No. Most of them are freestanding."

Kitty leaned forward. "Tell me more. Where did you train?"

Aaron looked down at the toes of his combat boots. "I did a year at art school, but ran out of money. As soon as I left school, I got drafted. After 'Nam, I wandered around for a few years, worked as a roadie, got into trouble. Eventually, I started working again and ended up here."

An hour later, Kitty was sitting cross-legged in the center of the floor of the abandoned elementary school's art room. Aaron sat across from her, so close that their knees nearly touched. On the other side of the room, near his welding equipment, hung a heavy leather apron and a pair of gauntlet gloves at the end of a line of paint-strewn pint-sized smocks.

Kitty fondled a wine bottle shaped sculpture made up of four separate bottles that had been broken, then fused back together. "This is exquisite. What do you call it?"

There was a hitch in Aaron's voice when he replied, "1972."

"Why?" She ran her finger across the joint between a green section and a clear section like a raised scar.

"'72 was the year I stopped drinking." He took the bottle from her hands and spun it on his forefinger.

I never thought to commemorate the year I stopped drinking. I guess it hasn't even been a whole year. Maybe I will at some point, assuming I make it another year.

"I get it now. You were broken and got fused back together."

"Exactly," Aaron replied. He grinned at her. She noticed that his eye tooth was chipped. She wondered if it was a casualty of his drinking days or if it was from a childhood accident. Aaron seemed to be the type of man who had been a rough and tumble boy.

Aaron looked at Kitty in a way that made her uncomfortably aware that they were alone. She liked the sensation that look gave her. This was the kind of man that Kitty wanted in her life; dark, artistic, stimulating. She was so done with the country club set, with their gin and tonics and fake attention. This guy was actually interested in her and very interesting.

Oh my god, what am I thinking? This guy is at least ten years younger than me.

Kitty got up and stepped over to one of the three sculptures Aaron was working on. The piece was a collection of scrap metal vaguely in the shape of a man and pierced with Jack Daniels bottles.

"Is this a riff on St. Sebastian?"

Aaron got up and stood a little too closely behind her. Kitty wondered if he could hear her heart pounding. In that moment, she felt very much alive. "Very good. That's St Francis over there."

Kitty stepped away, ostensibly to look more closely at the sculpture of Saint Francis. It was unfinished but she could already make out soup can birds alighting on the arms and something resembling a rabbit near the feet. "Are these marigolds around his feet made out of traffic cones? Why found objects?"

"I don't know. Why does anyone do anything? These will eventually end up in a mediation garden out back, so they have to be weatherproof and I like the idea of making beautiful things out of garbage. It seems appropriate for a shelter."

Kitty couldn't argue with that. Art didn't conform to logic. "How did you construct the cross that's hanging in the chapel upstairs?"

"I failed a few times before I got to what I had in my head." He played with the buttons of his pink oxford shirt. There were burn holes in the sleeves and the collar was frayed. "It was easy enough to find the bottles. At first I walked around downtown and bummed them off the drunks that sleep under the highway overpasses. Then I found out that the city has these drop-off recycling centers."

"Yes, I know where those are." When Kitty was drinking heavily, she had gone to one of the drop-off centers to dispose of her empties because she couldn't let her neighbors see her put them out in the monthly Overlook recycling drive.

"So, you've seen the huge dumpsters filled with glass bottles? One day, I happened to be there when the guys came to empty the dumpsters. I got talking to them, they were both fellow vets, and they let me come back with them to the recycling plant." Aaron's face lit up like a kid remembering a trip to Disneyland. "It was amazing. They have every shape and color of glass bottles I could ever want."

"You said it took you several attempts to get the cross the way you envisioned it. How so?"

"It took me awhile to figure out how to make it strong enough but still be transparent."

"Traditionally, people used lead or copper to join the pieces."

"I didn't have access to either of those things, so I played with the

73

materials I did have."

"Fascinating. What did you try?"

"Well, first I tried wood epoxy, but that couldn't take the weight of the glass, so I started experimenting with cement. I ended up using tile grout." Aaron smiled a crooked grin. "You'd be surprised what gets thrown out at the end of a construction job." Kitty recalled the piles of trash the construction crews left on the curb when a new house was built. Thinking of Overlook pulled her back to reality.

She stood up and hooked her pocketbook over her shoulder. "I'm very interested in what you're doing here. I think other people would be too." Kitty took a few steps toward the door. "I don't remember if I mentioned it, but I curate the new exhibit space for the Arts Center downtown." Aaron stopped smiling at her like a hyena and cocked his head. "I'd have to run it by a committee of people first, but I'd like to display some of your work."

Aaron took a step back. "Far out! Like an official show?"

"I don't know how official it would be," Kitty said. "We aren't a New York gallery, but we do get a little bit of press." She rustled around her bag for an Art Center brochure. "Why don't you give me a call in a few days and we can talk?" She turned and walked away. *Oh my god, I hope he calls.*

nine

Now that they were a one car family, Kitty had to fit in her hours at the Art Center around Becky and Bobby's schedule. She was beginning to regret leaving the Volvo beside that boat ramp. It had been six weeks. She'd assumed someone would have found it by now and alerted the authorities, but no one seemed to care that Seth was gone; sadly no one seemed to have even noticed. From the outside, Seth appeared to have such a full life; a nice home, a nice job, a nice wife. She had cracked open the thin veneer over his hollow reality, as well as his skull.

A week before graduation, Becky dropped her off at the Arts Council. Kitty needed to use the postage machine and hoped to talk to the director about getting a raise. She was willing to work more hours and take on more responsibilities, if it meant more money. When she went into the office to see if she could speak to him, the receptionist pointed to a pile of boxes in the corner of the room.

"Thank goodness you're here. That's all for you."

After the success of her quilt exhibit the year before, word had spread that Kitty was curating an exhibit of North Carolina pottery. Now, random potters were sending her samples of their work in hopes of being featured in the exhibit. The pieces were, for the most part, gorgeous, but she had nowhere to store them. She didn't have an office, just a box stashed in a cabinet in the conference room. Most of the pieces were sent back to the potters C.O.D. She'd made arrangements with the figure-drawing instructor to stash the few suitable pieces in his classroom.

"Some of the boxes are real heavy. Want me to get someone to help you carry them to the conference room for you?"

"No, I can manage," Kitty replied. She was glad she was wearing slacks and a simple knit blouse. Going through all the boxes and moving the ones she wanted to keep would be sweaty work. "Is there a hand truck in the storage room I can use?"

"Sure, shug. I'll get one of the security guards to find it."

Kitty took three small boxes from the top of the pile. "Is Mr. Prescott in? I need a minute to talk to him about a few things."

The receptionist twitched her nose and looked away. "I heard about your husband walking out on you."

"He's left me in a real bind. Do you know of any full-time positions, here or close by?"

"Mr. Prescott will be in after lunch, but they don't like hiring single women for those positions. That type of position usually involves travel."

Heaven forbid a woman travel by herself. She might talk to a man.

Kitty carried the boxes to the conference room and searched for the old X-Acto knife she'd pilfered from the print shop. The potters usually put so much reinforced packing tape on the boxes, scissors were useless. The first box contained a hand-thrown tea cup in shades of olive and gold, like half the other boxes she'd received. She taped the box back up, slapped a return-to-sender sticker on the top, and put it to the side. The next box was pretty much the same.

The third box had been hand-delivered. Instead of reinforced shipping tape, it was closed with red and white cotton string like an Italian bakery would use to tie up a box of cookies. A torn envelope with her name on it was tucked under the strings. Kitty's breath caught in her throat as she opened the box and the contents caught the light. She slid her fingers down the side of the cardboard and pulled out a dented hubcap filled with layered shards of pale green and brown glass soldered together to form blossoms. The leading edge of each petal was left jagged and raw. The box could have only come from one person, and Kitty already knew Aaron well enough to know he'd intentionally left the edges dangerously sharp.

At the bottom of the box was a piece of torn notebook paper. It read: I can't sleep for thinking about you, so I made this. These flowers will never fade away.

Kitty sat down hard in the chair behind her and cradled the hubcap in her palms. The flowers were exquisite, but it was the thought of Aaron spending a sleepless night creating them for her that made her feel lightheaded. Seth had never done anything remotely that romantic. She considered calling him to thank him for the gift, but she didn't trust herself not to say something foolish. Aaron made her feel as impulsive as a teenager.

She opted to send him a note instead. She found a handmade notecard cast off by the printmaking class and scrawled:

Thank you for sending the glass hellebores (I assume they are hellebores). They are exquisite. I hope you chose that flower for its color, rather than its meaning in the language of flowers - scandal. It's a bit scandalous to know the thought of me kept you up.

I hope to see more of your work soon.

Fondly,

Mary Katherine

Kitty blushed at her words; however, she didn't rip up the note. She licked it shut before she changed her mind about sending it. As she turned it over to address the back, she realized she was sending such an intimate note to a man whom she'd met only once. She didn't even know his last name. She did feel scandalous. As she tucked the flowers back into their box and tied it shut so no one could see her private piece of art, she wondered if Aaron knew that hellebores were poisonous at the root.

★★★

Four hours later, there was a knock on the door of the conference room. Kitty scooted around the pile of boxes destined to go back to the post office and swung the door open with a broad smile. Her face fell when she saw it was her daughter.

"Expecting someone else?"

"Mr. Prescott." Kitty pulled out a chair from around the conference room table and motioned for Becky to sit down. "I was hoping to talk to him before you came to pick me up. How was the graduation rehearsal?"

"Boring. We practiced lining up and slowly walking in a straight line."

"I think you can handle that." Kitty carefully taped a box shut and smoothed a label over the top. "Anybody say anything about graduation parties? You must be one of the few kids going off to an Ivy League school." She added the box to the pile. "I'd think you'd be the belle of the ball these days."

"No way!" Becky got up and walked to the window. With her back to her mother, she said, "People are kind of blowing me off these days. I don't know if it's the fact that I'm going to Brown in the fall, the whole Dad thing, or what."

"Oh sweetie, that can't be true. You're just feeling self-conscious."

Becky spun around. "Mom, I am not just feeling self-conscious. Nobody wants me around anymore. They're always whispering behind my back about how Dad ran off with some tramp." Becky rubbed the back of her neck. "Someone even thought he'd gone to live with Mrs. Kaur."

"Marni? He would never!"

"I know that, but it's not such a crazy idea. They did have an affair last year."

Kitty shook her head with a frown.

"Don't be such a spaz, Mom. Everyone knew."

Kitty turned to place the box in her hand on the pile against the wall. Not only had killing Seth not solved any of her problems, it had created a whole new set of them. "Can we talk about this later? I need to arrange for all these to be taken down to the loading dock. Then I really do need to talk to Mr. Prescott about expanding my responsibilities here, or picking up a few more freelance projects, or something. I don't know how I'm going to pay next month's bills." She tucked the box from Aaron in her tote bag and walked out of the conference room. "Why don't I meet you in the car in a few minutes?"

Twenty minutes later, Kitty slid into the passenger seat of the Bug. Paul Simon was singing about the Fifty Ways To Leave Your Lover on the radio as Kitty kicked off her pumps. A red line cut across the tops of her feet where they had swollen over the edge of the shoes. Kitty would have to keep wearing them. There was no money to shop for a more comfortable pair.

"Did you talk to him?"

"For all the good it did me. He can't, or won't, help me." She rubbed her ankles in an attempt to get the blood flowing in her feet again.

"Typical man. He loved it when I was an over-educated housewife wanting to work a few hours, but now that I need to provide for a family, I'm something to be ashamed of. I went in there looking for a raise. Now, I'm worried he's going to fire me."

Becky turned the car off and shifted in the driver's seat. "Okay, that's it!"

Kitty looked up at her. When did she start sounding so much like Rose?

"I wasn't going to say anything about this because I thought you'd need me at home this summer, but Coach Campbell offered me a job at a camp this summer."

"That's kind of last minute. Don't camps start right after Memorial Day?"

"They started last week, actually. Coach told me they had to fire the head lifeguard and asked me if I could go up and work until the Fourth of July."

"I don't know, Becky. Where is this camp?"

"Somewhere in northern Virginia." Becky looked out the windshield and loudly exhaled in exasperation in the way only an eighteen-year-old could. "And, as if you're not wondering, they'll pay me. Coach said he could even get Bobby a spot as a junior counselor. I don't think they'd pay him, but he could go to camp for free in exchange for watching a cabin-full of little kids and working in the arts and crafts cabin or something."

"Does Coach think we're so destitute that we need charity?" Kitty looked around to see if anyone was looking before hiking up her skirt and slipping off her pantyhose. There was no way she was going to cram her feet back into those pumps. She would have to go home barefoot.

Becky started the car and let it idle. "We are destitute, Mom."

"Don't be so dramatic. We have a roof over our head and we're not going hungry yet."

"You just said, you can't pay the bills and Dad isn't sending you checks or anything." She shifted the car into reverse then pulled out into the afternoon traffic.

The idea of Becky leaving home months sooner than planned broke Kitty's heart, yet she saw the advantage of her taking the job.

They needed the money. As it was, Becky was going to have to pay for all her school expenses out of the trust fund Kitty's father had set up for his grandchildren. Kitty wasn't going to be able to give her anything for incidentals. This job would give Becky some wiggle room. Also, with the children gone, the weekly grocery bill would be cut in half. "If you did take the job, how would I get you up there?"

"I'm sure I could go up with the Campbells. Mrs. Campbell does something with the horses there."

"That would solve our car problem."

"So, you'll let me go?"

"Do you want to go?"

Becky frowned as she pulled onto the expressway. "Honestly, yeah." Kitty was pushed into her seat as Becky shifted into overdrive. She drove like a man, confident and unafraid. "I am so over Magnuson. I just don't want to be here anymore."

"Gee, thanks Becky."

"Now who's being dramatic?"

Kitty sighed and watched the trees zoom by. *She really is sounding more and more like Rose every day. Maybe it would be for the best if they spent less time together.*

"Let me think about it."

★★★

That evening, instead of going on her usual after-dinner jog while Bobby watched reruns of The Six Million Dollar Man, Kitty sorted the stack of bills they'd received into piles on the floor of her home office. She wasn't sure where to start. In all the years they'd been married, Seth never talked to her about money. He gave her a handful of cash every week to cover groceries and incidentals, and if she wanted something more, she wrote a check. Seth had a good job. They lived in a lovely home. Money wasn't an issue.

She started by collecting all of Seth's pay stubs and putting them in chronological order, then did the same with their mortgage statements and utility bills. As she suspected, Seth's salary more than covered their reasonable mortgage payments and living expenses. *Okay, then. We're fine. Becky doesn't need to take that job. She can stay here until it's time to leave for Rhode Island in August.*

She leaned against the wall and opened their most recent bank statement from NCNB. The balance was only $200. *How could that be? I haven't paid the mortgage or electrical bill yet.* She glanced at the remaining piles. *Could there be a savings account somewhere? Would Seth have had investments?* Kitty seriously doubted her big galoot of a husband would ever play the stock market. That would be too much work.

Daisy trotted into the room and lay on her neat piles. Kitty rubbed the golden retriever's belly for a few minutes while she thought of what to do next. She remembered the envelope that Seth's secretary had slipped in the file box she had brought home from his office. Perhaps he corresponded with his broker from the office. That could explain the lack of funds in their checking account. She gave Daisy one last belly rub, and went to find that box.

The envelope didn't solve Kitty's bank account dilemma. It added to it. Seth had two additional credit cards billed to his office, rather than their home. The charges on the American Express card all took place in the Charlotte area, so it wasn't difficult to see why he'd hidden it from her. Still, Shelly hadn't used it for more than rent and utilities. The other credit card had no new charges on it, however it had a balance of $4,000. *Wow, I can't even pay the interest on that.* She upended the envelope on the desk, hoping there was treasure at the bottom. An envelope from Wachovia Bank slid out and fell to the floor. Kitty heaved a sigh of relief. *Thank goodness, there's another bank account.*

She picked it up and slipped her thumb nail under the flap. It wasn't a statement for a savings account statement, or even an additional checking account. The envelope contained a mortgage statement. Her scalp tingled as though she'd been plunged into cold water. She read the statement through three times before it sank in. Seth had taken out a $20,000 second mortgage on their house and was six months behind on the payments.

Kitty ran to the kitchen extension and called Quentin Tate. "Hey, Kitty. How you doing?"

"Quick question. If I were to sell our house, what would you say I could ask for it?"

"Well now, prices in Overlook have been holding up pretty well and this would be a good time to sell, before the redistricting plan goes in." He paused for a moment and Kitty could hear him flipping through sheets of paper. "You could probably ask $40,000, although it could take a while to sell it. I hate to ask such a personal question, but have you heard from Seth?"

"Not yet," Kitty said.

"I know you're just asking a question, but do you know if the mortgage in Seth's name or in both of your names?"

She knew the second mortgage was in just Seth's name, since she hadn't known about it ten minutes ago and had certainly never signed any bank documents about it. She pulled the phone cord around the desk to reach the pile of statements for their primary mortgage and opened the top statement. "How would I know that, Quentin? Would it say it on the statements?"

"Do you have one there? Look at the top of the page; is your name under Seth's?"

"No." Her stomach flipped in her belly. "What does that mean for me? Do I have to keep paying the mortgage?"

"You should talk to a lawyer," Quentin replied. "I know in a divorce people need to keep paying until the divorce is final or they agree to sell the house and split the equity."

"About that, what exactly is equity and how does that work?"

"It just means the value of the house versus how much you have it mortgaged for."

"Of course," Kitty said with a little laugh. "I knew that. The terminology trips me up sometimes."

"You've lived there for quite few years so you'll probably have at least $10,000 in equity if you were to sell. Kitty, I don't mean to pry, but what are you planning to do? I can give you the names of some good lawyers."

"Thanks, Quentin, you're a peach. I think I'll give Seth another month or two to come to his senses. I'm sure it will all work out." They ended the call with empty promises to get together and hung up. Kitty lay down on the floor next to the dog. "What are we going to do, girl? I'm sinking deeper and deeper into debt and I can't even sell this place." The dog nuzzled against her shoulder. "Got any money squirreled away in your doghouse?"

★★★

That evening, Kitty decided that they weren't going to buy anything more than the bare necessities - milk, eggs, bread. They could eat out of the cabinets for at least a few weeks. She went out to the garage and took a quick inventory of the deep freeze. There was enough meat in there to last her a month. Then, they would live on rice and beans if necessary. When Becky came home, Kitty pulled her into the laundry room. "Have you spoken to Coach about working at that camp again?"

"Not yet. Why?"

"If you go, do you really think you could take Bobby with you?"

"Seriously? Is that what you want?"

"It's not what I want at all." Kitty opened the dryer and started folding towels. She needed to do something with her hands to hide how upset she was. "I looked at the bills while you were out, and... well, we're broke. I don't know what I'm going to do, but if you can make some money for yourself, I say go for it." She tossed a towel in the basket at her feet. "If Bobby is out of town too, then I can take any little curating opportunities that come along without worrying about leaving him alone all the time."

Becky opened the laundry room door. "Hey, Bobby! Mom says we can go."

Kitty slammed the door to the dryer. She hated when her children seemed to have a better perspective on their family situation than she did. She was the mother. She needed to look out for them in life, not the other way around.

By that weekend, the arrangements had been made. Bobby could make a few dollars as a junior counselor helping out in the camp kitchen and live in one of the cabins with the younger campers. Becky would be head lifeguard and live in a bunk house with the other staff. They would be home for a week in July, then perhaps go back for another few weeks.

On Saturday morning, Kitty and Becky carried Bobby's bag out to the front steps and dropped it beside Becky's overstuffed duffle bag. Kitty stuck her head back in the foyer and yelled up to Bobby, "Did you pack enough undershirts? What about hiking boots? Are there hiking boots in this bag?"

"They're on my feet, Mom," Bobby yelled back. "I couldn't find them 'cause someone's been messing with my closet."

"That would have been me," she called back. "You'd grown out of half the things in there so I packed them up for the charity box."

"He thought you'd sold them," Becky said.

Kitty tried to smile. "We're not that broke yet."

"Are you going to be all right with us gone all summer?"

Kitty unzipped Bobby's bag and inspected its contents. "Don't you worry your little head about that."

"Really, Mom? Don't worry my little head?" Becky leaned in so that she was nose to nose with her mother. "Aren't we a bit past that at this point? In the last two months, I've gotten into an Ivy League school that I am terrified I'm not smart enough for and my father may as well have been abducted by aliens. Oh, and yeah, my mother is sending me and my little brother out of town because she doesn't have the money to feed us."

"I'm doing the best I can, Rebecca."

"Dream on, Mom. You are so not!" Kitty zipped up Bobby's bag and walked away. She told herself that as much as Becky's words stung, she needed to act like the adult. Becky was lashing out because she was scared, although she suspected her daughter meant every word.

A battered red pick-up truck with Meadowlark Farm painted on the side pulled into the driveway. The engine knocked and pinged for a moment after Coach Campbell turned off the ignition. Kitty hoped the truck could make it all the way to Virginia. A mannish woman in her fifties with a grey braid looped over her shoulder sat in the passenger seat. Kitty had met Coach Campbell many times at swim meets and awards nights. She hadn't ever given any thought to his marital status. He was a coach and nothing more in her mind. He rolled down his window and stuck his head out. "You ready to boogie, Becky?"

Mrs. Campbell opened her door and gracefully jumped down. A typical horsewoman, she was small, but had a powerful physical presence. She wore dungarees, a man's shirt, and boots as if she had walked off the set of a cowboy movie. Kitty half expected the woman to ask where the young'uns were 'cuz they had some rustlers to track down. Instead she spoke with a quiet, almost patrician voice. "I hope you like The Beatles, Rebecca, because the eight track player is stuck again. Maybe you can help me get the cartridge out."

"No problem, Willow," Becky said. She flung the bags into the bed of the pick-up and pulled herself up into the cab.

Kitty descended the steps as if she were coming outside for the first time that morning. "Hello! You must be Mrs. Campbell. Thank you so much for letting Becky and Bobby drive up with you."

"Our pleasure," Willow replied. "I always enjoy hanging out with Rebecca and it will be a big help to have a third driver."

"Will you stop for the night? Let me give Becky money for a room."

"Not necessary," Coach Campbell said across the front seat. "It's not that far so we'll drive straight through." He hooked a thumb over the bench seat. "Willow rigged the space behind the seat here with a sleeping bag and stuff so the kids can stretch out if they get tired."

"I get sleepy driving to horse shows and I don't like to leave the horses alone, so I usually find a rest stop and take a nap back there."

"You pull a horse trailer all by yourself?"

"The truck does most of the work," Willow said with a wry smile. "I just steer."

Kitty saw why Becky liked this woman. She was gently funny without making Kitty feel insulted. She exuded a sense of calm confidence Kitty rarely felt off the tennis court.

"Who's taking care of your horses while you're away?"

"Most of them are partial boarders so their owners come and muck out their stalls. It would probably be better for my business if I stayed here all summer, but I've been running the equestrian program up at the camp for over thirty years now. I love it, and I do what I love. It's that simple."

Bobby ran out the front door and gave his mother a fleeting kiss before scrambling into the truck next to Becky. Kitty could still feel the dampness from Bobby's lips on her cheek as the Campbell's truck roared out of Azalea Lane. Her children had flown the nest.

Kitty sat down hard on the front steps and stared at three blades of grass growing from a crack in the brick walk.

Is it that simple?

ten

Kitty left her solitary bowl on the drain board after a meal of boxed macaroni and cheese. Without the children, she didn't have the energy to cook real dinners or run the dishwasher. One box of artificial cheese and pasta could feed her for days and cost a matter of pennies. She no longer bothered to clean either. She had cancelled the cleaning service the day Becky and Bobby left for camp so the laundry was piling up, the carpeting on the stairs needed vacuuming, and the plantation shutters were riddled with spiders' webs.

She was brushing orange cheese powder off the counter when she was startled by the phone. The house had been silent all day. Before she could say hello, Betty Oliphant from across the street yelled, "Is everything okay over there? A police car is in your driveway!"

Kitty felt the blood drain from her face. Her eyes went to the windows overlooking the lake. She couldn't see any police boats out on the water or flashing lights. She pulled the phone cord across the kitchen to see out the dining room windows. A single policeman stood in her driveway. They'd send more than one man if they'd found a body. Lumps of dread turned to happy butterflies in her chest.

Finally! They found the car.

"Gotta go, Betty." Kitty hung up before her neighbor could say any more.

Stay calm. Don't look guilty. Stay calm.

She tugged on the fingers of her rubber gloves, then reconsidered. It would have a greater effect if she answered the door with bright yellow appendages. As she walked toward the front door, she slipped on her silly housewife persona like a housecoat. When the bell rang, she counted to thirty before she opened the door. The police officer standing on the front porch barely looked old enough to be out of the police academy.

"Oh my goodness, Officer! Is something the matter?"

"Is this Seth Haskell's residence?"

"Yes." She steadied herself against the door as if about to faint. "He isn't home right now. But can I help?"

"When do you expect him?"

Kitty looked over the policeman's shoulder. Betty Oliphant stood in her front yard talking to Eileen-from-across-the-street. Kitty was happy to see Eileen looking very pregnant after hearing about her repeated miscarriages. She waved to them and made the universal sign for making a phone call before turning back to the policeman.

"I'm not sure. He's…away."

The officer shifted from one foot to the other. "Are you Mrs. Haskell?" Kitty nodded. "When do you expect your husband home?"

"I don't really know how to answer that question." She slowly tugged her rubber gloves off one finger at a time like a burlesque dancer. "It's a bit embarrassing to admit this, but I haven't seen Seth in weeks and, well, I think he's left me."

The young policeman nervously pulled a small notebook from his shirt pocket. "When did you last speak to your husband, ma'am?"

"April fifteenth?" *Did I remember that too quickly? No, I should have that on the tip of my tongue. I'm supposed to be upset.*

The officer nodded and wrote the date down in his notebook. Kitty leaned on the doorjamb. "Excuse me for asking, Officer, but what is this about? Is Seth in some kind of trouble?"

"We found a car registered to a Seth Haskell at this address."

"Oh?"

"A 1972 Volvo wagon, green, license plate …" He looked down at his notebook. "… LB 2289."

"That's Seth's car," Kitty replied. "What does that mean? Was he in an accident?" She reached out and grabbed the policeman's sleeve. "Is he hurt?"

"Mrs. Haskell," the policeman said, stepping back. "The car doesn't appear to have been in an accident."

Kitty arranged her face in what felt like a confused expression.

"Okay, then why are you here? Was it stolen?"

"The vehicle received several parking tickets before it was eventually towed to an impound lot." The policeman flipped to a page in his notebook. "The vehicle was illegally parked on a boat ramp near Copperhead Island—"

"Where?"

"—With a boat trailer attached to the back. Does your husband own a boat, ma'am?"

"Yes," Kitty said with a carefully modulated undertone of frustration. "Seth took it when he left. Or maybe he sold it. Either way, the boat's been gone since April too." She looked at the notebook in the policeman's hand. "Was the boat with the car?"

"I don't think so, ma'am," he said. He cleared his throat and looked down at his notes. "Can you think of any reason your husband would go boating on Lake Wylie? Does your husband have known associates in the Charlotte area?"

Kitty bit her lip and tugged at the hem of her blouse. She worried she was acting unstable, rather than worried. "I don't know anyone on Lake Warbly—"

"Wylie."

"—but Seth might. He travels all over the state for work. He works for a golf equipment company. Are there golf courses in that area?" Kitty hated to sound so stupid, yet felt it necessary to spread the brainless housewife act like a sweet frosting on a less than palatable cupcake.

The policeman shifted uncomfortably toward the steps. "So you don't know why your husband's car and boat trailer would be on Copperhead Island?"

Kitty waited until she was sure she could speak without her voice giving her away. "I really can't say. Why is that important?"

"I want to make sure I have all the facts, ma'am. There was evidence of alcohol in the car, it was parked next to a lake, and now you're telling me he may be missing."

"Missing?" Kitty slid down the doorjamb and sat down hard on the front steps. Caught off guard, the policeman was too slow to catch her. "You mean like missing, missing?" The policeman dropped his notebook and moved to help her up.

A voice from behind him shouted, "Leave her!" as Betty Oliphant ran across the cul-de-sac and up Kitty's driveway. She pushed him aside and scooped Kitty up. "What's happened? Is it Becky? Bobby?" Kitty could hear the glee of getting first dibs on a juicy piece of gossip before any of the other Lookers.

"Please step back, ma'am," the young policeman said.

"What's happening? Is it Becky?"

"No," Kitty said. "Seth. They found his car near a lake." She let Betty hold her up. "They think something might have happened to Seth."

"I didn't say that," the young policeman protested. He backed halfway down the steps. "I'll have the Charlotte police look at the car again. Make a few phone calls." He was at the bottom of the steps before he remembered to pull his business card out of his pocket.

Betty stepped down and took it from him. "Thank you, Officer. I think I'll take Mrs. Haskell inside now and help her calm down." She led Kitty back inside and into the formal living room. Kitty eased onto the closest side chair. Her blood felt bubbly in her veins. The plan was finally playing out. Someone had found the car. With any luck, the police would put the pieces together, and assume something terrible had happened on Lake Wylie.

Betty sat down on the settee and put her hand on Kitty's arm, her cheeks flushed with excitement and the short sprint across the street. "What's happened?"

"They found Seth's car near a lake. It had the trailer attached, but no boat. It sounds like he'd been drinking. They think he might have taken the boat out on some lake—"

"Did they find him?"

"No, just the car."

"Without a body, how will you know for sure?"

"I don't." Kitty pulled her arm away before she slapped Betty for her impertinence. *What a thing to ask? What if I really was a grieving widow?* "Geez, Betty, they just found the car."

Suddenly, the front door burst open and Stacia ran in. She pulled up when she saw Betty and composed herself. "Eileen called. She said the police were here. Is everyone all right?"

"Everyone's fine.

"They found Seth's car parked next to a lake," Betty said. "The police can't find him. He might be dead!"

Kitty stood up and looked pointedly at Betty. "Thanks for running to my rescue, Betty. I'm fine now." She walked to the still open door. "I'm sure you were doing something important when you came over. I'd hate to keep you from it."

Betty took the not-so-subtle hint and walked out. Kitty watched her walk across the street and go up to Eileen's front door to start the gossip train moving. As soon as she closed the door, Stacia said, "They found the car? So, what's the next step? How can I help?"

★★★

Now that the police had found the Volvo, it was time to move on with phase two of their plan - making Seth's disappearance official. The first call Kitty made was to her children. Becky was out of breath when she came to the phone. "What's going on, Mom? Did Dad turn up?"

"I'm afraid not, sweetie. But, I do have some news about him. It looks like he took the boat out on Lake Wylie at some point. The Volvo got towed from a park or something, along with the boat trailer, but I don't know much more than that."

"How long was the car there?"

"A few weeks maybe? The policeman who came by said it had several parking tickets on it." Becky was quiet. Kitty pictured her leaning against the wall in the snack bar in her red lifeguard suit staring at the floor with her serious look on her face. That expression would eventually leave a permanent furrow in her freckled brow if she wasn't careful.

"How's camp?"

"Good," Becky replied. "Bobby has a girlfriend. She works in the kitchen, so he's always volunteering to help bus the tables in the mess hall."

"He never volunteered to do dishes around here. I guess I need to install a pretty girl in the kitchen in order to get some help from him."

"Mom," Becky whispered into the phone. "What does it mean that they found Dad's car next to a lake?"

"I don't know, sweetie. I hope it's as simple as he simply left it there and drove off with someone else. I hope it's not something more serious."

"Like going out on the lake and smashing into something? Remember that time Mr. Sugg hit that rock and smashed up his boat?"

"I thought about that too," Kitty said. "I didn't want to mention anything so frightening."

"Well, I will. We need to consider that Dad might have pulled some bonehead move and got himself drowned."

It frightened Kitty how cold Becky was being. Not so much because she seemed so unfeeling about the possible loss of her father, but because of how much she sounded like Rose. Kitty didn't want Becky to be like her aunt. She wanted Becky to be optimistic about the world, a little trusting, and kind. It was too late for Kitty and Rose. It wasn't for Becky.

"You know what, sweetie, let's not jump to any conclusions just yet. You just concentrate on your job there at the camp and plan for your first year at Brown. We'll let the police work out what happened to your father."

"Sure, Mom. We'll just keep pretending nothing's wrong. Dad's simply on a very long business trip, right?" Becky mumbled something to someone at the camp. "Look, I've got to go. Call me if you hear anything more, okay?"

"I love you, sweetie. Enjoy the lake and remember to put the zinc ointment on your nose."

Kitty hung up the phone and thought how wonderful a vodka tonic would taste at that moment. She could keep up the facade with strangers, but Becky always saw through her. It was unsettling how much they were alike.

The second person Kitty called was her brother-in-law, Joe. As the in-house counsel for the Roman Catholic Diocese of Norwich, Connecticut, he worked famously long hours. Seth used to joke that Joe wore his Armani suits like a hair-shirt. She tried to make her voice sound breezy when she was transferred to his office. "Hey, Joe. It's Kitty."

"Wow, I haven't heard from you in ages? Is everything okay?"

"Not really. Have you heard from Seth lately?"

Joe cleared his throat as if he were weighing his words carefully. "We had a bit of a falling out. I haven't talked to him in several months."

Kitty knew all about their disagreement. When Seth had confided in Joe about their marital troubles, Joe had admonished him to clean up his act. Kitty wasn't sure if Joe even knew about Seth's involvement with Shelly Sullivan. She couldn't remember when Seth got tired of Joe telling him to honor his commitments, and stopped taking his brother's calls. Either way, Joe's disapproval would have motivated Seth to misbehave all the more.

"Why?"

"He's gone AWOL, and now the police are looking for him. They were just here."

"How long has he been gone?"

"Almost two months."

"I'm sorry my brother is such a difficult man. We all have our crosses to bear."

Kitty rolled her eyes. *Save me your patronizing mumbo jumbo.*

"Actually, Joe, I'm really worried." Kitty inhaled a fake sob. "See, they found his car. Beside a lake. And his boat is missing."

"Hold on, Kitty. What are you saying?"

Kitty took a deep breath. "That's the thing. The car was there for weeks, but there's no sign of Seth, or his boat."

Kitty heard the rustle of papers. "I'll be on the next plane down there."

"What? No!" Kitty took a breath. She wanted to sound worried, frantic even, but she didn't want to seem panicked enough to warrant him coming to North Carolina. "That's very sweet of you, but I'm okay."

"Fiddlesticks, with Dad gone and Mom in the nursing home —"

Evelyn is in a nursing home? When did that happen? Seth should have told me that. Now I look like the insensitive daughter-in-law.

"I'm all the family Seth has."

"You don't need to do that. I know you have a lot on your plate with the diocese."

"It will be difficult for them to get by without me, but they can spare me for a few days to take care of family business."

"No, really, I'm fine. I've got it under control." Kitty genuinely felt panicky now. She didn't want Seth's pedantic brother scrutinizing her husband's death any more than Seth had wanted him judging their lives. She searched for a good excuse for him not to come down and play the concerned brother. There was no way around it. They would both lose face if he didn't.

If Joe was going to come down to North Carolina like an avenging angel, she would need to hide the fact that Seth had been sleeping in the guest room. Even though everyone knew that Seth was a cheater, Joe would assume it was somehow Kitty's fault that Seth had strayed if he knew they slept apart.

Kitty pulled several trash bags out from under the kitchen sink and climbed the stairs to the guest room suite. Kitty hadn't been in there since Seth's death. A stack of clean boxer shorts sat on the foot of the bed. His toothbrush still sat next to the sink as if he would be back at any moment. She lifted the wastepaper basket from between the toilet and the wall and brushed everything on the countertop into the trash.

She recalled the last time she had been in that bathroom. She'd found the receipt for Seth's visit to a downtown STD clinic. All the rage and disgust she'd felt the year before came flooding back. Even the persistently itchy sensation returned, making her unconsciously squirm. She pulled Seth's towels off the bar above the toilet and tossed them in the trash bag. There was no point in keeping them; she would never use them again.

After scrubbing down the entire bathroom with bleach, Kitty moved back to the guest bedroom. She opened the bottom drawer of the high boy and slid out a stack of Seth's sweaters. She held each one up and inspected it for moth damage or pulls before placing it in a clean garbage bag destined for the charity box. Only Seth's favorite threadbare Carolina blue golf sweater went in with the trash. She regretted spending so much time and money buying him new sweaters every year. He never wore most of them.

She pulled out the drawer of pajamas and dumped them unceremoniously in the trash. It was such a satisfying experience that she pulled the drawer of boxer shorts and socks from the frame and upended it over the bag. A pair of brown socks flew under the bed like a rodent. She knelt down to retrieve it and recalled how she had done a similar thing while tidying up before the housekeepers came to clean. Seth would tease her about cleaning up the house for the cleaners.

Kitty sat back on her heels and thought about their old housekeeper, Renee, and her part in the demise of their marriage. If Renee had not told Debbie Manning and the other Lookers that Seth was sleeping with Kitty's tennis partner, Kitty may have lived out the lie that they were a happy couple for the rest of their natural lives. Instead, the Lookers all knew each other's secrets until it got to the point that Kitty and Stacia had to team-up to get rid of her. Renee had the Lookers in the palm of her rubber glove until the two friends started a rumor that Renee was selling drugs to the children of Overlook. Every one of the Lookers fired her within a week. Stacia had hinted at Renee's dishonesty to enough important people that she couldn't get work anywhere in Magnuson and had reportedly filed for bankruptcy. If Renee hadn't been such a hateful woman, I may never have found out about Marni, Seth would have continued to carry on with his women, and Renee would still have a thriving cleaning company.

Well, I guess I got the last laugh there.

Kitty stood up and opened the walk-in closet. Several of Seth's suits still hung there in dry cleaning bags. They got thrown on the bed along with a barely worn dress coat. Someone more deserving could wear them now.

She moved on to the heap of shoes on the floor of the closet. Seth had a nasty habit of kicking off his shoes and leaving them where they fell. She fished out the nearly new pair of Topsiders she had bought him for Father's Day. The insoles had yet to conform to his foot. She raised a shoe to her nose; it still had that new leather smell.

These cost an arm and a leg. I wonder if I could still take them back almost a year later. No, I can't do that. What if someone saw me?

When the dresser and closet were empty, she dragged the trash bags down the stairs and shoved them in the backseat of the Bug. She then went back upstairs to put clean sheets on the guest room bed and fresh towels in the bathroom. The room truly was a guest room again.

eleven

ver since she had received the glass flower, Aaron was never far from Kitty's mind. His art spoke to her in a way that words could not. She found it exhilarating to remember how his crooked smile sent bolts of electricity down her spine. Perhaps the young artist merely wanted her to be intrigued by his artwork; however, Kitty found him magnetic. Seth's old suits gave her an excuse to see him and thank him for the gift in person.

She found Aaron in the future meditation garden behind the shelter spreading gravel. His sculpture of St. Sebastian had already been installed at the far end of the path. Kitty stopped along the curb and rolled down her window. "Hi," she called. He stood up and impatiently wiped his brow with the bandana hanging out of his back pocket, until he recognized Kitty.

"Ah, Mary Katherine!" A wide smile burst across his face.

"Is this a bad time? I hate to pull you away from your project."

"Nonsense, the guys have got this. Right, guys?" The group of men grumbled agreement and returned to tossing shovelfuls of gravel between the future flower beds. Aaron leaned on the open window frame. He smelled of stone dust and honest sweat. "What brings an angel in green to our humble establishment today?"

Kitty had spent the morning at the Arts Center interviewing candidates for the new exhibit space, so she was dressed in a forest green sleeveless shift with tiny daisies around the neck that showed off her toned arms and legs. Green and white sandals finished off the outfit. She could have changed before driving to An Open Hand; but she didn't. She wanted Aaron to see her as a stylish woman rather than just a mom.

"I wanted to thank you again for the incredible glass flower you sent to my office." Their faces were close enough that Kitty could see the fine lines beginning to form around Aaron's eyes. They were charming and gave his face character, rather than detracting from his relative youth.

"I didn't know your home address, so I took a chance and sent it to the address on the brochure you gave me."

Kitty felt her blood rush up her neck and flush into her cheeks. The idea of Aaron coming to her home seemed so gloriously wrong that she could barely fumble out the words. "I...I have some more things to donate. They're nice suits. Armani I think."

Aaron rocked back away from the car and thumped the roof with his hand. "What a trip! Mary Katherine is bringing Armani to the homeless."

"Was it inappropriate to bring them here?"

"Not at all." Aaron opened her door and helped her out of the car. He watched her appreciatively as she bent to pull the bags from the backseat.

"Do they need suits? I thought they'd come in handy when one of the guys has a job interview."

"Good idea."

Kitty stooped to pull a box from the floor of the car. "I also brought this pair of shoes for Tomás." She handed Aaron the barely worn Topsiders. "My husband has small feet and Tomás is going to need good shoes when he goes to the new language immersion magnet school next year."

"What's a magnet school?"

"It's part of this whole new redistricting plan they're pushing through. To attract more kids from the northern and southern parts of the city, they're converting some of the schools downtown into magnet schools, one for the arts, one for math and science, and one for languages. It was in the paper the other day. Attendance won't be based on a child's address anymore so, as long as Tomás can show he lives somewhere in the Magnuson city limits, he can attend the school, no matter how often he moves."

"You're an angel!" Aaron hugged her. She froze. Aaron stepped out of the hug, but the electricity between them was still palpable. "Sorry."

Kitty stepped back. "That's okay." She fussed over the few specks of dirt on her dress to keep herself from throwing her arms around him.

Aaron picked up the bags and bound around the car. "Come on. We can put these in the office, then go find Tomás." He suddenly stopped and looked back at her. "Or maybe we should wait until his dad gets back. He'll want to thank you personally. How's your Spanish?"

"Terrible. My Portuguese is pretty good though."

"Portuguese? You're a surprising woman Mary Katherine. What's your last name again?"

"Haskell."

"You're Mrs. Haskell? Like in Leave It To Beaver? Rad."

Kitty followed Aaron in through the front of the building. He stopped outside the main office. "Hey, do you mind chilling out here for a minute? I'm all grubby."

"Sure." Kitty turned away in case her face showed how much the thought of Aaron cleaning up affected her. She walked over to the bulletin boards that had once displayed children's art projects and bus schedules. It now held lists of job fairs and places to get job training. She ran her fingers over the place on her arm where Aaron had left a sprinkling of stone dust as she paced the dim hallway imagining Aaron in the shower.

Aaron returned in a clean shirt, his hair damp. "Why are these rooms marked emergency shelter? I thought the whole building was a shelter."

Aaron crooked his finger for Kitty to follow him. "We have sixty beds down here for guys who need a place for one, maybe two, nights. They can show up here any time between five and eleven and we give them a place to sleep - no questions asked."

They stopped outside a room that contained rows of narrow cots like barracks. There was no hope of privacy. Each made-up bed had a thin pillow and a zip-top bag with a toothbrush and basic toiletries in it. The room was swept clean and was quiet now; however, Kitty imagined it was noisy at night with twenty men snoring and snorting in their sleep.

"Can the men get a hot shower while they're here?"

"If they get here by nine o'clock, they can get a shower and we provide a hot breakfast in the morning. Sadly, these guys have to be out by nine the next morning and can't stay more than two nights in a month."

"That seems a bit cruel. Where can they go?"

"The social workers who come in funnel some of the guys to the VA, or refer them to the mental hospital over in Raleigh. Some of the guys apply to stay upstairs."

"What's upstairs?"

"Transitional housing. Tomás and his father live up there." Aaron resumed his quick walk down the hallway and stopped in front of the double doors to the stairwell. He took a set of keys from his pocket and tossed them between his hands.

"Whole families can stay here?"

"No women, so we don't get many children."

"Where is Tomás's mother?"

"No idea. I don't think he knows either. I gather she has, or at least had, a drug problem." He unlocked the doors to the second floor.

"You lock the people in?"

"We lock the other people out. These doors open from the inside. The people on the transitional floor don't need any Tom, Dick, or Harry going upstairs and rifling through their things."

Kitty nodded pensively as they climbed the stairs. "How do they support people long term? Does the shelter get money from the state?"

"It's an experimental model so they qualify for a grant from HUD. And, several local foundations and churches give them small grants." Kitty recalled Pinnacle Pointe Presbyterian having a special collection for An Open Hand at one point. That was how she had first learned about the shelter.

"Most of our transitional residents go on to find permanent housing well before their ninety days are up."

"Ninety days isn't a very long time to get yourself back on your feet."

"No, it's not. Affordable housing is getting harder and harder to find. More and more of the old mill houses are getting torn down. They were a good place for a single guy to live."

Kitty thought about the hillsides covered with triple-deckers in

Worcester, Massachusetts where she lived right out of college. She had a cheap, safe apartment with friendly neighbors.

She paused as they turned along the wide landing with its stained glass window depicting water flowing over a dam. The old school had some lovely architectural details. "It's nice, isn't it?" Kitty's pulse raced a bit when Aaron brushed up against her hip as he climbed to the second floor.

Each of the classroom doors on the second floor had three names written on the inset window in grease pencil. Jazz music trickled faintly from a room to the left. They walked halfway down the hallway and stopped outside a room marked Brown, Lance, Gomez. Aaron knocked.

"Come in," a deep voice said from inside the room.

That's not Tomás.

Aaron opened the door into a sunny room divided into quadrants. The curtains surrounding two of the quadrants were pulled back to reveal Tomás and a hefty black man with dreadlocks trailing down his back. They were playing cards on the floor. A pile of pennies sat in front of each of them.

"Don't tell me you let this little card sharp trick you into playing with him," Aaron said.

"I'm down fifteen cents," the man said with a grin. "Hello, ma'am."

"James this is Mrs. Haskell. You remember her from the other day, Tomás?"

"She had that big box full of shirts. No stains or nothing. I took a few for Papa."

"I brought you some shoes. I noticed yours had split across the toes."

"Look at those," James said as he nudged Tomás to get up. "You'll be all fancy looking in those."

The little boy pulled himself up and took the shoes from Kitty. "Thanks, lady."

Am I being patronizing? I didn't intend to make this little boy feel like a pauper. Kitty felt nauseated. "They might be little big."

"We'll make them work, ma'am," James said. "Try them on, Tomás. Let the lady see." Tomás pushed his feet into the boat shoes and strutted up and down the walkway like a peacock. It saddened Kitty that a simple pair of shoes could make the boy so happy.

"Did Joe say when he'd be back today? Mrs. Haskell thinks she has a spot in a school for Tomás."

"He shouldn't be too much longer. They were finishing up the curbs in that new subdivision."

"Tomás can hang out with me if you need to go downstairs and get the kitchen going." Aaron turned to Kitty. "James here is a cook and is in charge of the kitchen here."

"At least I learned a trade in Vietnam."

"Don't let James fool you. He turns cans of vegetables and cheap cuts of meat into something you'd order in a fancy restaurant."

Kitty smiled at James. "Cooking for a crowd requires a lot of creativity. A good beef stew is delicious and costs next to nothing."

"Don't I know it," James said as he gathered the cards up.

"I should get going. I have some errands to run." Kitty heard how lame her excuse sounded. She didn't have any reason to go home at all. Her husband was gone for good, her children were gone temporarily, and she refused to use the dog as an excuse for anything. She pulled a piece of paper from her purse and wrote Stacia's phone number down. "If he has any questions about the new magnet school, this woman should be able to answer them." She turned to leave.

"Wait up," Aaron said, "I'll walk you out. Theoretically, women aren't allowed up here at all."

"Breaking your own rules, are you?"

Aaron slid down the bannister and jumped in front of her on the landing. She bumped into his chest and bounced off. He caught her by the shoulders and kissed her lightly on the lips. "I'm a rule breaker from way back."

Kitty was so surprised, she kissed him back. When she pulled away, her entire body trembling.

"I'm sorry," Aaron said. "I shouldn't have—"

"No! I'm sorry. I...I..." She brushed a kiss across his cheek then rushed down the rest of the stairs and out of the building before she did what she wanted to do, and would probably regret.

twelve

Stacia stormed into the Magnuson Police Department like a yellow jacket intent on a dropped popsicle. She would get Seth Haskell declared dead like only a member of the Tate family could, through fear and intimidation.

The Tate Municipal Building had changed. The high oak counter at the back of the marble-clad entry had been replaced by a steel wall with a reinforced glass reception window. A bum slept in his own filth in the corner. She joined the short line behind a weepy woman. By the time the woman finally gave up pleading to see her son in the drunk tank, Stacia was buzzing with impatience.

The young female officer behind the glass flipped to a fresh page in her logbook. "Next!"

"Stacia Tate Curran to speak to Sargent Lafferty."

The officer looked up. "We don't have a Sargent Lafferty here, ma'am."

"Yes, you do," Stacia said. "John Lafferty. Big barrel-chested guy? He's played poker with my daddy every Thursday night for decades."

The young woman shook her head with a small smile. "I know who you're talking about. I knew John when I was a cadet. He retired ages ago. I think he's down in Florida now."

"He can't have retired. I danced with him just——"

Stacia realized that it had been almost twenty years since she last saw Sargent Lafferty. He would be in his seventies and long retired from the police force.

The officer looked over Stacia's shoulder at the growing line. "Was this a social call or is there something I can help you with?"

"I need to speak to whoever is in charge now. I think my neighbor is dead."

The young officer rolled her eyes and pulled a form from the vertical file at her elbow. "Fill this out and an officer will contact you if they need any further information."

"No, the police have already spoken to the man's wife. I need to speak to someone in charge so they know to make this case a priority."

"Fill out the form, ma'am, and an officer will contact you if they need any further information," the officer said in a deadpan voice.

Stacia pushed the form back through the slot in the wall. "Tell them that Stacia Tate Curran wishes to speak to them." She leaned forward and spoke slowly and loudly. "Tate, as in Lake Tate, and Tate Square, and the Tate Municipal Building that you are sitting in."

The young officer leaned forward as well. She narrowed her eyes and lowered her voice. "I don't care if you're Martha Washington of the Washington Monument, you need to fill out the form and an officer will contact you if they need any further information."

Stacia didn't know what to say. No one had ever dismissed her like that. The Tate name had always opened doors. People did what she wanted. She stood there, mouth agape, until the officer said, "Next!" and the man behind her shoved her aside.

★★★

Not only did the Magnuson Register publish Stacia's editorial outlining how the proposed redistricting plan would not benefit Magnuson's most vulnerable children and increase economic segregation, it was the lead article in section C. The newspaper's editor-in-chief wrote a response below the anonymous editorial praising it for its Christian values of tolerance and fairness.

No one else seemed to appreciate the sentiments behind the editorial. That Sunday morning, after the final hymn, the parishioners of Pinnacle Pointe Presbyterian gathered for coffee, cookies, and conversation in the Tate parlor. Weldon wandered over to Quentin and Stacia's father to talk about some rumors he'd heard about the coal plant adding another generator. Stacia stayed near the coffee table. She was avoiding Quentin that morning. He might slip and say something about the real author of the editorial. She took a cup from the coffee hostess and stood near the window. Now that Sunday school had ended for the year, dozens of children ran around the cemetery playing hide and seek. It had rained overnight. The children's feet would be muddy when they came in to drag their parents home. She leaned against the glass to see if she could spot her son. With Bobby Haskell away for the summer, Marcus had volunteered to watch over the younger children during the coffee hour. She was proud of him for helping.

Behind her, a man's voice said, "Did you catch the editorial about the schools in the paper this morning?" Stacia put her thumb on the edge of her coffee cup to keep it from clattering in her shaking hands. "Thanks to all that nonsense over in Charlotte a few years back, the school board is redistricting the whole city. Apparently, we aren't 'diverse' enough." The man made the word seem like an expletive. Stacia took a deep breath and resisted the urge to turn around to stare down her fellow parishioner. Once she knew who they were, she would never be able to see them in the same light.

"What does that mean exactly?" another voice asked.

"It means Magnuson is going to hell in a hand basket. They're going to start bussing."

Stacia heard the sound of high heels approach. "Thanks, babe," the second man said. A pale blue sleeve fluttered in Stacia's peripheral vision. "Bert was just telling me how they're going to start bussing the blacks out of The Heights. What a waste of our tax dollars. They can't be thinking of putting them in Oaks Primary, can they?"

"I don't know. I just heard about the whole thing this morning. We'll probably have to move out of Magnuson to get away from them."

"Perhaps that would be best," an all too familiar voice said. Stacia moved her head just enough to confirm that the pale blue sleeve belonged to Bitsy Magnuson-Evans, her childhood neighbor and adult rival. Bitsy's husband, Chip, stood beside her with his arm around her tiny waist. It was hard to believe the leggy girl who'd spent more time with her horse than her dolls, had grown into this adult-sized Barbie doll. Her skin had a plastic sheen and her bubble of blonde hair defied the laws of gravity.

"Good thing I sent my girl to Magnuson Country Day," Chip said. He took a sip of his coffee and made a face. "This coffee is cold." He shoved his cup in Bitsy's hand and walked away with Bert in tow. "Come on, I've got a cooler of beers in the car."

Bitsy watched her husband walk out the door before sidling up to Stacia. "Nice editorial."

Stacia took a step back and bumped into a side table. She put out her hand to stop it from tipping over. "Excuse me?"

Bitsy leaned over so their faces were inches apart. Stacia could see a thin raised scar along her hairline. "Don't worry, Stacia. I'll keep your secret."

"I don't know what you're talking about." Stacia glanced around the room for Quentin or Weldon so she could signal them to come save her.

"Sure you do. No one else in this town would use the word 'ergo' in a letter to the editor. Or, at all, for that matter." A rare genuine smile that showed her teeth graced Bitsy's face. The crooked teeth of her youth were gone and had been replaced with perfect white enamel. "I remember when you learned that word. You used it in all your oral reports at school, even when that big bully, Rupert McInnis, made fun of you."

"Rupert McInnis was a felon," Stacia snapped and moved away from Bitsy.

"Anyhoo, I liked the editorial, even though it's just going to get people riled. Better to let sleeping dogs lie." Bitsy straightened up to her full height and stiffly turned to look over her shoulder. Stacia wondered if she was developing arthritis in her neck. "Chip's back. Better go."

Bitsy slid away on her impossibly high heels. Stacia slumped into the closest chair and gulped down her entire cup of coffee. *Of all the people to figure out it was me. Bitsy!*

Don't other people use the word ergo?

She stared out the window in a daze until Weldon found her. She looked around and saw that most of the congregation had left. "You okay?" Weldon asked. "Eulalie and Brett will be at the house soon."

Stacia pulled herself up from the chair. "I'm feeling awful tired. I wish we weren't having a houseful today."

★★★

Later that afternoon Stacia's anonymous editorial was the main topic of conversation around the dinner table. "I think we should protest the redistricting plan like the editorial says," said Weldon's brother.

"I bet we could get the PTA and the mother's groups behind a protest," Stacia replied. It felt good to talk about her editorial with like-minded people, even if she had to pretend it was written by someone else.

"I don't think so, Stacia," Brett said indulgently. He ran his hand over his afro and tried to catch Weldon's eye. "I think the community can handle any protest on its own." Stacia bristled. When Brett said 'the community' what he really meant was 'the black community,' which she, as a white woman and a Tate, could never be a part. It didn't matter that she was married to a black man or that she was an advocate for all the children in the Magnuson school system, regardless of color; her help was unwanted.

"I agree with Stacia," Brett's wife Eulalie chimed in. "Bussing is going to hurt the white kids just as much as the black kids. The plan isn't going to make anyone happy." She paused and took a sip of her iced tea. "I bet the la-di-da ladies in the Oaks aren't going to want their precious little boys and girls going to school with the likes of the kids in the Heights."

"Exactly," Weldon said. "I'm sure a lot more people will be sending their children to private schools now." He put his large hand over Stacia's tiny one to signal that he wasn't finished talking. "And, that is their prerogative. The state has a responsibility to provide a decent education for all the children, black, white, rich, or poor. People can choose to take advantage of a public education, or not."

"But won't this undo everything your aunts worked for? Like Stacia's always telling me, a Mrs. Curran have run the schools around here for generations." Weldon and Brett's grandmother and aunts had all been teachers and prided themselves on raising the education level of the traditionally black schools to be higher than the schools the white farmers' children attended. "Now everyone who can leave the city schools, will," Eulalie said. "Who will be left to speak for the poor kids that can't speak for themselves?" Stacia was surprised at her sister-in-law's intensity. Perhaps she had been listening to what Stacia had been saying all these years.

"I agree. We're trading racial segregation for economic segregation." He draped a long arm around Stacia's shoulders. "But like I keep telling Stacia here, we are not responsible for taking care of all the children of Magnuson, just our two. That's why as soon as Stacia started poring over the charts and maps involved in the new plan, I called Bitsy Magnuson-Evans and got Marcus a spot at Magnuson Country Day School."

"You what?" Stacia exploded. "How could you?"

"It was easy. I talked to Chip after church a few weeks ago."

"I can't believe you!"

"He'll be fine. He won't be the only black kid there. The Richards kids go there and the Ortons are thinking about sending John there."

"Once the other kids meet him," Brett added, "it'll be fine. He's a good student and an excellent athlete. Once they see his ball skills, they'll be happy to have him."

"It's not that." Stacia stood up and gathered the empty plates. "Marcus is a great kid. Everyone will love him. It's Bitsy. She's going to hold the fact that you asked for her help over my head until we're both old and gray." Stacia knew it was petty of her, but she didn't like Weldon talking to Bitsy at all. Underneath her pretentiously polite facade, Bitsy seemed obsessed with Stacia. Ever since Bitsy's daughter had gone off to college, she'd been watching Stacia and her family in church. Stacia could still tell when Bitsy wasn't listening to the sermon, even though a lifetime had gone by since their days of playing tic-tac-toe on the backs of their bulletins.

thirteen

Kitty sat at the dining room table surrounded by Polaroids of insipid student watercolors and awkward sketches in preparation for her meeting with Molly Blevins and the life drawing instructor later that day. She tried to arrange the Polaroids into thematic groupings, but couldn't concentrate. Instead, she dragged her fingertips over the jagged surfaces of Aaron's glass flower and thought how his lips had felt on hers. In the two days since they kissed in the stairwell, she had thought of little else. She felt like a teenager again with all the same obsessive thoughts and riotous feelings, yet she also felt very much a grown woman. She ran her thumb along the copper vein at the flowers base and recalled the twinkle in Aaron's eye as he had slid down the banister seconds before he'd kissed her. She wanted more of that twinkle, a lot more.

Her train of thought was broken by the sun flashing off a car's windshield in the cul-de-sac. As a black Ford circled three times, Daisy jumped up from her place under the table and pressed her nose to the picture window. "Who is it, girl?" Kitty stood to get a better view. "That car screams unmarked police car. Those Oliphants have always seemed a little dicey."

The car circled one more time before pulling into the driveway. Kitty stepped back from the window as fingers of panic tickled her stomach. "It's not really the police, is it? They're not watching the house, are they?" The man behind the wheel shifted in his seat and peered up at the house. One black clad elbow poked out of the car window. "Oh boy, it's Joe." She laid the glass flower safely out of sight in the top drawer of the buffet and ran her sweaty palms over the hips of the simple wrap dress she'd put on for her meeting. She hoped Joe would see the navy and kelly green geometric design as appropriately conservative and overlook the expanse of bare leg below her hemline.

Kitty hadn't seen Joe in the years since she and Seth had been exiled to North Carolina. Joe and Seth had kept in touch with perfunctory phone calls on birthdays and Christmas. Seth's mother didn't deem them worthy of an invitation to Joe's ordination. The Haskells acted like Kitty was the first young woman to walk down the aisle while pregnant. Before Becky was born, Seth's father had found him a job in North Carolina and Seth's mother simply pretended Kitty and the children didn't exist.

The dog let out a warning bark as Kitty opened the front door. She pushed Daisy back into the dining room and waved to Joe. She plastered an anemic smile on her face; she wanted to look pleased to see him without looking too happy. "Joe? Is that you?"

Joe turned off the car and rolled down the window. "Praise the Lord, Kitty. I assumed you were the daughter when you first opened the door. You're as slim as a rail."

She wondered how Seth had been describing her to his brother in their infrequent conversations. She skipped down the stairs and crossed the lawn to where Joe was parked in the center of the driveway. "Why didn't you tell me you were coming this morning? I would have picked you up at the airport."

Joe climbed out of the car with a grunt. "I like to have my own car when I travel." He was no longer the happy-go-lucky fraternity boy she'd known in 1957. In a priest's black shirt and pants, he looked like every other priest Kitty had ever known. His lush brown head of hair had been replaced by a spotted scalp and a fringe of gray. He'd gained weight, which obscured his handsome face and his nose was reddened by broken capillaries. Kitty wondered if he drank.

He stepped forward and barely embraced her. The front of his shirt never actually touched any part of her before he looked beyond her to the still open front door. "Where are Seth's children?"

Seth's children? Like he's been oh so involved in their lives.

"Becky and Bobby are away at camp." Joe raised his eyebrows. "I felt it best to maintain as much of their routine as possible." Kitty nodded at the rental car blocking the driveway. "As a matter of fact, if

110

you'd come very much later, you would have missed me as well. I need to get to work."

"You mean your little art projects?"

Kitty crossed her arms over her chest and squeezed her hands in her armpits. *Play nice, Kitty. If anyone could make a whole lot of trouble for you, it's Joe. Smile and nod, smile and nod.*

"Seth told you about my position at the Arts Center? Did he also tell you that my exhibit got written up in The New York Times?" Joe's eyes widened as he took a step back.

She took a deep breath of humid air. They would have a thunderstorm that afternoon. "Do you have a bag? Can I help you carry it in?"

Joe shambled to the back of the car and popped the trunk. At that moment, Betty Oliphant walked out to her mailbox and pretended to be checking the mail.

Gee, Betty. Could you be more obvious? The mail doesn't come for hours yet.

"Hey, Betty," Kitty called. "Expecting a letter?"

"Fine, just fine," the older woman replied eying Joe lifting his suitcase out of his rental car. "Company coming to stay?"

Kitty took Joe's elbow and led him across the cul-de-sac. "Betty, I'd like you to meet my brother-in-law, Father Joseph."

"A pleasure to meet you, Betty," Joe said in an eerily low voice, very different from his naturally sharp tone. The difference between Joe Haskell and Father Joseph was jarring.

"Joe's here to help me through this—." Kitty covered her mouth with her hand and looked up as if fighting back tears. It was sickening how easy it was to play the grieving widow with Betty.

"Of course, we're all so worried about dear Seth," Betty said disingenuously. "Is there any news?"

Joe put his heavy arm around Kitty's back and pulled her toward her house. "It was nice meeting you, but I think I should take Mrs. Haskell inside." They walked back across the cul-de-sac and paused to pick up Joe's suitcase. Kitty could not have asked for a more dramatic way to get the rumor mill humming than Betty seeing a priest come and stay. She would be on the phone telling all The Lookers within five minutes of Kitty closing her front door. As much as she was unhappy that Joe was visiting, the appearance of a family circling the wagons in a time of crisis was invaluable in moving the plan along.

"I'm sorry about that," she said, once they were inside. "The neighbors around here are super nosy."

Joe parked his suitcase inside the door and sighed. "Proverbs says - 'Whoever goes about slandering reveals secrets, but he who is trustworthy in spirit keeps a thing covered.'"

"How very apt. Are you sure you haven't met Betty before?"

"There are busybodies everywhere, Kitty dear. That woman should fill her time helping the poor and sick."

"That reminds me," she said picking up Joe's bag and starting up the stairs. "After we get you settled, I'll call my sister Rose, and have her join us for dinner."

Joe slowly followed her up the stairs. Kitty wondered if Seth was aware of how sedentary his former football star of a brother had become. "Your sister lives in the area?"

"Yes, as I told you on the phone. She's been very helpful these past few weeks." She glanced at her watch. "I hate to say hello-goodbye, but I really do need to get to work. I have people waiting for me."

"That's fine. I'll just freshen up. Then, I want to go down to what you people down here call a police department, and find out why they haven't located my brother yet."

Kitty shook her head and lugged the suitcase into the guest room. "I'll write down the address for the police station before I leave. There are clean towels in the bathroom. If you think of anything you might need, I'll leave the number of the Arts Center. They can take a message." Kitty quickly left a message for Rose to come by after her shift and ran a bit of lipstick over her lips. She wanted to get away from Joe as soon as possible. His presence made her both uneasy and sad. In the last eighteen years, Seth's fun-loving brother had become a pedantic snob.

She gathered up the photos still on the dining room table and stuffed them in her carry-all. "If you go out through the garage, the door will lock by itself. See you later."

"Drive slow and hurry back," Joe said. Kitty's heart twisted in her chest. Seth used to say that to her when they were first married.

Welcoming Joe and getting him settled made Kitty ten minutes late for her meeting. As she rushed down the hall to the conference room, the life drawing instructor stepped out of the studio classroom. "Sorry I'm so late, Thad," Kitty said. "I hope I'm not cutting into your prep time for your three o'clock class."

"No problem, Kitty. I was just tidying up the studio so my classes can have a clean workplace today." She recalled Molly griping that Thad was overly dramatic about her leaving the studio messy. Now, that Kitty had been working at the Arts Center for several months, she saw that Molly annoyed the people at the Arts Center as much as she annoyed Stacia and the Lookers. Molly didn't follow the rules. She didn't file her paperwork when she was supposed to or collect tuitions on a regular basis. Her classes didn't start or end on time which left crowds of waiting students loitering in the halls. She was, in short, a hair in the administration's wet paint.

"Still I appreciate you taking the time," Kitty replied. She felt her jaw tighten as she opened the door and saw Molly sitting in the conference room nursing a cup of tea. Instead of piling the boxes left for Kitty in a neat pile, Molly had pushed them to one end of the table to make room for her portfolio. Several boxes had fallen on the floor. Kitty hoped the pieces inside were still intact. Even if Molly didn't take her job at the Art Center seriously, Kitty did. Molly would have known that if she paid closer attention. Kitty didn't simply make cupcakes for a PTA bake sale; she made cupcakes that looked like butterflies taking flight. She didn't merely decorate her house; she made the rooms blend one into the other across a color palette. The family room was done in ecru with navy and orange accents that echoed the watercolor prints in the breakfast nook and the trim on the navy raw silk drapes in the dining room. The silhouette of Kitty's clothes changed with current fashion, but remained within a palette of greens and browns that complimented her auburn hair and freckles.

"Okay, now that we're all here, let's get to it." Kitty pushed Molly's things aside and laid out the Polaroids.

"Hey!" Molly steadied her mug. "You almost knocked over my tea."

Kitty ignored her. "I have some ideas on how we can display the students' work." Over the next half hour, Kitty explained how the pieces from the watercolor, acrylics, and oils classes could be spread out between the small exhibit space and the hallways so they both looked appealing and allowed everyone's work to be displayed. Molly grumbled when her pet students didn't get the prime spots, but with Thad there and the director of the Arts Center wandering in and out of the conference room several times, she accepted Kitty's ideas.

After the meeting, Molly pulled Kitty aside. "So, have you heard from Seth? I hear there was a priest at your house this morning."

That was quick. I didn't think Molly was that tied into the grapevine.

"Nobody's heard anything from Seth so his brother is here for a few days to help sort things out." Kitty picked up a Polaroid and slip it into the file folder. "I'm beginning to think Seth's never coming back."

A smug smile tugged at the sides of Molly's mouth as she unwrapped a fresh tea bag and stepped over to the hot plate in the corner of the room. Kitty recalled their conversation on the deck just after Seth's death. Molly had implied that it was her fault Seth left. She'd let the comment slide at the time, because his death had still been new and she was coming down from a massive sugar high. Kitty now had all her faculties, and enough distance, to be offended by Molly's attitude. It was people like Molly who had made her feel it was her fault that Seth cheated on her. She had implied that Kitty was being difficult when she was furious with Seth for giving her the clap. Seth wasn't a toddler who wandered away whenever he saw a shiny new toy; he was a grown man with the ability to know right from wrong, and he had done wrong. He had known that and he had cheated anyway. He had done what he wanted, when he wanted, and Kitty had been expected to stand by and say nothing.

A bitter taste filled her mouth as she took a good long look at Molly. The woman she had once considered a quirky artist who eschewed the staid mores of society with her lack of makeup and bohemian clothes now appeared feckless. Molly wasn't bucking the system; she was lazy. No wonder Stacia disliked her so much. She didn't follow the traditional rules their mothers preached to them, yet she wasn't progressive in her thoughts. She had neither comforted Kitty with a casserole and gin nor encouraged her to forge her own independent path. Molly knew Kitty was upset about Seth leaving and hadn't warranted five minutes of her time.

"The police think he may have been in a boating accident, but they can't be sure without a...a...a body."

Molly held her tea under her nose and inhaled the steam. "Oh

Kitty, I'm so sorry for you."

The urge to grab the X-Acto knife off the table and plunge it into Molly's eye was so strong it terrified her. She scooped the rest of the photographs into the file and rushed out of the room before she did or said something awful. "Wait, Kitty. I'm sorry," Molly called after her, but it was too late for I'm sorrys.

fourteen

Driving out of the city, Kitty barely registered the road. Her brain was still buzzing from her encounter with Molly. How could she have not seen what a hypocrite Molly was? How could she be such a fool? All those afternoons they had walked their dogs and poked fun at The Lookers for being stuffy and closed-minded had made Kitty think of Molly as a maverick. She was wrong. It was much simpler than that. Molly was jealous; she was jealous of the other Overlook moms, with their pretty lives and pretty houses, who were included in Stacia's clique when she was not. And Kitty had been her stooge, feeding her pieces of information about the other Lookers for Molly to chew on like bits of gristle.

She roared into the cul-de-sac and almost hit Joe's rental car. *Just like his brother. He parks right in the middle of the driveway so no one else can get in or out.*

And close the garage door, you idiot. I know you weren't born in a barn. I've seen that mausoleum in Newton your parents call a house.

Kitty reversed out of the driveway and parked behind Rose's Gremlin. *Oh good, Rose is here.* She got out and stooped over to collect her carry all and realized she hadn't seen Rose since the children had left for camp. She'd barely seen anyone in the last few weeks. No one had come by to make sure she was coping and she hadn't wanted them to. She'd thrown herself into working on her projects at the Arts Center and applying for freelance positions. She'd eaten nothing but ice cream and cereal for days.

The sound of voices from the backyard greeted Kitty as she walked up the driveway. Rose and Joe were sitting on the deck with a bottle of

Seth's 'good' red wine on the table between them. She was surprised they were out there. The blaring afternoon sun reflected off the bricks and made sitting on the deck unbearable. No one sat outside at this hour. It just wasn't done.

She climbed the steps and sat on the arm of the teak chaise. The wood felt like a burning branch through her skirt, making her hop back to her feet. "Are you two catching up?"

Rose looked flushed. "Joe was just telling me about how surprised he was with the airport over in Winston-Salem."

"Yes," Joe said. "You ran out of here so quickly I didn't get to tell you about my journey." He poured himself another glass of wine. Kitty wondered if it was still good or if it had turned to vinegar. Seth wouldn't have known the difference; he bought wine by the dollar amount on the bottle, not by the grapes inside. She wondered if Joe knew any better.

Rose bounced out of her chair. "I've already heard the story, so why don't I go check on dinner? I found a dish of your delicious macaroni and cheese in the freezer and a batch of your chocolate chip cookies. How clever of you to freeze the dough as individual cookies." Rose nearly ran for the door to the kitchen. "I'll just go set the table in the dining room."

"Thank you, Rose," Kitty said as her sister disappeared through the door. It had been a long time since Kitty had seen her sister so rattled. Had Joe said something to make Rose think he suspected their involvement in Seth's death? Or was he just insufferable? She turned back to Joe. "Was there a problem with your flight this morning?"

"No, I was pleasantly surprised. That Piedmont Airlines is almost a real airline. The airport had moveable gates and everything."

"What did you expect? A grizzled old farmer coming out to get the suitcases with a wheelbarrow?"

"Honestly, yes. I didn't expect the South to be so modern. I didn't see one cotton field driving over here."

You provincial ass.

"Maybe you're thinking of Mississippi. This area grows more tobacco than cotton." She tucked her fingers under her thighs to keep from grabbing the wine bottle and pouring the dark liquid down her throat.

How am I ever going to get through this visit? He's only been here for a few hours and I already want to start drinking again.

"Did you make it downtown or did you stay here and settle in?"

"As tired as I am, I'm only here for two shakes of a lamb's tail. I felt it best I take the bull by the horns and get to the bottom of the situation on behalf of the family." Kitty nodded and smiled. She was still feeling keyed up from her argument with Molly and didn't trust herself to be civil. Joe didn't seem to notice her silence.

"I was at sixes and sevens for a bit finding the police department. I was looking for the standard sheriff's office, but a lovely young colored woman gave me directions to the Tate Building."

Kitty's toes curled inside her sandals. She hoped he didn't offend the woman who gave him directions. At one time she would have made excuses for Joe in her head; he doesn't have much interaction with black people, he means well, he's old-fashioned. She wasn't willing to do that anymore. She would call a spade a spade, as Joe would say. He was a bigot.

"That Tate Building is magnificent. Did you know that Magnuson was founded by two Scotsmen?"

Kitty recalled Stacia telling her how her great-grandfather and his business partner, Elias Magnuson, had built the three hydro-electric plants that created Lake Tate and made the city of Magnuson prosper. "I'm familiar with the story of the Tates and the Magnusons."

"You read the plaque in the lobby too?"

"Stacia Tate Curran is one of my closest friends and we go to church with Bitsy Magnuson-Evans, so..."

Joe raised his eyebrows as he took another sip of wine. Kitty hated how her association with the old families of Magnuson made Joe think more of her. She was tempted to introduce him to Weldon Curran just to see him squirm in the dissonance, but she wouldn't do that to Weldon and Stacia. Joe's intolerances were as deep and murky as the man-made lake where his brother's body was now decomposing.

"Were you able to speak to someone at the police station?"

"After waiting for an age, I spoke to a Sergeant Blount. He told me it's an open case, but they hadn't devoted any manpower to it. I put an end to that!" Joe smirked as he upended the rest of the wine into his glass. "They'll be putting a man on it first thing in the morning."

Kitty imagined Joe pompously throwing his weight around the Magnuson police station, demanding they devote all their attention to the possible disappearance of his brother, and cringed. She had to live in Magnuson. What would people think of her?

"When will the children be home from camp? I was hoping to see them while I was here."

"I'm sorry, they won't be home until the week of the fourth." *Thank God.*

"Does Rebecca have a job lined up or is she doing a course?"

"She's going to Brown in the fall." The mention of Becky going to Brown made the old rage boil up inside her again. She picked up the empty wine bottle and weighed it in her hand. Kitty thought how easy it would be to kill Joe the same way she had killed Seth, and dropped the bottle on the table.

What are you thinking? You can't go killing off the whole Haskell family over Becky's right to an independent future.

"Is that a local secretarial school?"

"No," Kitty laughed. She flexed her wrist as if brushing away an annoying bug. Joe may have been myopic, but he wasn't worth the risk. She took a deep breath and plastered a smile on her face. "Brown University. You know, the Ivy League school in Providence? Didn't you apply there?"

"But—"

"She's a girl?" Kitty stood up and tossed the bottle in the recycling bin. Joe would never know how close he had come to meeting his maker that afternoon. "Women can enroll there now."

Joe rolled his eyes. "What does Seth say about her going there? I can't believe he thinks that's a good use of his hard-earned money."

"He didn't." Kitty left it at that. She was afraid to say more and make Joe suspicious. She was willing to let him think his brother too weak to prevent his daughter from pursuing her dreams.

Rose appeared at the door. "Do you want to come in and tell me which placemats you want to use?"

Kitty turned to look at Rose. Something was up. She had never asked Kitty's opinion on anything quite as trivial as placemats before. Rose was always ready to criticize Kitty's choices, but never deferred to them. "Excuse me, Joe," she said. "I better go in and help my sister.

120

You sit tight and enjoy the North Carolina sunshine." Joe dismissed her with a thin smile and looked out over the lake.

Kitty followed Rose into the dining room. "What's the matter? Did Joe say something to upset you before I got home?"

"No, we were having a wonderful conversation. I'd forgotten how charming he was." Kitty smiled to herself. She'd forgotten how well Rose and Joe had gotten along the few times they had met around the time of her wedding. "Joe's not the problem, you are. First I get here and the house is a disaster."

"It's not that bad. I just need to pick up a little."

"There is no food in that refrigerator. What would you have served Joe for dinner if I hadn't pulled that casserole out of the freezer?"

Kitty pulled a set of rattan placemats out of a drawer and tossed them on the table. "I would be figured something out?"

"Never mind that, look what I found when I was looking for the corkscrew." Kitty froze as Rose lifted the glass flower out of the buffet. "What is this?"

"A piece of art made from reclaimed materials," Kitty said, trying to sound as didactic as possible. "It's the next big trend in folk art. Artists are making art from garbage and industrial waste as a commentary on our throwaway society." *I am so full of it!*

"Yeah right. Look at you, you're blushing like I caught you in bed with a man." Rose stepped back and stared at Kitty. "Holy shit, Mary Katherine! That's it, isn't it? You're sleeping with one of your artsy people."

"No, I'm not!"

"Really?" Rose waved the note that came with the flower in Kitty's face. "It's just a matter of time though, isn't it?"

Kitty leaned on the edge of the table. She felt faint as she realized that Rose was correct. It was just a matter of time before she slept with Aaron. She certainly wanted to and she assumed he wanted her too. Who was she kidding? He was a man.

"Maybe, maybe not. It's really none of your business."

"Yes, it is," Rose snapped. "I helped you get rid of Seth. As soon as I did that, everything you do became my business. And that Stacia woman's too, for that matter."

121

★★★

The phone screamed through the house in the middle of the night. The image of Becky floating face down in a cold Virginia lake flashed through Kitty's brain before she even opened her eyes. She pulled herself upright and swatted at the bedside table for the phone. "Becky? What's wrong?"

"Mrs. Haskell?" a thin high voice asked.

Kitty dropped the phone and fumbled with the bedside lamp. "Becky!"

"Who's Becky?" Kitty slumped back against the headboard with her hand over her mouth as the bedroom came into focus. Her children were fine. "Hello? Hello? Are you still there? Seth?"

"Who is this?" Kitty demanded. She heard movement downstairs, then a crash, and a moment later, Rose ran in. "What's happened? I heard the phone ring." Kitty was a bit surprised that the phone woke Rose at all. She had passed out on the couch after she and Joe finished off two more bottles of Beaujolais.

"Close the door! I don't want to wake Joe." She turned to sit on the side of the bed before talking into the phone again. "Who is this?"

The high-pitched cry of an infant keened across the telephone wires. The initial surge of adrenaline she felt on answering the phone quickly turned to shaky nausea.

"Who's Becky?" the voice asked. She sounded at the edge of hysteria.

"I said, who is this? Why are you calling me in the middle of the night?"

"I'm trying to reach Seth Haskell."

"Who are you?"

"My name's Shelly Sullivan. I know your husband."

Kitty felt faint. She knew exactly who Shelly was and whose child was crying in the background. She took a deep breath and shook the cobwebs out of her brain.

"Really? Do you work with Seth?" Kitty needed a second to think. Maybe she could stall a moment while pretending she didn't know who Shelly was.

"Seth and I are lovers."

So much for the naive wife act. I can't keep that up if she's going to be so damn direct.

Kitty waved her hand at Rose. "It's her!" she mouthed.

Rose's mouth fell open. "The bimbo?"

Kitty stifled a laugh as she pulled her sister over to sit beside her on the bed. She smelled like red wine and dog hair. They held the earpiece between their cheeks. "What? What did you just say to me?"

"Seth and I are lovers," Shelly said. Rose rolled her eyes.

"When was the last time you saw your lover?" Kitty asked, "because I would like to give him a piece of my mind."

"Not for months. He promised to—" Shelly's voice cracked. "Is he there?"

Kitty almost felt sorry for the girl. Almost. "I haven't seen my husband in over two months. When was the last time you saw him?"

"April fifteenth."

"I'll need to speak to the police about that. I'm sure they'll want to have that noted in Seth's missing person's file."

"I've already told them that. A cop showed up at my door this afternoon. They asked me all sort of questions about Seth, and the hospital keeps sending me these huge bills, and the baby won't stop crying, and my credit card keeps getting declined. The cop said they might charge me with credit card fraud."

Kitty and Rose looked at each other with wide eyes. They hadn't discussed how long it would take for the banks to start closing down Seth's accounts. If Shelly's credit card was being declined, it wouldn't be long before Kitty's card would be useless.

A door slammed in the background. Kitty could barely hear the baby crying anymore. "I can't go to jail, Mrs. Haskell. I just had a baby."

"Did you just close a door on a crying baby? Why aren't you picking that poor thing up?"

"He's Seth's."

"How unfortunate for you," Kitty replied. Rose clamped her hand over her mouth and turned away from the phone.

"The cop said Seth was missing. They think he might be dead."

"So why are you calling me in the middle of the night?" Kitty was fully awake now. "And why do you have my husband's credit card? Are you some kind of a grifter?"

"He's going to marry me!" Shelly screeched. "I don't know where you're hiding him, but he doesn't love you. He loves me. He's going to marry me."

Oh no you don't! You can't go around saying things like that to the police.

"You woke me up to tell me that? He tells all his women that he'll marry them."

"All?"

"Sorry, honey. Did you think you were the first girl to fall for Seth's charms? I may have been his first stooge, but I certainly wasn't his last."

"But I have a baby."

"Speaking of which, will you please go pick up that poor child? He sounds frantic." Kitty heard Shelly drop the phone and open a door. The cries stopped immediately. When Shelly returned, Kitty could hear the baby trying to catch his breath.

"What am I going to do?"

"Are you sure it's Seth's?" Rose said from the other side of the bed.

"Who's that? Is someone else there? Seth?"

"Hush up," Kitty said. "You'll frighten the baby." She took a deep breath. "Seth isn't here. Is it your fault he abandoned me and the children?"

"Children? He never said anything about having other children."

How dare he not tell this woman about Becky and Bobby. "We have two children. Rebecca and Robert."

"He hasn't seen his little ones since April?"

"They're not that little. Bobby is fourteen and Becky starts college this fall."

"That can't be right. Seth isn't old enough to have a teenager." The baby made a faint cry followed by the snuffling sound of a baby drinking. Kitty imagined Shelly nursing her newborn in the middle of the night and wondering about what happened to Seth. Kitty might have made this call too in her position. "Do you think he's coming back?"

"No, I don't think so. He's probably found someone else to play with." She wasn't enjoying it, but Kitty needed to make Shelly stop thinking that Seth would ever return for her. "The party's over, honey. You're no fun anymore, now that you have a baby. He may have promised to marry you, but I'm the only one he actually ever did."

Lucky me.

"Don't expect to ever hear from him again. And don't ever call here again!" With that, Kitty slammed down the phone. She took a few breaths before turning to Rose. "What do you think? Will she call again?"

Rose shifted on the bed. "She's definitely a loose end." She stared out the window into the dark for a moment. "What was all that about credit cards? Did I miss something?"

"He had credit cards. The bills went to his office." Kitty decided to not mention the second mortgage. That was too embarrassing to tell anyone about. "I'm not paying them. I can't."

Rose thought about that for a moment. "Didn't you say that this Shelly had been calling Seth's office right after the 'incident'?" Neither one of them could bring themselves to refer to the night Kitty killed Seth as anything more specific than 'the incident.' Euphemism was the Sweeney sisters' defense mechanism of choice, followed closely by feigned ignorance. "Then the secretary——"

"Suzie."

"——probably gave the police the woman's name. Even if they weren't suspecting her of anything more than being a kept woman, now that they've found the car and Joe has made such a fuss, they're bound to suspect her of something."

"What though? Illegal parking?"

Rose stood up and pulled Kitty to her feet. She led Kitty down to the kitchen. "I don't know exactly, but we could come up with something."

"I guess," Kitty sighed. She opened the refrigerator and took out the orange juice. "I can't stop thinking about that crying baby. It was one thing for that woman to be pregnant, but now there's a real live little person crying in the night while his mother is making frantic phone calls. It broke my heart to hear him crying like that."

The next morning, Kitty laid out a breakfast of bacon and eggs for Rose and Joe. She couldn't eat anything herself. Shelly's phone call had left her too agitated to eat like a normal person. If she were alone, she could have gorged on the whole pound of bacon and been calmed by its fatty pork goodness. Instead, she primly sipped at a cup of coffee while Joe and Rose chatted about the new nursing home the diocese was building.

"It sounds like a wonderful facility," Rose said.

"We'll need experienced nurses. Would you care for a position? You're obviously a seasoned nurse, and it's unlikely you'd run off get married at your age. After all, you are family of sorts."

"You'd have to make it worth my while," Rose said with a laugh. "I make a good salary here."

Joe leaned back and looked at Rose. "I'll double it." He smiled. "Why don't you come up next week? Look at the building. I'll have caught up from this trip by then. You can stay with me for a few days while you think about it."

Rose blushed and took a sip of coffee. "I guess that would be all right. Like you said, we are family and I have plenty of vacation time saved up."

Kitty sat back and looked at her sister and her brother-in-law. Were they flirting with each other? Could Rose have fallen for the Haskell charm again? Her thoughts were interrupted when the doorbell rang. The fresh-faced young officer who had come by to question her about the car stood on the front steps. He seemed to have matured years in the last week. "May I come in?"

"Certainly," Kitty said, and stepped back to let him enter the foyer. Joe and Rose joined her.

"Do you have any news, young man," Joe said. It annoyed Kitty that her brother-in-law was taking command of the situation, but she didn't protest. It was best for her to play the naive wife of a missing man in that moment.

"Yes, sir. We've looked into the matter of Mr. Haskell's absence and have ruled him a missing person."

"What does that mean?" Kitty said. "What are you saying?"

"I'm sorry, Mrs. Haskell, but it appears your husband had a boating accident. He was drinking when he took his boat out on an unfamiliar lake and probably hit a rock and, I'm sorry, but we have to assume he drowned."

Kitty gasped and clapped her hand over her mouth. She felt like such a phony acting surprised, but it seemed like the right thing to do. Rose stepped over to her and put her arm around her shoulders. She could feel her sister's heart racing through her blouse.

"Drowned?" Rose said. "How awful. He's such a good swimmer."

Joe stepped in front of Kitty and Rose. "What does it mean to be a missing person?"

"Just that," the officer said. He handed several forms to Joe. "In the absence of definitive proof—"

"A body, you mean," Rose said.

"—Seth Haskell is considered missing and presumed dead."

"Presumed dead?" Joe slapped his hand against his thigh. "We can't have a funeral if we don't know he's actually dead?"

"So what's next?" Kitty asked. "How do we know if he's actually dead? Or does he stay missing forever? What am I supposed to tell the children?"

"I'm sorry, ma'am. I should have said. Your husband will remain officially missing for seven years. Then you can file the paperwork to have him declared legally dead." Kitty knew exactly what that meant - no money. Without an official death notice, she couldn't collect his life insurance or inherit any of Seth's assets, like the house. The mortgage payments would continue to pile up, but she had no way of selling the property. It would have been better for Seth to have divorced her. She would at least have got half of everything.

Killing Seth may have been a mistake.

The officer moved toward the door. His work there was done. There was no need for him to linger. Joe opened the door for him as if it were his house. "This is unacceptable," he said.

The officer ignored Joe and addressed Kitty. "In the meantime, will you need any assistance getting the car towed back to Magnuson?"

"I don't think so," Kitty replied. "I can manage."

fifteen

itty and Rose's plan did not address what to do with the car and boat trailer after it was found. She already had Becky's Bug. She neither needed nor wanted the Volvo back, to say nothing of the car insurance payments. The sooner she put the Volvo and its role in covering up Seth's death behind her, the better.

Kitty had no experience with the buying and selling of cars. Seth had taken care of things like that when he was alive, so she asked Rose to go with her to Charlotte. Kitty also wanted to talk things through with Rose before she left for Rhode Island. They'd only been on the highway for a few miles before Kitty said, "I'm surprised you're taking Joe up on his offer to show you the new hospital. You just moved down here and you're thinking about going back?"

Rose looked out the window. "Living in North Carolina hasn't been all I thought it would be. The patients aren't the same as they were up north, and you and Seth didn't turn out to be how I expected."

"I guess not," Kitty said. They drove for another few minutes before Kitty looked over at Rose dozing in the passenger seat. "But why work with Joe? Won't he remind you of Seth all the time?"

"Maybe. One of the things I want to find out is how much Joe is actually involved with the hospital. He's a lawyer, not a doctor."

"Okay. I just thought you'd stick around to help me out. I'm broke. I thought you could move in with me and Bobby after Becky leaves for school."

"Nope." Rose pulled a lifesaver from her purse. "Maybe artist-man can pay your bills for you."

"It's not like that, Rose."

"Mark my words, this one will be trouble too. You always were a sucker for a winning smile." She popped the mint in her mouth and talked around it. "I'm not helping you hide any more bodies."

"I got rid of the body. If you want to nitpick, you just helped me with the cover-up."

"My point is, you have terrible taste in men," Rose replied. "I don't want to stick around to see how this one blows up on you."

"Aaron's not like that. He's—"

"Ack. Shut up, Kitty!"

Low clouds glowered over the highway for the rest of their journey, yet didn't appear motivated to release their loads. Kitty exited the highway and followed the directions the impound lot had given her over the phone.

At the end of a long street on the seedier side of town, two room houses devolved into plywood shacks. Kitty preferred to pretend streets like that didn't exist. The lot was no more than a field of cars surrounded by a ten-foot chain link fence topped with razor wire. She immediately picked out their Volvo and boat trailer from the Plymouths and Fords, many missing their wheels, and drove through the gate. At the back of the lot, she pulled up to a building that could generously be called a shed and walked inside. Rose awoke from her nap when the car stopped and trailed in behind her sister.

"Yoo-hoo," Kitty called to the man sitting behind a pane of reinforced glass. He had his hand deep inside a bag of potato chips. She waved her fingers when he looked up from the baseball game blaring on the small television on his desk.

"What you want?" the man said. He didn't appear intent on leaving his baseball game.

"I need to pick up a car?"

"Tag?"

Kitty told him the license plate number. He reluctantly wiped his greasy fingers across the leg of his coveralls and found the file on his desk. The clerk flipped and through the file and slid a pile of parking tickets along with a bill for storing the car through a slot in the window. Kitty felt as if she was going to vomit when she saw the total at the bottom of the invoice. There wasn't nearly enough left in the checking account to pay the fines. Rose wordlessly took the invoice from her fist, opened her purse, and handed the clerk a stiff $100 bill.

"I'll pay you back," Kitty whispered.

"Yes, you will."

"Where can a person sell a used car around here?" Kitty asked the clerk. He shook his head like he couldn't believe how stupid she was and pointed across the street. She turned. Directly across the street behind another chain link fence was Byrd's Salvage and Auto Sales.

"Can I take my car now?"

"Hope you got keys. 'Cuz we ain't towing it anywhere." Kitty and Rose left without keeping the man from his potato chips and television any longer.

At the car, Kitty stood beside the open driver's side door with the keys hanging from her finger. She couldn't get in. The car still smelled of whiskey and panic.

Rose pushed Kitty aside and sat behind the wheel. "Meet me across the street." The trailer fishtailed behind the Volvo and nearly tipped as Rose turned out of the parking lot too quickly. At that moment, the clouds decided to release their burdens. Kitty's thin dress was immediately soaked through and her hair plastered to her head. She quickly slipped her feet out of her suede pumps and trudged across the dirt lot in her bare feet. After the initial shock of getting wet, she enjoyed the feeling of mud between her toes and warm rain on her skin.

By the time she arrived at the salvage yard, Rose had taken care of the sale. Kitty need only sign the paperwork and collect the money. Mr. Byrd gave her more for the old Volvo and trailer than seemed fair to Kitty, yet she wasn't about to complain. She suspected Rose had given him quite a sob story about why Kitty was selling the car, and played along. She timidly let him walk her through what she had to do to cancel her insurance and notify the state that she no longer owned the car.

Once they were back in the Bug, Kitty peeled off a $100 bill from the wad of cash Mr. Byrd had handed her, and handed it to Rose. "What did you say to him to get me such a good price?"

Rose looked up from searching the glove compartment for a paper napkin and blushed. "You don't want to know. But I have to say, it didn't hurt for you to show up looking like a drowned rat."

Kitty ignored her sister as she rubbed the back of her neck. She felt too good to let Rose get under her skin. She had enough money to cover several months of her living expenses. She pulled out of the salvage yard and drove off without looking back at the station wagon that had been such a large part of her life as Becky and Bobby's mother.

The sisters stopped at a drive-in burger stand and ordered greasy cheeseburgers and chocolate shakes. While Kitty's clothes and hair dried, they talked about everything but what was on their minds. Shelly Sullivan lived in Charlotte. It wasn't until Kitty had pulled out of the parking lot and didn't get on the highway that Rose laughed. "Shouldn't we call and tell Shelly we're coming?"

"I don't think so," Kitty replied. She loved her sister, yet she hated the way she could read her mind. "I think I'd like to surprise her." At the next traffic signal, she pulled the Rand McNally book out of the map pocket and dropped it in Rose's lap. "I found her address in the phone book. It's on an index card in my pocketbook. Think you can find the place?"

After a few false starts and wrong turns, they found Shelly's sad little apartment complex at the end of what had once been a nice street. Kitty got the impression the builder had intended the apartment complex to be bigger. There wasn't a blade of grass in sight. Kitty parked next to an overflowing dumpster and they made their way across the mud-streaked parking lot.

At the top of the dreary enclosed staircase, Kitty hesitated outside Shelly's door. The smell of garbage and fried chicken were overwhelming in the tight passage.

"What are you waiting for?" Rose asked. "Knock before someone sees us."

Kitty wanted to lay eyes on Shelly Sullivan, nevertheless when it came right down to it, she was afraid of what she would find. "We should go. What if she's movie star gorgeous? Or hideous? Would that be worse?" Rose pushed her aside and knocked on the door. A soap opera clicked off and the sound of steps approached. When the door swung open, Kitty couldn't see Shelly's face. She could only make out a pair of faded jeans and part of a Led Zeppelin t-shirt.

"Holy crap!" Rose gasped and stumbled out of Kitty's line of sight.

Shelly was in her mid-twenties, with long auburn hair and a slim frame. A sprinkling of freckles danced across her upturned nose and clear blue eyes sat under sparse brows. It was like looking at an old photograph of herself. Kitty's heart twisted in her chest. For the first time since she killed Seth, she remembered that she once loved him. *He really was trying to start over. He wasn't trading me in for any old floozie. He found a younger version of me.*

"Can I help you?" Shelly said.

Kitty stepped out of the shadows. "I'm Kitty Haskell."

"Oh," Shelly said. She pulled her shoulders back and stood up straighter. "Won't you come in?"

Kitty and Rose stepped inside and stood awkwardly in the tiny living room. The apartment resembled a sorority house after a party. Dirty clothes covered the couch and chair. The remnants of a pizza congealed on the floor and a pile of plates threatened to teeter into the sink. Shelly pushed a pair of pajamas off the couch. They landed beside a laundry basket of baby clothes. "Would you like to sit down?"

"I'll stand," Kitty replied. The stench of dirty diapers made her eyes water. She walked past Shelly to a bassinet in the kitchen area where the baby was curled up in the corner. There were no blankets or toys in sight. His tiny hands stuck several inches out of the sleeves of the heavy blue sleeper. "This child needs to be changed."

"I changed him a few hours ago."

"A few hours ago?" Rose grabbed the young woman's arm and began lecturing Shelly on proper diapering techniques. Kitty leaned over and lifted the baby out of the crib. The diaper had leaked through the sleeper on to the thin sheet. Kitty held the baby in her hands like a turkey and walked further into the apartment. There were no changing supplies in the cramped bathroom. She pushed open the bedroom door with her hip in search of a changing table.

The bedroom was that of a girl, not a mother. A flimsy nightgown hung on the back of the door. The large bed had rumpled, cleanish flannel sheets. Museum prints for Manet and Pissarro exhibits covered the walls. There was no changing table and no crib.

Kitty looked down at the baby. "Where are all your things, little man?" He looked back at her with serious blue eyes. She took the baby back into the bathroom and considered the mildew covered shower enclosure while she sat on the toilet to pull the wet sleeper off the baby.

"Sink bath it is," she sighed. It was difficult to avoid getting her dress dirty, but Kitty managed to strip the baby down and wipe him off with toilet paper. Kitty dropped the soiled sleeper and heavy diaper on the floor and gave the inside of the sink a quick wipe with the hand towel. "I'd like this to be cleaner, but beggars can't be choosers." She turned on the taps and wiped the baby down with the cleanest looking face cloth she could reach. The baby had yet to make a peep. He continued to study her throughout the short bath. When she wrapped him in the only towel in reach and cradled him in the crook of her elbow, he gave her a charming little smile.

"Oh yeah, you are definitely Seth's child. You've got his rakish grin." She tickled his soft cheek. The baby started to root for her finger.

Kitty stepped back into the living room where Rose seemed to be making some kind of chart on the back of a pizza box. Shelly blinked at her as if she were about to cry.

"Where do you keep the diapers?"

Shelly looked away from Rose and stared wide-eyed at Kitty. "You look a little like me," she blurted out.

"You look like her," Rose said. "She's the original. You're the cheap knock off."

"Where are the clean diapers?" Kitty repeated slowly. "Baby? Diaper?"

"Over there." Shelly flicked her finger in the direction of a paper shopping bag sitting on a kitchen chair. Shelly didn't move to take the baby from Kitty or retrieve a diaper for her. Kitty wondered if she was on drugs. She was certainly dimwitted.

The baby fussed when Kitty moved toward the make shift changing area Shelly had set up on the kitchen table. Kitty's stomach flipped to see the trash can full of dirty disposable diapers so close to the sink full of dishes. She doubted Shelly had ever used the table as an eating surface, but it still was not a proper place to change a baby.

"Wait a minute, Kitty. Don't put him down yet," Rose commanded as she stormed out of the apartment. Kitty held the baby's naked little body against the front of her dress. He nuzzled into her neck. A rush of emotions rose in Kitty's chest. She remembered holding Becky and Bobby's little bodies when they were this age. Those sleep-deprived, hormone-laden days of perpetual feeding and changing her babies were some of her fondest memories. She loved being a mother.

"What's his name?" Kitty asked.

"Steven," Shelly replied. She still hadn't moved any closer to Kitty. "Seth picked it."

"After his favorite uncle. He wanted to name Becky, Stephanie. Rebecca is a much more solid name."

Rose returned with a newspaper. "When I did my nursing school rotation with the health department, Sister Agnes taught us that the pages of a newspaper are near enough to sterile." Her eyes danced as she swept the damp towel and soiled changing pad off the table on to an empty chair and spread the classified section of the newspaper over the table. Kitty was reminded of how passionate Rose had been when she first became a nurse. She'd lost that spark over the years of working in the delivery room. Rose took the baby from Kitty and laid him down on the paper. "Okay young man —"

"His name is Steven," Kitty interjected.

"Of course it is." Rose rolled her eyes. "Seth was going to get a kid named Steven by hook or by crook." Rose examined the baby closely, rotating his hips and peering in his tiny ears. "He looks good. A little thin, but okay." Rose deftly slipped a disposable diaper under Steven's bottom and peeled back its adhesive strips. She held her hand on his squirmy body like a seasoned expert as she reached into the laundry basket under the table for a clean onsie. Once the baby was dressed, Rose turned to Shelly, still standing in the middle of the living room staring at them.

"This baby is hungry. When was the last time he nursed?"

"There are bottles made up in the refrigerator. I made them with boiled water like the can says." Shelly spoke as if talking to a teacher or police officer. "I only nurse him at night. He has formula during the day because I have to go back to work in a couple of weeks." Rose turned the flame on under the saucepan of water still on the two burner stove, and retrieved a bottle of formula from the refrigerator.

"What do you do?" Kitty asked. *Obviously not housecleaning.*

"I'm an art teacher." She looked at her hands. "At least for now. I don't know how much longer I can tell them my new husband is away on business."

"That's the least of your problems, honey," Rose said from the kitchen. She tested the formula on the inside of her wrist and returned to swirling the baby bottle in the simmering water with one hand while holding the baby in the other.

"Let me guess," Kitty said. She stepped around Shelly and started picking up the clutter around the apartment. "You have a degree in Art History."

"Fine Arts," Shelly said.

Kitty examined a stained sleeper. "You don't seem very well set up for a baby. Where's the regular crib? I thought it would be in the bedroom."

"I had this one in the bedroom, but I can't sleep with him crying next to my head. He's fine out here."

Kitty recalled how she and Seth had argued about moving Becky from the bassinet in their room to her crib in the nursery so he wouldn't hear her crying in the night. Kitty had slept on the floor next to the crib until Becky was sleeping through the night. When Bobby came along, Kitty set up a cot in the nursery to save her aching back.

Rose tested the formula again and was satisfied. She brought the baby back into the living room and seemed about to hand him to Shelly, then thought better of the idea and sat down on the low couch. Steven immediately began rooting for the bottle. "He's got a good appetite. That's a good sign."

Shelly watched Rose, which allowed Kitty to get a better look at Shelly. The resemblance was remarkable. Shelly's hair, pulled back in a loose ponytail, was the same carefree light auburn Kitty's had been when she was Shelly's age and she had a similar way of standing on one foot and then the other.

"He's always hungry," Shelly said as she tossed a tiny sock into the basket in the hall. A deep ridge formed on her forehead as she furrowed her eyebrows. "Then he just poops it all out and is hungry again."

She's not as young as I initially thought. That peaches and cream complexion is going to get blotchy and lined before this child is walking. I didn't start getting wrinkles until Bobby was riding a bike.

"He's a baby," Rose said with a snort. "They do that."

Kitty sat down next to Rose and stroked Steven's bare foot. "But where is the crib?"

"We never bought one. It seemed silly to buy one until we moved.

Seth promised that we would have a quickie wedding then move into his house."

"My house." Kitty corrected her without taking her eyes off Steven's instep. "It's my house. I am still his wife."

Kitty looked at Shelly's pink toes sticking out from her bell bottoms. *She shouldn't be walking around in bare feet on this filthy carpet.* The carpet was disgusting. There were stains here and there and bits of food embedded in the pile. It was no place for a child to be crawling around.

Rose popped the bottle out of Steven's mouth and sat him up on her lap with a practiced hand. "What exactly did you expect Seth to do?"

"He promised to take care of Steven and me." Shelly sounded so desperate, Kitty felt bad for being so harsh with her.

"Seth's promises aren't worth a whole lot. He promised to be faithful to me," Kitty said. "A lot of good that did me." She took Steven from Rose and put him over her shoulder to burp him. "You're on your own now, honey. Just like me."

"But, um, don't you have alimony from your first husband?"

"Alimony? What are you talking about?"

"You must have been married before. Seth isn't old enough to have a kid in college."

"How old did you think he was?"

"Thirty-seven?"

"Try forty-nine. He's two years older than I am." Shelly's face fell. "Yeah, he lied to you. Haven't you figured that out yet? He was lying to you about everything."

Steven expelled a loud burp in Kitty's ear and nuzzled into her neck. "Let me guess, Seth must have told you all sorts of wonderful things about me. Did he say something like I am too smart for my own good? Or that I know all kinds of useless things about art and philosophy and history, but can't balance a checkbook?"

Shelly blushed and looked away. "Something like that."

"Did you know that Seth thinks it's a waste of time to educate young women? Women like you, for instance."

"No way!"

"He doesn't think our daughter deserves to go to Brown, because she'll just get married and have kids anyway."

"Brown? Wow."

"She's very bright," Kitty said with pride.

She repositioned Steven to her lap and took the bottle from Rose. "Really now, did you really think he was going to leave his wife and children? What makes you any different from all the other pretty little girls Seth has led down the garden path?" Rose stood up and rounded on Shelly. "I'm sure it was fun for him to come here and play house for a while, but you're a fool if you thought he was actually going to marry you! That was a bold assumption, even for a gold digger like you."

Shelly seemed to wake up a bit. "I'm not a gold digger!"

"Were you having an affair with a married man?"

Shelly seemed to shrink again. "Well, yeah."

"Did you know he was married when you got yourself pregnant?"

"Yes, but —"

"Are you aware of the existence of birth control?"

"Of course, but —"

"Exactly. How are you not a gold digger then?"

Kitty wasn't sure if the emotion clouding Shelly's face was rage from Rose taunting her, or pent-up frustration with having her situation so plainly stated. Shelly stabbed her finger toward the door. "Get out of my place! You can't come in here and lecture me on being a good mother. What do you know? This is between me and Mrs. Haskell."

Rose walked to the door. "I'll be in the car. I wouldn't want to offend this delicate flower any further."

"I'll be there in a sec, Rose." Kitty stood up and pushed Steven into Shelly's arms. He immediately began to cry.

"You're leaving? But what am I going to do?"

"I don't know what you're going to do. It's really not my problem." Shelly was so pathetic; Kitty hoped she didn't seem pathetic to other people.

Shelly put the baby down on the couch and sat down with her head in her hands.

"No!" Kitty ran across the tiny room and scooped up the baby again. "He could roll off."

"No, he won't. He can't do anything. I think he's defective."

Kitty covered Steven's ear with her palm. "Don't say that. He's perfect." She rubbed her thumb across the baby's skull. "He'll start rolling over any day now. You just need to give him a chance to get strong enough. Are you giving him some belly time every day."

"All he ever does is lay around on his stomach. It's the only way he'll sleep."

Kitty gritted her teeth. "You put him down on his belly?"

Shelly looked at her blankly.

"Didn't anyone warn you about crib death? Isn't your mother helping you? Don't you have sisters?"

"I don't have any family. My parents died when I was a kid, and my brother was killed in Vietnam." Shelly started to cry. "You have to help me. I can't do this all by myself. Where's Seth?"

As if Seth would have been any help. He didn't change a diaper or stay up rocking a colicky baby. He never paid any attention to either of his other children until they were walking.

Kitty looked around for a place to put Steven down. There wasn't a clean surface anywhere and the crib sheet was still dirty. She tried to hand the baby to Shelly. She wouldn't take him. "I can see you're feeling down," Kitty said. "It gets better eventually."

"This is nothing like I thought it was going to be." Shelly began to weep. "He just keeps crying and I'm so tired. I can't do this."

"Have you spoken to your doctor about having the Baby Blues?"

"He said to get more fresh air and it would pass."

Kitty could imagine what that conversation had been like. Doctors seemed to think new mothers weren't able to know when there was something wrong. She'd felt overwhelmed after Bobby was born, and she had both her mother and her sister helping her for the first few months. Kitty hadn't had to worry about money or keeping a roof over her head either.

"I just need to get some sleep. I'm sure I'll be okay if I just got some sleep."

"That's not very likely," Kitty said with a little laugh. Kitty stripped the sheet off the bassinet with one hand while deftly holding Steven with the other. "I don't think I slept more than a few hours at a time until Bobby was six."

When she looked back at Shelly to ask her where a clean sheet might be, she was staring glassy eyed out the window. "I can't do it. I can't."

There was a desperation in Shelly's voice that frightened Kitty. It sounded very much like the desperation she had felt herself at times. She was afraid Shelly could do something rash and live to regret. Kitty held the baby a bit tighter to her chest.

"Please, I can't do this all by myself."

"I don't know how I can help you. Seth left me nothing but debts." Steven started to fuss. Kitty rubbed his little back until he quieted down.

"How did you do that?" Shelly stood up and watched Kitty soothing the baby. "I don't know how to do that. I don't know how to be a mother."

"It's not something you learn how to do from reading a book. You just do it. You just love them more than anyone else in the world, more than yourself." She looked up at Shelly and recognized the exhausted look in her face. She needed a break. "Look, you have my number. If you get in trouble and need advice, give me a call. Okay?"

Tears ran down Shelly's freckled cheeks as she nodded. Kitty gave Steven one last pat on the back and rushed out the door before she gave in to the impulse to stay and take care of them both.

She walked back to the car and climbed in without a word. She blinked back tears as she drove away from the dingy apartment complex. She hated leaving Steven there.

Rose looked over at her with a little smirk. "You are such a sucker for a cute baby." They navigated their way back to the highway and drove for an hour before Rose pushed the cigarette lighter in on the dashboard. She fished a cigarette out of her purse and held it to Kitty's clenched lips. When the lighter popped out, Kitty held its glowing surface to the tip of her cigarette. After three long drags on the cigarette, Kitty said, "I don't like leaving him there. She's half out of her mind."

Her hand shook as she lit another cigarette off her first and pressed the butt into the tiny ashtray. She made a mental note to clean the car when they got back to Magnuson. Becky had kept it spotless and now there was ash in the carpet. She pushed her hair behind her ear and twisted her diamond stud.

Rose flicked Kitty's hand away from her ear. "What?"

"What do you mean, what?"

"You would be a terrible poker player. You fiddle with your earrings when you're trying not to say something. How do you think Mother always knew when you were lying about not getting an A on a test?"

"No mystery there. She didn't think I was capable of doing well enough to get an A."

"You would twist that pair of gold hearts in your ears like they were television knobs."

"I loved those earrings," Kitty said. "I lost one of them somewhere along the line. I kept its mate. I thought it could resurface in an old pocketbook or be stuck inside a sweater."

"Okay, so what are you not saying?"

She cracked the rear window to let the smoke out. "I was just thinking how none of this would have happened if I hadn't stopped drinking."

Rose raised her eyebrows and wagged her head back and forth as if she didn't disagree.

"No really. If I hadn't stopped drinking, I would never have been so hard on Seth. We would have gone on like before, and he would never have looked for a new me. I could have gone on being his Kitty instead of being such a drag all the time."

"You were always a drag."

"If I was still drinking, I could have ignored things and Seth would've stayed home and never met Shelly. If I hadn't changed, he wouldn't have ruined that poor woman's life."

"You don't know that. He cheated on you when you were half in the bag all the time. You just didn't care."

"I cared. I didn't talk about it, but I cared." Kitty took a deep drag and blew the smoke out the window. It didn't help enough. She needed something to fill the growing need in her belly – a drink, or something sweet and gooey. A drink. "I should have learned to handle Seth better. Now I've ruined all our lives." Kitty changed lanes to get around an old pick-up driving thirty miles an hour. "That little boy doesn't deserve what's happened to him. He deserves a better life than that woman can give him."

"He's a baby. He doesn't know anything different."

"But we do. We know." She changed back into the center lane and settled at a steady speed. "No child should live like that. There wasn't even one teddy bear or special blanket."

"Did you see the inside of that refrigerator," Rose said.

"Filthy?"

"Empty. The whole top shelf was bottles of formula. She must make twenty up at a time. But the rest of the fridge was pretty much empty. There was a half-gallon of milk and some orange juice but no meat or vegetables."

"I saw a bunch of pizza boxes and some cartons from a Chinese restaurant in the trash."

"Yeah," Rose said thoughtfully. She looked up at the roof of the car as if trying to recreate what she had seen in the apartment in her mind. "The pizza boxes were at least a week old. The cheese was hard and mold was beginning to grow on the tomato sauce. The stuff in the trash was old too. I think Miss Shelly is not eating much of anything right now. She was awfully thin for a nursing mother."

Kitty shook her head slightly. "I find it hard to believe she would stop nursing like that. I nursed both the kids for at least six months." Kitty took another drag off her cigarette and flicked the ash out the window. "I don't think she loves that little boy at all."

"Be serious, Kitty. The child has been secondary all along."

"People take no responsibility for their actions anymore." Kitty quickly looked over at Rose, threw her head back, and laughed hysterically.

sixteen

tacia came in from her morning swim to find an illegible note on the kitchen counter. "Did you take this?" She asked Weldon.

"It was me," Marcus yelled from the patio.

"It was I," Lana corrected him. "It was I."

"Okay, Emily Post," Marcus said through a mouthful of Cheerios. "It was I." Stacia smiled to herself as she freshened up Weldon's coffee and poured a cup for herself. It was nice to hear her children teasing each other again. There wouldn't be too many more years before Lana stopped coming home during summer break, then Marcus would go off to school himself.

She held the note at arm's length. "I can't read this. Who called?"

"That tall lady that's always so mean to you. Betsy?"

"Bitsy?" Stacia put her coffee cup down and stared at Marcus. "What did Bitsy want?"

Marcus poured more cereal into the puddle of milk still in his bowl. "She wants you to come over for tea at two. Something about the school."

"My goodness," Stacia said with a lightness she didn't feel. "I've been summoned to the inner sanctum." Chip Evans frequently bragged about the Chicago firm he'd hired to design their masterpiece of modern architecture and the time Architectural Digest featured the house in the magazine, but he and Bitsy never entertained.

"You'll have to wear your fanciest flip-flops," Lana said. She poured coffee into a cup and held it under her nose. Stacia wondered exactly when her little girl had grown into this willowy woman that drank coffee and corrected people's grammar. If she tamed that hair back in a tight chignon, she'd look just like Von did at that age. Stacia paused as she realized Lana was already older than her Aunt Von had been when she died. *How did I miss that? Where did the time go?*

"Bitsy will probably make your mother take her shoes off and wear paper booties before going inside," Weldon said from behind the newspaper.

"Poor Bitsy," Stacia sighed. "It's hard to believe the quiet girl who lived across the street from me grew up to be the brittle woman we know now."

Lana sat down beside her father and picked up the business section of the paper. "Were you friends?"

"We spent a lot time together. Her mama and my mama were real good friends. Happy Magnuson came by every morning for coffee, even when Mama got sick." Stacia had to pause and hang on the side of the sink for a second. She still felt the loss of her mother like a hole in her heart.

"Kind of like the way I know Becky because you and Kitty are friends?" Lana tossed the paper aside and picked up the comics. "Was Happy happy?"

"No," Weldon said. "She was a lot like Bitsy - mean as a hornet." He flipped the newspaper around to show Lana an article. "Check this out, they put the article about the uprising in Soweto on the bottom of page six."

Stacia left her husband and daughter to debate world events and went upstairs to change. She hadn't thought about Happy Magnuson in years. Happy had died while Stacia was concentrating on recovering from the five surgeries that eventually allowed her to walk again, then she and Weldon had moved all over the country for several years while he was in the service. By the time they returned to North Carolina, Bitsy was married to Chip and they were both mothers. Stacia paused on the stairs as she realized that she and Bitsy were nearing the age their mothers had been when they died.

★★★

In the area of Magnuson known as The Oaks, the stately homes stood back from the broad shaded avenues like a line of debutantes, beautiful and aloof. Until Overlook and a handful of other exclusive neighborhoods were built beside the two lakes that cradled the

Magnuson city limits, anyone who was anyone lived in The Oaks.

Stacia waited at the light on Center Street to turn left onto Loralei Lane. There hadn't been a light there when she'd ridden her bicycle every afternoon to her ballet lessons. She studied the white pillared monstrosity that had been the Magnuson home when she and Bitsy were little girls. It was now the headquarters of the Magnuson Junior League. The side yard had been converted into a parking lot and the front porch had been retrofitted to accommodate wheelchair ramps. It was hard believe a family had ever lived there.

When the light changed, she made the turn and pulled into the driveway of her childhood home, a stone and brick Craftsman style house with a deep front porch and stone portico on the side. A bicycle was propped against the side of the house. Stacia was glad her brother and his children had moved in with their father. Ever since her sister-in-law had walked out on him, they'd leaned heavily on each other for support.

Stacia had a few minutes before she needed to meet Bitsy and wanted to drop in on her father. She didn't get over to the old house as often as she should. She spoke to her father several times a week and saw him at church on Sundays. He was still in excellent health and kept himself busy helping care for his other grandchildren.

Mr. Tate was washing the breakfast dishes when Stacia came in. "You caught me with my rubber gloves on," he said.

Stacia kissed her father on the cheek. "We wouldn't want you to get dishpan hands, Daddy." She pulled a dish towel from a drawer and lifted a plate from the sink. "Here, let me dry. Did the children get off to their day camp okay this morning?"

"We almost had a disaster. Tim couldn't find his swimsuit and was in tears." Mr. Tate handed another plate to Stacia. "If you'd told me twenty years ago my retirement would involve getting children ready in the morning and washing dishes, I would have worked 'til I dropped."

Stacia swatted him with the dish towel. "Hush up. You love having children in the house again." She picked up another plate and carefully dried it. "Where was Bud during the swimsuit disaster?"

"He'd already left for the office. Keep it under your hat, but Magnuson-Tate is thinking of buying the hydroelectric plant below Lake Wylie."

"Really? There's a hydroelectric plant on Lake Wylie?" Stacia wondered if Kitty knew that and if that could become a problem if they ever dragged the lake looking for Seth's body.

"What brings you by this morning?"

"I'm visiting Bitsy."

"Really? Getting in that house is like getting in to see The Great and Mysterious Oz."

"You've been reading The Wizard of Oz to Tim at bed time, haven't you?"

Mr. Tate put down his washcloth and turned to his daughter. "He's very careful with the books in your room. He knows they belong to you."

"They belonged to Mama long before they belonged to me." She lifted the stack of dishes and slipped them into the cabinet. She looked around the kitchen. "How's everything around here? Do you still need Weldon to come by and look at the shower valve upstairs?"

"He talked Bud and I through it the other day. We weren't using the right kind of wrench."

"I'm surprised you and Bitsy are getting together. Weldon told me how you reacted when you found out that he asked Bitsy to get Marcus into Magnuson Country Day School."

"I'm still pretty freaked out about him calling her. I assume that's what she wants to talk about. How much do you bet she wants me to be on the PTA over there?"

"You do have years of experience."

"I'm too tired. I'm finished with PTAs and school boards. If the city wants to destroy itself, I don't need to be a part of it."

"So you're just going to take your ball and go home?"

"Pretty much." Stacia checked her watch, then kissed her father goodbye before rushing out the door. "Gotta boogie, Bitsy's waiting."

★★★

The Magnuson-Evans lived beyond the paved portion of Loralei Lane. After the line of black iron mailboxes ended, Stacia continued to drive between dense walls of camellias for another half mile until she came to a polished pink granite obelisk with the number forty-two chiseled into each face. Stacia slowed and coasted into a clearing carpeted with white pea stone. Bitsy's distinctive white Cadillac sat inside an open garage next to the sleek glass and steel structure. Stacia could see clear through the house to a stand of birch trees around what appeared to be a patio. She wondered if there were blinds cleverly hidden behind the steel roof supports.

She checked her lipstick in her Jeep's side view mirror before walking between the squared off boxwood borders along the raked stone path. There wasn't a leaf or an errant blade of grass. She won't have been surprised if someone silently emerged to rake away her footprints while she was inside.

The door swung open before Stacia had a chance to ring the bell. Bitsy appeared as if out of nowhere. Her powder blue silk jumpsuit and oversized sunglasses made her hair seem even more Barbie doll-like than ever. "Stacia, honey," she drawled.

"It was such a surprise to be invited to your home." Stacia heard the disdain in her own voice and took a breath. *Be nice. Don't show weakness, but act like a Tate.* "We probably could have talked about the school over the phone."

"I actually wanted to talk to you about something else." Bitsy wound the hem of her voluminous sleeve around her finger. "In private." In the direct sunlight, Stacia noticed deep wrinkles around Bitsy's mouth as she glanced over Stacia's shoulder. "Did anyone see you drive in?"

"I don't know, why?"

Bitsy seemed to flutter more than step back to let Stacia enter. "No reason."

Everything inside the house was white – the floors, the walls, the furniture. The only color in the entryway was a single enormous poppy blossom on the central table. There were no shoes by the door, no keys in a bowl, no sign that people lived there. The house reminded Stacia of a set from A Clockwork Orange. It had been several years since she and Weldon had seen the film, however she wouldn't soon forget it.

"How's Chip?" Stacia asked.

Bitsy propped the door open with a porcelain statue of a dog. "He's away for a few days with the National Guard."

Stacia shuddered in the air conditioning. "Is Judy enjoying her summer so far?"

"She's staying in Nashville for the summer." Bitsy blinked rapidly and looked toward the stairwell to the lower floor as if Judy could suddenly appear. "She wants to take a few extra classes." Stacia cocked her head. *Why would Bitsy lie like that about Judy taking classes? I was only making small talk.*

Bitsy turned toward the pristine kitchen. The tips of silver slippers peeked out below the wide legs of her jumpsuit. "I made tea. Would you like some?"

"Please."

As Stacia wandered deeper into the house, she recalled reading about how the architect had achieved the illusion that made the house notable. A sunken living room created the effect of being able to see through the house and out the back wall. Polished black steps led down to a black marble floor below while plush white carpeting cascaded over the edge to a white velvet horseshoe. Stacia paused at the top of the steps, suddenly feeling off balance. The architect had used the same types of depth perception sleights of hand the stage designers had used when she played a doll coming to life in the ballet. As she'd spun across the stage, she appeared to change size.

Bitsy returned with a lacquered tray containing tall water glasses and a diminutive tea set in the palest of celadon. She seemed to float down the three steps rather than walk and poured two cups of pale green tea. It smelled like rose petals and newly mown grass.

Stacia took a cup and sat opposite Bitsy on the deep cushions. "Did Chip bring these back from Korea?"

"The spoils of war." Bitsy took a sip from the tall glass in front of her. She pushed a sugar bowl in the shape of a flower across the table. "You still put a pile of sugar in your tea?"

Stacia smiled and spooned two scoops of sugar into her cup. "Some things never change." A wry smile flitted across Bitsy's face as she stared into her glass.

Stacia glanced out the wall of glass at the back of the house. A line of birches were stationed like sentinels around a slender pool set flush with the geometric stone patio. At the far end of the patio, a stylized stone monkey sat on its haunches. At first glance, the pool area appeared peaceful but the longer she looked at it, the more uncomfortable she felt. She wouldn't have been surprised if the monkey's eyes were implanted with video cameras like in a Bond film.

"Do you swim often?"

"It's Chip's pool," Bitsy said with a shrug. "He does laps every morning, rain or shine, all year round. I never go out there." She flicked a nonexistent piece of lint off her knee before taking another sip from her glass. Stacia suspected it wasn't filled with water. Perhaps the giant sunglasses covered bloodshot eyes as well as making a fashion statement. Bitsy's hand shook as she laid the glass down on an ebony coaster and stiffly crossed her legs. "Are you still swimming in those little races of yours?"

"Not as often as I was a few years ago. There aren't as many opportunities to compete at our age."

"You always were more athletic than me. Do you remember when I fell off my bike and broke my arm?"

Stacia carefully put her tea cup on the coffee table. The porcelain was as thin as paper. "When we were nine?"

Bitsy nodded and took another sip from her glass. "Remember how the other kids just kept going like nothing had happened?"

"Not really." Stacia wasn't sure where this conversation was going: certainly not toward her letter to the editor or Magnuson Country Day School.

"I do." Bitsy refilled her cup. "You circled back and helped me back to the house. Then you went back and got my bike while my mother took me took to the hospital."

"I did? I don't remember that."

"You're always so helpful," Bitsy said. She looked away as if thinking of something else.

Stacia took another sip of the delicious tea and waited for Bitsy to get to the point.

"That new place for women the church had a benefit for. Is it up and running yet?"

"Not as far as I know. I can check with Kitty. She was on the Women's Circle committee."

"No, I don't want to talk to anyone else. Only you."

"Me? Why? I'm not even on that committee."

Bitsy swung her head around to look directly at Stacia. "I need your help."

"Okay." Although she'd been looking forward to getting a look at Bitsy's mysterious modern enclave, Stacia wanted to get out of there.

Something was wrong. Bitsy had lost the breathy quality in her voice. "What do you need?"

"You know lots of people. People not from here."

"I guess I do." Stacia frowned. "People relocate in and out of Magnuson all the time these days."

"I need help relocating."

Stacia rolled her eyes and stood up to leave. "Quentin would know more about that than me. Why don't you ask him?" As she moved toward the stairs, her teaspoon caught on the rickrack trim at the bottom of her dress and flew across the table.

Bitsy automatically reached out to catch it. The sudden motion forced her voluminous sleeve back to expose mottled green and yellow bruises along her twig-like forearm.

"Goodness gracious, did you take another tumble off your bike?" Bitsy's earlier question seemed to make more sense now.

What little color Bitsy had drained from her face as she retracted her hand into the deep sleeves. "This was a mistake," she said quietly. She pulled her legs up onto the couch and hugged her knees to her chest. "You need to go."

The fine hairs of the back of Stacia's neck stood up as her internal radar blared. She reached over and pulled back Bitsy's sleeve. A bruise in the shape of a man's hand marred Bitsy's upper arm.

"What is this?"

"Just a bruise." Bitsy tried to pull away, but Stacia was much stronger. "It's nothing, really."

Stacia looked around the immaculate house. There wasn't a speck of dust or a piece of lint anywhere. It was perfect. She had a sinking feeling in her stomach. Stacia didn't let go of Bitsy's wrist as she moved to sit beside her and gently lifted the sunglasses from her face. Bitsy's left eye was swollen shut. The bruises were more than a day old. The skin around the eye was still purple, but the edges had begun turning yellow. Stacia had seen her on Sunday in church, so the bruises were less than five days old.

Stacia put the sunglasses down on the coffee table and paused for a moment. She was tempted to leave and never say another word about this to anyone. It could be their little secret. Stacia was getting very good at keeping secrets.

She could feel Bitsy quietly sobbing next to her, yet her mind was filled with Happy Magnuson's booming voice. Happy had been unflinching in the face of Mrs. Tate's debilitating illness and bound into their kitchen every morning with a smile. It would break her heart to see her Bitsy battered and bruised like this.

Stacia slowly pulled Bitsy into her arms. "Tell me. Tell me everything."

seventeen

Bitsy pulled away from Stacia's embrace and reached for her glass. Stacia grabbed it out of her hand and took a sip. It was gin. "Are you drunk?"

"I was nervous."

"I thought after you took that tumble at the church fair and Chip was so—"

"Embarrassed?" Bitsy snatched the glass and drained it before Stacia could grab it back. "Disappointed? Is that the word you're searching for? You have no idea how disappointed he can get." She rubbed the base of the glass over the back of her wrist.

"How long?" Stacia asked. "Judy was a little girl when you fell down that time. Even then?"

Bitsy turned her head and stared out the window at the line of birch trees standing guard around the pool.

"That nose job a few years ago? He broke your nose, didn't he?"

Bitsy nodded.

"All the make-up. I should have known."

Bitsy wiggled her fingers toward the long scar running over the Stacia's knee, which was a daily reminder of her car accident. "Some of us aren't so proud of our scars."

"I'm not proud. I don't want to forget."

Bitsy continued to stare out the window. "I do."

Bitsy flinched when Stacia reached out and touched her shoulder. She suspected it was bruised as well. "The eye lift?"

"Broken cheekbone."

"Why didn't you leave him?"

"I've tried." Bitsy looked at the empty glass in her hand and sighed. "He always found me."

"You're not helpless. Run away."

Bitsy swung her head around to look at Stacia, and winced. "It's not that simple," she said rubbing her neck.

"You have money." Stacia leaned back. "Please tell me you haven't signed over your money to that man."

Bitsy's brow furrowed unevenly. "I don't think so."

Stacia stood up and gathered up the tea set. "We should clean this up and get you out of here." The muscles in her legs and back were twitching with anger. She needed to move. "Quick, go pack a bag."

Bitsy ran up the three marble steps to the foyer and disappeared down the stairs to the lower level. After a few minutes, she stumbled back up the stairs with the largest suitcase Stacia had ever seen. She rushed from the kitchen and took the suitcase from Bitsy. "Give me that." The suitcase was nearly as big as Stacia. "All we need is to have you go flying down the stairs and breaking your neck on the day you finally get up the nerve to get out of here." She carried it into the foyer.

"For your information, I've tried to leave many times. Three years ago, I was gone two whole weeks before he found me."

"The year you took Judy to Paris?" Stacia stopped and thought back to that summer. Bitsy and her daughter had been gone for over two months. When she returned, Bitsy had a stylish short hairdo that made her look like she had just walked off a runway. Stacia raised her hand to side of her head. "Your hair."

"Broken skull. They had to shave the side of my head."

"But Judy—"

"She went to Paris that summer, just not with me. My sister took her. That's why I made a run for it." She wiped her nose with her sleeve. "It got worse after Judy went away to school. He used to have to wait until she was out of the house."

"Does Judy know what he does to you?" Bitsy nodded. Stacia felt like a coward. She couldn't bring herself to ask if Chip hurt Judy as well.

"Where do you want me to take you? I'm sure one of the shelters—"

"No! Not anything in Magnuson. I can't let anyone know."

"How about a hotel?"

"I don't have any cash and I can't use my credit cards or write a check. He'll find me. He always finds me."

"I have money. How much do you need?"

"I don't know. I'd need a car, and a place to sleep, and—"

"Hold on, first things first. We need to get you out of here." Stacia carried the suitcase out the door. "Where did you ever get this thing? Were you planning on taking a cruise around the world?"

"It was Mama's. She stored her winter clothes in it and kept it under the bed." Bitsy hung on to the foyer table. The alcohol was hitting her. "I've had it packed and ready to go for about six months. I couldn't use any of the pieces Chip bought. He'd notice if anything had moved in the spare room."

Stacia bent to move the porcelain dog away from the door. Bitsy lunged forward and caught the door before it could close. "Don't close the front door. I held my finger against the lock when Dorrie went out to get the paper, so the alarm wouldn't go off when you came." Stacia now understood why Bitsy seemed to appear out of nowhere when she'd arrived. She'd been waiting with the door slightly ajar.

"Is Dorrie the girl? Where is she now?"

"Sleeping downstairs." Bitsy smiled a genuine smile that showed a chip in her lower incisor. "I put two of my sleeping pills in her morning coffee, so I don't think she'll be waking up for a while."

"Doesn't she see what Chip does to you?"

"Chip pays her to look the other way and lets her live here so she can keep an eye on me when he's out of town." It made Stacia's blood run cold to think of Bitsy living in that house for one more second with a prison guard as a maid.

"Come on, let's go," she said. Bitsy retrieved her handbag from a mirrored chest of drawers and teetered outside. Stacia helped her to the Jeep then returned for the heavy suitcase. She looked at their footprints and the tire marks in the gravel driveway.

"When she comes to and finds you gone, will Dorrie call Chip right away?"

"I don't know. Probably."

"Then let's make it a little bit harder for them to figure out how you left." She got Bitsy into the backseat of the Jeep and drove out to where the pavement began, then returned to the garage. She found a

155

rake and smoothed out their footprints and the tracks left by her tires. Then, she slipped off her shoes and walked across the gravel in her bare feet so she didn't leave footprints. All those years of walking across the Overlook pool's gravel parking lot were finally paying off. As far as Dorrie would be able to tell, Bitsy had disappeared without a trace. She hoped that would slow Chip down enough for her to figure out what to do with Bitsy.

Stacia drove past their childhood homes as though she was transporting explosives. "I can't thank you enough for this," Bitsy said.

"Why me? Why ask me for help?"

"No one else would believe me. I know you don't like Chip, even though everyone else loves him." Stacia looked in the rearview mirror and saw Bitsy's eyes dance in her pale face. "And you're the only person who knew me before."

"What about your sister? Couldn't she help you get away from Chip?"

"Liza? She thinks Chip hung the stars just for her. She'd call the men in white coats before she'd ever call the police." Bitsy looked out the window at the majestic trees lining their street. "I tried once. Years ago, when Judy was a little girl. We'd all gone down to Emerald Isle and rented a big house on the water. Liza kept teasing me about not getting in the water until I finally told her that I couldn't because I had an enormous bruise on my thigh from where Chip had thrown me against the bedside table. No bathing suit, no matter how matronly, could've covered it up and make-up would wash right off."

"What did she say?"

"She teased me in front of Chip about making up stories in order to stay under the umbrella. He punched me so hard that night, I think he broke a rib."

"Didn't you try again? She's your sister."

"Of course I've tried." Bitsy's hands shook as she hung on to the head rest. "Dozens of times, but Chip's got it in her head that I'm making up stories to get attention. How can I fight against that?"

Stacia unconsciously drove north toward Overlook while she tried to absorb everything Bitsy had told her. "It still doesn't make sense to me. Why call me? You and I haven't been close since we were little girls."

"Like Mama used to say, you're good people." Bitsy leaned back. "I knew, even if you didn't help me, you wouldn't tell Chip."

Stacia laughed under her breath. It was true. She wouldn't have. Bitsy could still embarrass her by publicizing who wrote the controversial letter to the editor. Also, if Stacia did nothing, she would look callous if Chip ended up killing Bitsy and it came out that Stacia knew about the abuse. Although Bitsy was frightened and a drunk, she was sharp. She had little to lose by confiding in Stacia.

"Still, I was pretty sure you would help me. I remember what you did when you got in that car accident. Most people would have saved themselves, but you crawled to that house to get help."

"Lot of good it did," Stacia said under her breath. "They all still died."

"You tried though. If you would crawl to a house to save a car full of black girls, I thought you'd probably help me. We've known each other for almost fifty years."

Stacia was too kind to say it, but she would have traded Bitsy's life ten times over for even five more minutes with Von. She'd failed to save Von and the other girls that night, and had spent a lifetime trying to make amends.

They stopped at the bridge over the Lake Tate dam. Stacia looked out at the spot in the lake where she had watched Kitty kill Seth. Bitsy was right to assume she would help. She had helped Kitty keep her secret. She always helped, whether people asked for it or not, whether they deserved it or not. Her guilt about surviving that car accident was a hole in her heart that she promised herself she would fill with good deeds. Or, was it a scab she liked to pick at to know she was still alive?

She looked over at Bitsy and wondered if she had gone too far this time. Chip was a dangerous man. "Why leave today? Why didn't you call me yesterday, or last week?"

"Judy called last week. She's dropped out of school to go live with some boy in California." Bitsy played with the window crank. "She promised to go back to school if I promised to get out of that house, so I have to do this even if he finds me and kills me. I have to. Judy can't end up like me."

Stacia rolled her eyes. "You sound like Kitty, putting all your regrets on your daughter's shoulders. She's just a kid. Let her make her own mistakes." The light changed and Stacia let the clutch out to inch forward.

Kitty. Kitty can help Bitsy.

"I have an idea."

Bitsy looked at her, hope in her eyes. "Really?"

Stacia shifted into a second gear. "You are going to hide out at Kitty's house until we come up with a better plan."

"I can't do that! She'll tell Chip."

"Kitty won't tell. She's different than other people. She'll understand." Stacia shook her head at the absurd turn her day was taking. "And she's very good at keeping secrets."

eighteen

Stacia felt the weight of eyeballs on her as soon as she pulled into Kitty's driveway. Nothing on Azalea Lane ever went unseen. Until that moment, she'd capitalized on the Lookers curiosity to keep track of what was happening in Overlook. Now she craved a modicum of privacy. "Stay down," she said to Bitsy who was crouched in the back seat. "I don't want that Betty Oliphant seeing you."

She jogged up to the front door. As she waited for Kitty to answer the door, she looked across the street and saw Eileen watching her from the second-floor nursery window. She waved. It had only been a few months since Stacia had found Eileen clinging to her mailbox in the throes of yet another miscarriage and had discreetly helped her navigate the difficult days afterward. They hadn't seen much of each other now that Eileen was expecting again and didn't need Stacia's help.

Eileen had the decency to step back so Stacia could no longer see her snooping, which is more than Stacia could say for Betty Oliphant who stood in her open doorway. Living across the street from Kitty Haskell was prime real estate for a gossip those days. Betty had reported to the other Lookers when police cars and heretofore unheard of relatives had shown up in Kitty's driveway. They would have to keep Bitsy well hidden from Betty's prying eyes.

She rang the bell again and finally heard footsteps from inside the house. She was beginning to fear Kitty was working at the Arts Center that day. As soon as Kitty opened the door, Stacia pushed past her. "Is there anyone else here?"

"No, why?"

Stacia sprinted into the kitchen and opened the door to the garage. "Do you have an automatic door opener?"

"No, what's the matter?"

"Help me open the garage door." Stacia went to the heavy door and pushed it up like it was made of paper. She was already climbing into her Jeep when Kitty rushed to catch the door as it hit the top of the track and bounced back.

"Close the door behind me," Stacia shouted over the noise of the engine.

Kitty did as she was told and closed the door behind the Jeep. "What's wrong? Why are you acting like this?" She jumped when she saw movement in the back seat. She leaned closer to the window. "Bitsy!" Kitty stepped toward the open driver's side window and stared at Stacia. "What is going on?"

"You're going to have a house guest." Stacia hopped down from the Jeep and helped Bitsy climb out. She was unstable on her feet as she leaned on the fender. "Bitsy's going to stay here for a few days."

"Is she drunk?" Kitty whispered.

"As a skunk," Bitsy replied.

Stacia pulled the enormous suitcase out of the back of the Jeep and carried it into the kitchen. "And don't give me any sass about her staying."

"But—" Kitty took Bitsy's elbow and helped her inside. Bitsy wobbled through the kitchen and lay down on the family room couch.

"She's staying and you're not going to let anyone, and I mean anyone, know that she's here."

"Why here? Why me?"

"You owe me," Stacia said.

Kitty jerked her head back as if Stacia had slapped her. She couldn't argue. She did owe Stacia. She could have her locked up with a simple phone call. They both knew it.

"But, why? What's going on?"

Stacia walked over to Bitsy and pulled off her sunglasses. Kitty recoiled at the mottled skin around Bitsy's eyes.

"Who did this?"

Bitsy closed her eyes and moaned. Kitty lifted her head and tucked a pillow under it.

"Who do you think?"

"Chip? Really?"

Bitsy didn't resist as Stacia leaned over and pulled her sleeve back so Kitty could see the other bruises.

"What about the rest of her?"

Stacia rubbed the back of her neck. "I didn't have the heart to look."

"Oh, Stacia, I'm so sorry. Of course she can stay here." They walked into the foyer out of earshot of Bitsy on the couch. "Did she do something to set him off?"

"No, apparently it's been going on for years. Remember when she changed her hair." Kitty nodded. Everyone at church had noticed when conservative Bitsy had cut her hair so radically. They had all chocked it up to the influence of Paris fashion.

"He'd broken her skull."

Kitty gasped.

"You have to help her."

"Why didn't you take her to a hospital? Or your house?"

"She's afraid. He's found her before and beaten her even worse." Stacia gave Kitty a meaningful look. "And she's afraid of what people will say. You, of all people, understand what that's like."

"Yes, yes I do," Kitty said. "A lot of good that ever did me. Pride goeth before the fall."

"Amen to that."

★★★

Stacia was up and out of the house at dawn the next morning. She didn't understand how other women kept so many secrets from their husbands. She had almost told Weldon Bitsy's story four different times between coming home the previous afternoon and that morning. She didn't keep secrets from him, at least not important ones. She would leave specific details out of conversations, but she had never kept anything more important than the knowledge of a neighbor having been caught shoplifting from Weldon. Now she was keeping her involvement in covering up a murder and her hiding a battered woman from him.

She was afraid of what Weldon would do to Chip if he found out. Ever since Weldon came back from Korea, he had a sore spot for any man that raised his hand to a woman. Weldon didn't like to talk about his time in the service. Stacia had probed the point but she could never get anything out of him beyond a stream of expletives about a GI from Arkansas doing something awful in a bar in Seoul.

Stacia wished she could ask for Weldon's help. Of the hundreds of women Stacia had helped over the years, none of their problems had been this serious. She needed to take care of the Bitsy situation, and right quick. She didn't immediately know how to handle things. Should she contact the police? After her last experience with them, she doubted it. Years ago, she could have trusted the police to exact some down-home justice on Chip and keep the Tate and Magnuson names out of any police reports. Now, the police department was a maze of documentation and impersonal automatons who didn't care that her family name was on the front of the building they worked in. She was no more than a middle-aged woman in a short dress to them.

She left a note for Weldon that she was going to go to the grocery store and do some errands. That would give her a few hours to check up on Bitsy without Weldon worrying where she was. She did go to the store and bought a watermelon as well as some staples for Kitty. When she had been at Kitty's house the day before, she had noticed that her friend had very little food in her fridge and suspected she was quickly running out of grocery money. Bitsy would need to be fed and most likely had expensive tastes. Kitty was a genius in the kitchen, but she couldn't make her signature cakes without milk and eggs.

Stacia parked in Kitty's driveway and walked around the back of the house to enter through the sliding doors from the deck. She didn't want to risk Betty Oliphant seeing Bitsy answer the door. She needn't have worried. Through the glass door, she saw Bitsy and Kitty asleep on the couch. A bottle of whiskey lay on the coffee table.

Stacia shook her head and heaved a heavy sigh. *This is awful. I hoped Kitty would keep Bitsy sober, not join her in the bottle. I can't deal with a drinking Kitty on top of a murderous Kitty. There is no telling what kind of shenanigans she could get up to if she's drinking again.* She eased the slider open and stepped inside. Kitty opened her eyes and sat up. Bitsy didn't move.

"What time is it?" Kitty put a hand to her forehead. She was still dressed in the clothes she'd been wearing the day before.

Stacia hoped she had a headache, and a blinding one at that. "It's almost eight thirty. I brought you some eggs and bread."

Kitty turned a bit green at the mention of eggs. She stood up and wandered toward the kitchen. "Coffee?"

"What happened last night? I thought you'd quit drinking."

Kitty slowly made the coffee as if every motion was a laborious task. "I did. I hadn't had anything to drink for almost a year, but then Bitsy found Seth's whiskey, and then she started telling me about all the awful things Chip has done to her, and the bottle was right there, and I could tell she needed to tell me about it, but it was so terrible, and the bottle was right there, and—" Kitty leaned her head against the cabinets.

Stacia walked across the kitchen and shoved her aside so she could finish making the coffee. "That can't happen again. I need you to be on your game."

"I know," Kitty said. "I can't live like that again. I'd be sure to slip up and get myself arrested or killed." She straightened up and smiled. "Can you stay with Bitsy for a bit? I think I know someone who might be able to help Bitsy, and us, get out of this mess."

"Who?"

"No one you'd know." A smile tugged at the corners of Kitty mouth. "Just an artist I met."

nineteen

Aron bore witness to human tragedies every day; perhaps he could help her and Bitsy. She quickly showered the dregs of Seth's liquor out of her hair and stood naked in front of her closet. Nothing in her closet seemed earthy enough for the shelter. Her thoughts were muddled until she remembered that most of Becky's clothes were still in her room. She slipped on her underthings and walked down the hall to raid her daughter's things. She found a simple pair of faded Levis which were a bit loose, but would work if she wore one of Becky's thick belts. None of Becky's t-shirts and peasant blouses flattered Kitty. She wanted to look good when she saw Aaron. The thought of the younger man sent tingles down her spine. She questioned if she was really going to see him for advice on how to deal with Bitsy, or if Bitsy was an excuse to run to him.

She went back to her own closet and found the simple white silk blouse she usually wore under her green suit at Christmas time. It would work, especially if she left the top few buttons open. She had seen Lauren Hutton wearing something like that in a perfume ad. With a simple pair of loafers, Kitty looked less like a suburban mom and more like an attractive woman.

The front door of the old school was unlocked when she arrived at An Open Hand. Inside the building, she took another moment to remove her sunglasses and let her eyes adjust to the dim entrance hall light while she determined how much she could share with Aaron. The last thing Bitsy needed would be to have the Magnuson name dragged through the mud if the public discovered she was a battered woman. The offices of An Open Hand had once been the administrative offices of the school. A large curved reception desk held brochures for local social service agencies and soup kitchens. To the right, Kitty spotted Father Mike hunched over a ledger book in what must have once been the principal's office. Instead of making her presence known, she slipped down the stairs to the basement and along the hallway to the art room. Aaron stood in the center of the room with a blow-torch in one hand and length of metal tubing in the other. The statue of St. Francis was almost complete. Kitty stepped inside and waved her arms until Aaron saw her.

"Hey, pretty lady!" He had a huge grin on his face as he extinguished the torch and pulled off his leather apron. There were scorch marks on his forearms and some fresh burn holes in his shirt. "Did you hear back about showing some of my pieces, or have you got more clothes to drop off?"

"Neither I'm afraid." Kitty spread her hands out in front of her. "I've come completely empty handed today."

She felt Aaron eye her curves as she walked around the sculpture. The form-fitting jeans and simple silk blouse seemed to elicit the desire effect. Kitty felt a flush steal up her neck. "Could you have come by just to see little ol' me?"

"I need some advice." She looked away as she remembered getting drunk with Bitsy the night before. "On a couple of things."

Aaron moved as if to embrace her, but stopped short. His smile faded as he said, "Sure, sure. Let me get a chair." He stepped into the teacher's office off the art room and pulled a straight back chair into the room. Through the doorway, she could see the edge of a cot with an army blanket neatly folded across it and a small desk covered with books. Kitty hadn't realized until then that the art room was both Aaron's studio and bedroom. He sounded resigned as he turned off the light in the small office. "Can I offer you a cup of coffee? I have a thermos around here somewhere."

"No thanks. A glass of water would be nice though. I'm very thirsty this morning."

"Of course you are. You're coming off a bender. You smell like one of the guys upstairs when they're drying out."

Kitty dropped into the chair and rubbed her temples. "I'd been so good, but then...it was so awful...I can't tell you."

Aaron retrieved a half empty bottle of Coke from the other side of the room and squatted in front of her chair. "Drink this. The sugar and the caffeine will make you feel better."

"I'm so embarrassed. I had no idea you'd be able to tell."

"People can usually tell, especially if they have a problem themselves."

Kitty remembered Stacia saying something very similar to her. Everyone knew she drank. She was fooling herself to think she'd ever kept it a secret.

She felt her cheeks burn as she wiped her tears away. She wondered if they smelled of whiskey too. "Did you know that I drank when you kissed me?"

"I recognized you as a kindred spirit from the way you responded to my art that first day." Aaron pushed the Coke bottle into her hand and encouraged her to drink it. "Most people smile politely and move on, but it touched you deeply, so I figured either you have a problem with the bottle or are close to someone who does."

"Both." She drank down the Coke in one swallow. It did make her feel a bit better. She couldn't remember the last time she had drank a sugary soda; they had so many empty calories.

"Your husband?"

"My father. My sister too, I guess."

"What happened? I couldn't smell it on you the last time." Aaron took the empty bottle from her and put it on the floor before shifting his weight forward to lean his forearms on her knees. "And I pay attention, especially to pretty ladies that show up in my life like complicated angels." Kitty wiped her eyes and tried to assess what she was feeling. Her emotions were a jumble. Part of her wanted to be offended, part of her wanted to beg for his help, and part of her wanted to rip his clothes off.

"You have no idea how complicated."

"I like complicated. Who wants vanilla when you can have Rocky Road?"

"I'm a bit more Rum Raisin today."

He smiled at that and wiped a tear off the tip of her nose. "So what happened?"

"Well, a friend came over. And, she's going through a really hard

167

time. Really awful. So awful. And, she started drinking my husband's whiskey, and that reminded me of the mess I made of my marriage, and how my kids are away, and how much I miss them." She took a breath. "Suffice to say I fell off the wagon."

"And now your ass is killing you from where you landed in the road?"

Kitty laughed at that. It was nice to be honest with someone and have them understand her.

"How long had you been sober?"

"Not long. Only a few months, really. Less than a year. A lot has happened in that time though, so it felt like a long time."

"Especially when the bottle was calling to you every day."

Kitty nodded and relaxed back into the chair. It was hard, yet extremely comfortable.

Aaron rocked back on his heels. "Can we back up a second? Did you say your friend was drinking your husband's whiskey?" Kitty nodded. "He lives with an alcoholic and he keeps whiskey in his house?"

"First of all, he's gone now so it's my house, not his, and he didn't know I have a problem."

"Yes, he did."

"No, he didn't."

"Unless he's deaf, dumb, and blind, he knew. Don't kid yourself, Kitty Cat, everyone knew."

Kitty shoved him. "Don't call me that!"

Aaron teetered back and landed on his backside. He put up his hands in a gesture of surrender. "Oooh, I hit a nerve there."

Kitty crossed her legs and struggled to calm down. "It's just that I hate it when people call me Kitty Cat. It's so demeaning. I'm a grown woman."

"You go by Kitty."

"I didn't choose the name. My husband started calling me Kitty when we were first dating, and it just kind of stuck."

Aaron stood up and pulled her up out of the chair. "If you could choose your name, what would people call you? Mary?"

"There are way too many Marys in the world."

Aaron was standing entirely too close to her for her to think straight. "Kate? Kathy?"

"No, I don't like Kathy at all."

"Prudence? Martha? Deandra?"

"Kay?"

"Kay is pretty. Definitely an adult's name."

"I am an adult."

"Then act like one. Pull yourself together and stop blaming other people for your actions." Aaron leaned against the doorframe. "You said your friend was drinking. She didn't force you to take a drink too, did she?"

"No, but her stories were so awful and—"

"You seem to blame your ex for having the whiskey in the house. You could have thrown it out, especially after he left. Why were you keeping it?" Aaron rubbed the stubble on his chin. "Part of staying sober is removing the easy temptations from your life. Don't keep liquor in the house, for Christ's sake."

"What about when other people are there and they want a drink?"

"Don't let people drink in your house. It's your house."

"Thank you for the advice," she replied stiffly. "I'll keep that in mind." She sat back down and clasped her hands in her lap. "Anyway, the reason I came was to ask your advice about my friend. Like I said, she's run into a bit of trouble with her husband. He beats her." She took a deep breath as she remembered Bitsy recounting the time that Chip had broken her arm then wouldn't take her to the hospital to get it set. "She needs to get away from him. What can I do to help her? Is there some place she can go?"

"That's not really my area of expertise." He glanced around the room as if mentally flipping through file cabinets. "There's a shelter for battered women in Virginia. She's a friend of yours? Does she have any money?"

"Some," Kitty replied.

"I don't know if she would be happy there then. It's safe but it sounds more like a prison than a hotel. Has she considered checking into a hotel under a false name?"

"Believe me, she's tried that. More than once. He always finds her."

Aaron looked at Kitty with soft eyes. "I'm beginning to see what's going on now. Your friend shows up on your doorstep after running away from her husband and you two end up crying in your cups together. Am I right?"

"It's a bit more complicated than that, but pretty close."

"And now you show up here looking for my advice." Kitty nodded. "You're a good egg, Kay. A good egg."

Kitty felt her heart skip in her chest. She couldn't name what she was feeling, yet she knew that hearing Aaron compliment her made her belly feel warm and her feet feel cold at the same time. Her brain was pleading with her to get out of there before she did something stupid while her body was telling her to move closer to Aaron. She stood up and moved toward the door. "I should be going. I can't leave my friend alone for long."

Aaron stepped between her and the door. "You can't leave yet. We haven't talked about the elephant in the room."

"I promise. I will dump all the liquor down the sink as soon as I get home."

"That's good, but you know that's not what I'm talking about." He took a half step forward so they were inches apart. He smelled like soap and fire. "We need to talk about that kiss."

"Do we have to?"

Aaron ran his thumb along the shoulder seam of her blouse. "Look, I am very attracted to you, but…if you just want to be my friend."

Kitty closed the space between them so the front of her blouse pressed against his shirt. A small piece of her was appalled at her forwardness, but it was consumed by the fire engulfing her. Just like that night in the boat, Kitty felt a surge of power and clarity that enervated every cell of her body.

She raised her chin to look into Aaron's eyes and whispered, "I make an excellent friend, but I want more." She put her palms against Aaron's chest and pushed him through the doorway, then she kissed him.

Perhaps it was the remnants of the whiskey-soaked evening with Bitsy, or the closeness of the tiny office, or simply raw adrenaline-fueled lust, but Kitty made it abundantly clear how much more of Aaron she wanted. Her brain didn't interfere with her body until they were both spent and Kitty recognized her jeans were on top of the small desk and she had his leather apron wound around her ankle.

"Holy crap!" She pushed Aaron off of her and reached for the jeans.

"Holy crap, indeed!" Aaron tossed her panties to her. They were ripped and unwearable. "You weren't kidding. You do make an excellent friend."

"Oh my, oh my, oh my!" Kitty pulled the jeans over her hips and stuffed the ruined panties in her purse. She didn't know what to say when she looked up to see Aaron watching her button her blouse, a huge grin on his face. The details of what they had done were a blur, but she didn't regret it. "Oh my!" she gasped again and sprinted out the door without stopping to find her shoes.

twenty

Stacia felt odd sitting on the settee in Kitty's parlor when she was not there. She couldn't remember if she'd ever been in the parlor before and admired how well Kitty had put the room together. She flipped through the pristine copy of Ladies Home Journal on the coffee table, although she didn't register what she was looking at. She was still reeling from the events of the last few days. Happy Magnuson's face swam in front of her eyes. It would have broken her heart to see her daughter so misused. Stacia needed to help Bitsy, but she didn't know how.

She got up and went to the kitchen to find the kettle. Making a pitcher of tea always made her feel better. Kitty's kitchen was well-organized, so she easily found everything she needed. As she filled the kettle, she looked over at Bitsy still asleep in the family room. She and Kitty had talked at a regular volume for several minutes before she left, and Bitsy hadn't moved a muscle. Perhaps her own home made her so nervous, that anywhere she wasn't in constant physical danger was relaxing.

While the water came to a boil, Stacia took Daisy out to the deck and made sure the dog had fresh food and water in her bowls. She rubbed Daisy's ears. "What do you think about all this craziness? Do you miss Seth and the kids?" Daisy leaned against Stacia's thigh, making her lose her balance and sit down heavily on the teak chaise lounge. Daisy put her head in Stacia's lap. "At least you appreciate me." Stacia wasn't sure if either Kitty or Bitsy appreciated her. Neither one kowtowed to her like the Lookers did.

Stacia rubbed Daisy's ears and thought how even the Lookers

weren't as deferential as they once were. She wondered if she was losing her edge as she thought back to the day Debbie Manning was rushed to the hospital. Blaire Morton had gotten all in a lather apologizing for where the paramedics had moved Debbie's car, as if Stacia would be more concerned with a parking violation than Debbie's health. *Is that what they think of me? Do any of them appreciate any of the things I do for them? Or, am I becoming one of those shrill old women who condemn people for not doing things the way we've always done them?*

By the time Kitty came in, the tea was cool and Stacia was as restive as a hummingbird. She kept coming back to the same questions: Had she lost control of the situation when she brought Bitsy to Kitty's house? Kitty was a loose cannon and Bitsy might be the spark to set her off again. Should she have taken Bitsy to a hotel and risked Chip finding her? Should she tell Weldon? Was she in over her head this time?

Kitty had an oddly triumphant look on her face as she opened the freezer and pulled out a tray of ice cubes. "Everything okay around here? Thanks for making some tea."

"Bitsy's still asleep. Did you talk to your friend?"

"Yes and no." Kitty ran her fingers under the waistband of her jeans to tuck a loose piece of her blouse in. "I wanted to find out what Bitsy's options are."

"You told her about Bitsy?"

"No details. I just asked a few general questions about shelters and what not." Kitty walked through the kitchen and put her pocketbook down in its spot on the foyer table. Stacia was continually surprised by how rigid Kitty was in her habits. No wonder she was such a natural athlete. It was too bad that discipline hadn't crossed over into her personal life.

Kitty padded back into the kitchen in her bare feet. "I simply said that I know a woman who would like to get away from her abusive husband. My friend knows far more about the social services available to people like Bitsy than I do." Kitty glanced toward the family room. "Speaking of Bitsy, where is she?"

"Right where you left her. How much did you two drink last night?"

"Too much." Kitty popped a few ice cubes into a glass and poured the remains of that morning's coffee over the ice. "But that's the end of that. If nothing else, I am going to get Bitsy dried out while she's here.

No one can think straight when they're drunk all the time."

"You would know better than I."

Kitty swallowed some coffee with a grimace. "That's true."

Stacia scooped ice into a tall glass and returned the tray to the freezer. "Before Bitsy wakes up, I want to talk to you about the next steps."

"Good, what's the plan? Bitsy can't stay here indefinitely."

"Why not? With Seth and the kids out of the house, you're here alone right now."

"The kids will be home next week. What am I supposed to tell them?"

Stacia hadn't thought about Becky and Bobby coming back. That complicated things. "Can they stay at the camp for a few more weeks?"

Kitty stared into the kitchen sink for a few seconds as if weighing the idea of postponing her children's return. "No," she said. She dumped the coffee down the drain. "I don't want to lie to them. Whatever plan we come up with has to include the kids."

"You can't expect Bobby to be able to keep a secret like this."

"Why not?" Kitty asked with a cynicism that didn't suit her. "He's had a lot of practice. He kept all of Seth's secrets from me over the years. Both of my kids are very good liars."

Stacia swirled the ice in her glass. "I don't know. I'm not comfortable bringing any more people into this than is absolutely necessary." She looked over her shoulder to where Bitsy still lay motionless on the couch. "Do you know what you'll do if Chip finds her here?"

"I don't know yet, but I don't want any of this to blow back on you." Kitty turned to Stacia. "You've done so much for me already. Let me take the heat for this if things get dicey. Hopefully, we'll come up with a workable plan and Chip will never figure out where she is."

"What makes you think you can get away with it?"

A sardonic smile spread across Kitty's face. "Stacia, I sank my husband's body in the middle of a lake and no one gives a damn; I think I can help one woman hide."

Stacia ran her hand through her hair and glanced at the clock above the door. *Is Kitty losing it or has she been this screwy all along? Maybe she just needs to get out on the tennis court and smash some balls.* She recalled the few times she'd found Kitty practicing alone at the Overlook Swim and Tennis Club. Kitty could hit the tennis balls with enough force to make them stick in the fence at the other end of the court. Until that moment, Stacia had admired Kitty's strength and precision; now she found the emotional intensity behind her forehand a bit unsettling. She moved into the breakfast room to put the counter between her and Kitty.

"I'll do whatever I can to help you keep Bitsy safe, but we need to stay on the right side of the law. I'm not you. I'm not comfortable committing felonies."

"I wouldn't say I'm comfortable with it, Stacia. It's not like I planned to knock off my husband or anything."

"Shhh, Bitsy's just in the other room. I still can't believe you let your sister know about all that."

"She can't believe I let you know."

"I wish I didn't. I haven't slept well in weeks." Stacia straightened the already straight placemats on the breakfast table. "Speaking of your sister, where is she? You can't let her find Bitsy here."

"She's in Rhode Island interviewing for a job. She'll be gone for at least another week."

"Good." Stacia paced around the breakfast nook. "Okay, what do we know? Chip won't be back for at least a few more days, and then he won't be looking for her in Magnuson. Think about it. When she left before, she always tried to get as far away as possible. He'll assume she's done that again." Stacia stopped and turned back to Kitty. "I know Chip. He's arrogant enough to assume that no one he knows would actually go against him and shelter Bitsy. Least of all, me. Or you, for that matter, because everyone knows that you're my friend—"

"He would say lackey," Bitsy said from the couch. She stood up and stretched her arms over her head. "Chip doesn't understand the concept of friendship. He sees everything as a chain of command, with him on top, or trying to get to the top."

Kitty went to the couch and helped Bitsy into the kitchen as if she were a delicate bird. "How are you feeling? Can I get you something?"

"I could use a drink. My head is killing me."

"Sorry, no can do." Kitty helped Bitsy to a chair at the table. "I am cutting you off. No more drinking."

"What? But—"

"No, booze never solved anyone's problems. It certainly hasn't solved yours." Kitty sat down in the chair next to Bitsy and took her hand in hers. "Last night was a mistake. I never should have let you drink so much, and I should never have drunk with you. I had been sober for months and was just getting my life together."

Stacia guffawed from the sink where she was getting Bitsy a glass of water.

"Well, I was," Kitty said. "I've had a few setbacks lately, but I'll figure everything out in due time."

Stacia put the glass down in front of Bitsy, who guzzled it down in one go. She took the glass back to the sink to refill it for her.

"Look, Stacia and I were just talking about how you're going to stay here with me for a while."

Bitsy nodded uncertainly.

"And while you're here we are going to get you sober. No more drinking. We're going to get you healthy and ready for the next stage in your life, because you are not going back to Chip. You hear me? We may not have all the details figured out yet, but we will. Together. You're not alone anymore."

Stacia paused at the sink and looked at Bitsy and Kitty with their heads so close together. The glass shook in her hand. Stacia was helping Bitsy get away from Chip, but her reaction was one of compassionate anger and duty. She didn't feel things with the same intensity as Kitty did. Listening to Bitsy's story had obviously affected her deeply. That worried Stacia. Kitty was dangerous when she felt things intensely, deadly even.

★★★

An hour later, Stacia walked into her own house and was thankful Weldon and the kids were out for the day. She didn't think she could hide what was going on at Kitty's house from her family at the moment. It was too much. She wasn't any closer to figuring out how to get Bitsy to safety, and Kitty's life was far too tangled for Stacia to unravel. She felt powerless to help either of them.

She changed into one of her bright swimsuits and made her way down to their dock. A nice long swim out to the island would calm her mind. She knew she should wait until Lana or Marcus could follow beside her in the boat, but she wanted to be alone. She wanted to talk the situation through with her best friend while she swam. Even though Von had been dead for nearly thirty years, Stacia still listened to her advice more than anyone living and breathing. By the time she was halfway out to the island, she had laid out the whole situation and Von's voice, so like Lana's, was clear in her head.

Why are you doing this? You are way over your head here.

"Bitsy needs my help."

Okay, so you helped her. Now walk away.

"I can't just walk away. They need me."

Stop it. They don't need you. Kitty said it herself. Let her take this one.

"But Bitsy asked for my help."

And you did help her. You've stuck your neck out far enough. Now just stop.

Stacia lifted her head and trod water for a moment. Could she do that? Could she just stop?

Why do you keep doing these kinds of things? What are you trying to prove by helping all these women?

"I'm not trying to prove anything," Stacia said. "I help people. That's who I am."

She lifted her arms above her head and let her body sink below the surface. The sun penetrated the clear water at an angle and reflected off something at the bottom of the lake. She wondered if it was one of the old buildings, now covered with algae and freshwater mussels, that her and Bitsy's forefathers had drowned when they dammed the river and created Lake Tate. "I have to help her. She's a Magnuson. The old families need to stick together."

So what? You don't owe her anything just because your mothers were friends. And breathe, for Christ's sake.

Stacia popped up and inhaled a deep breath. The island was still a quarter mile or so away. She could see several boats beached near the spot where her son and his friends hung out. She was glad Marcus had a place to relax and kick back during the summer. She and Von used to spend hours lying in the shade of the old oak tree in her backyard between dance classes. Those days were some of Stacia's fondest memories. She resumed swimming toward the island, however, she changed her trajectory toward the shaded inlet at the tip. As she regained her rhythm, her thoughts went to Bitsy.

Bitsy is no fool. You were the perfect patsy for her plan. She knew you'd help her, you help everyone. Stacia smiled internally and increased her pace. Oh don't go feeling all proud of yourself there. That wasn't a compliment. She's handling you with the same light touch she used to control those horses of hers.

"I saw the bruises. They were real."

I don't doubt that Chip is a brute. I'm telling you. You're putting Weldon and the children in danger by hiding her in Overlook. Kitty is great, but she is capable of things you would never dream of doing. She's liable to do anything, especially if she's started drinking again.

Stacia swam on for a few moments before Von's voice echoed again in her head. *And that sister. She's nuttier than a fruitcake. Who knows what she's liable to do if she finds out that Kitty is hiding Bitsy in her guest room.*

"What can I do? I can't call Chip and tell him where Bitsy is. He'd kill her."

Walk away, Von's voice whispered in her ear. *Walk away.*

twenty-one

After Stacia left, Kitty went to the liquor cabinet and started carrying all the bottles to the kitchen sink. Bitsy quietly sat at the kitchen table watching her, until her fourth trip. "You don't have to get rid of all that. I'll be good."

It broke Kitty's heart that Bitsy would put it in those terms. "It's not about being good or bad. It's about being able to think straight in order to get away from Chip." She turned to go back to the bar and get another armload of bottles. "You'll see everything differently when you're sober. Believe me, I know what I'm talking about."

"Okay, Kitty. If you think that's what's best." Bitsy poured a bottle of Chambord down the drain.

"That's the spirit. Keep going while I go out and find a sturdy box in the garage for the empties. We'll need to take them to the recycling center at some point." Kitty was out in the garage wrestling a box from behind the Christmas decorations when she heard the doorbell ring.

What now? Stacia wouldn't come to the front door after making such a fuss about not bringing attention to her comings and goings earlier. Daisy let out a warning bark from the foyer. And Daisy wouldn't bark at Stacia. She loves Stacia.

Oh no, Chip!

Back in the kitchen, Bitsy was gone. Kitty held her breath until she heard light steps moving overhead. They stopped in the master bedroom closet. Kitty hoped she'd stay there until she could deal with whoever was at the door. Daisy ran back and forth from the window in the dining room to the front door while Kitty pulled a knife from the drawer and made her way to the front of the house. "Hush, Daisy. Sit!" She peeked out the dining room window. There was no police car in the driveway, so it wasn't Officer Blount with more useless information about Seth's non-death. A wave of irritation flooded through her at the memory of how Joe and the police had left her in the lurch once they'd decided that Seth was missing, but not officially dead, as if she and the children could simply go into suspended animation for the next seven years.

She stood against the wall and pushed the drapes back with the blade of the knife. At first, all she could see was a worn leather satchel until the person stepped back to look up at the house. She recognized the tattered oxford shirt with singe marks on the sleeves. She had ripped it off Aaron's body hours before. "Aaron!" she gasped and ran to the door. She swung it open and pulled him inside.

"What are you doing here? Did anyone see you? Did you talk to anyone?"

"Hello to you too." Daisy sized Aaron up for a second, then jumped up to lick his face. Kitty felt that was a good sign. Daisy was an excellent judge of character.

"Daisy, down!"

Aaron gently pushed the dog away and patted her on the back. "Nice dog. Nice knife."

Kitty looked down at the knife in her hand and dropped it. "What are you doing here?"

He pulled her loafers from his satchel. "You forgot these." Kitty took them and tossed them into the parlor. She hadn't had a chance to fully process the fact that she had impulsively had sex with him a few hours before.

"About this morning. I don't know what to say. That's not who I am." Kitty realized she wasn't making any sense. "I'm sorry. I don't normally act so recklessly." She looked down at the knife stuck in the foyer floor as it dawned on her that reckless was exactly how she had been acting lately. The surge of passion that had made her have sex with Aaron that morning was related to the surge of rage that had incited her to knock Seth over the head, to say nothing of what she had been prepared to do with that knife. She covered her face with her hands.

"Hey." Aaron took a step back. "Do you regret jumping my bones?"

"No, not at all." She paused to let that sink in for a second before she looked up again. She didn't regret it. She had thoroughly enjoyed the sense of power she got from their lovemaking. She'd never felt that with Seth. She wanted more of that feeling. A lot more. And, now here Aaron was standing in her foyer with clear-eyed expectancy in his face.

"How did you find me?"

"There are only so many Haskells in the phone book. By the way, Bob and Jenny Haskell on Honeysuckle Lane are a lovely couple in their eighties, and were far easier to get to than this place."

"Did anyone see you?"

"Probably. I passed a bunch of people walking here from the bus stop."

"Buses come out here?" Kitty went into the dining room and looked out at the cul-de-sac. She couldn't see Betty or Eileen-across-the-street watching the house. Without a car, Aaron may have gone unnoticed. Workman invisibly moved around the neighborhood all the time. The Lookers were only interested in each other's activities.

She returned to the foyer where Aaron stood holding the formal family portrait she kept on the side table. "Your kids are beautiful. They're so grown up."

She took the silver frame from his hand and put it back in its place beside her wedding portrait. She wasn't sure how old Aaron was but he was definitely closer to Becky's age than her own. "That's because I'm old and decrepit."

He gathered her into his arms and kissed her. "You are far from being a frail old woman. I can attest to that."

A flame of desire reignited inside her, tempting her to lose herself in Aaron for a second time in one day, but he pulled out of the kiss and whispered in her ear. "Are your kids home?"

At the mention of her children, Kitty regained her footing. "No, but my friend is hiding somewhere upstairs. She disappeared when the doorbell rang. The kids, thank God, are at camp for a few more days. That gives me a little time to figure out what to do with her."

Aaron's eyes hardened as his expression became serious. "Which is why I'm here." He dropped his satchel on the floor and looked around the house. "Have you ever gone through detox?"

"No, not really. It was hard for me to stop drinking, but I was never an actual alcoholic."

Aaron ran his hand over the top of his head and smiled wryly. "We can talk about that statement another time, but—"

"Hold on, you can't meet her. She's a very private person."

Aaron shook his head. "I'm sure she is."

Kitty walked into the kitchen and closed the door to the garage. "I'm sure I can handle it. Look, we've already started to get rid of the liquor. We don't need any help."

Aaron looked at the line of bottles beside the sink. "There really is a friend?"

"Of course there is. She's upstairs somewhere."

Aaron's expression lost its playfulness. "Did you turn your back on her at any time after you started dumping out the booze?"

"Not really. I was out in the garage when you rang the doorbell, so she was in here for maybe five minutes."

He squatted down and opened the cabinet under the kitchen sink. After a moment of rustling through Kitty's back-up bottles of dish detergent and cleansers, he pulled out a short bottle of Amaretto. He held it up for Kitty to see. "It only takes a few seconds to squirrel away an extra bottle. You won't be able to take your eyes off her until every drop, and I mean every drop, is out of the house."

Kitty's jaw dropped, shocked by Bitsy's deviousness, yet also impressed with her resourcefulness. She went to the stairs. "Get down here. Right now!"

"Oh yeah, I see it now," Aaron said from the kitchen. "You're a mom."

"I told you, I'm old."

He closed the gap between them and put his hand on her lower back. It felt warm through her thin blouse. "Or it means you have successfully given life to two people and lived to tell the tale." Her heart fluttered in her chest. No one had ever said anything so beautiful about her being a mother.

Bitsy appeared at the top of the stairs. "Is he gone?"

"My friend is still here," Kitty called up the stairs as she leaned into Aaron's touch. "He actually came to see you."

"I can't let anyone see me!" Kitty glanced over her shoulder to the family room. The edge of Bitsy's hair piece peeked out from under the couch.

As much as she wanted to stay in contact with Aaron, she needed to get Bitsy presentable if there was any chance of him talking to her face-to-face. She stepped into the family room and knocked a magazine onto the floor. When she stooped to pick it up, she scooped up the hair piece with it. "I'll be right back," she said. "Maybe you could dump out the rest of the bottles while I strong-arm her into coming down to talk to you."

Upstairs, Bitsy was curled up in a ball in the doorway to the master bedroom. She looked like an egret chick, all awkward appendages and tufts of downy feathers. "I can't go down there. What if Chip sent him?"

"Chip didn't send him. He's my friend and he knows how to help people stop drinking and get back on their feet. He's very nice."

Bitsy shook as she rocked back and forth. "I can't. I can't."

"Yes, you can." Kitty wondered if she had seemed so pathetic when Rose had helped her shower and get dressed the night Seth died. Now it was Kitty's turn to be the rational one. She didn't like the role. She helped Bitsy stand up and walk into the guest bedroom. "Now sit right here for a second while I find something for you to wear." Kitty opened Bitsy's suitcase and found a simple knit dress. It was several years out of style, but she didn't think Aaron would notice. He didn't seem the type to notice women's fashion trends; he would know what he liked and stop there.

She eased Bitsy out of her soiled clothes and slipped the dress over her head. It didn't look too bad. With her hair pieces clipped into her patchy hair and a bit of rouge, she almost looked normal. Kitty didn't have the proper cover-up to fully conceal the scars on Bitsy's face, but she doubted it was important to anyone but Bitsy.

"Come on, let's go down and talk to him."

"Do I have to?"

"You don't have to do anything, sweetie. You are a free woman. But I'll be pretty pissed if you don't."

Bitsy smiled her chipped toothed smile that made her seem much more real than her usual dour expression. "Well, we wouldn't want to piss you off." She squeezed by Kitty in the doorway and started down the stairs. "Who knows what you'd do to me."

Kitty paused for a moment before following her. *What did she mean by that?* She shook it off as the ravings of a desperate woman, but wondered how much of her conversation with Stacia Bitsy had heard.

Bitsy walked into the kitchen. "Good afternoon, young man."

"Oh shit! Ms. Magnuson?"

"Aaron!" There was a few seconds of silence in the house before they both yelled, "Kitty!" in unison.

She launched herself down the stairs to find Bitsy rigidly standing with her face to the kitchen wall and Aaron staring at her back. "You told me you were helping a friend. You didn't tell me you were helping Bitsy freakin' Magnuson!"

"You know each other?"

"She gave me my grant."

"I just fund the grants. Someone else chooses the recipients." She turned to look at Kitty. "How do you know him?"

Kitty moved so they were within whispering distance. Bitsy was trembling as she leaned on the counter top. "He...I...it's complicated. Let's just say we met. Became friends. He gets me."

"Can we trust him?"

"I think so," Kitty replied, although she wasn't sure anymore. The situation seemed to be getting more complicated, rather than less. It was easier to talk to Aaron about the anonymous woman she was helping out, rather than the heiress who funded foundations and was known for her frosty demeanor.

Aaron rubbed his palms over his eyes and down his cheeks. He stared at Kitty and Bitsy for several minutes as if weighing his words before speaking. "Where is Captain Evans? Is he looking for her?"

"We don't know," Kitty answered. "If he's not looking for her now, he soon will be."

"He's away on exercises until tomorrow." Bitsy's chest heaved as she clung to the counter top. "Please, Kitty. I need a drink. Please."

Aaron opened the nearest cabinet and pulled out a coffee cup. He splashed some scotch in it and gently tapped Bitsy's arm. "Here," he said. "Just a few mouthfuls." She turned and took the proffered cup with a trembling hand.

"What are you doing?" Kitty asked. "What happened to drying her out? Helping her though the DT's?"

"That was before I knew all the facts," he replied. He gently took the glass from Bitsy and led her into the family room and over to the couch. Daisy jumped up beside her and put her head in Bitsy's lap. She was still shaking; however, she seemed to be calming down.

"I don't get it," Kitty said from the kitchen. "What the hell is going on here?"

Aaron went back to Kitty. "When you told me that you were helping a friend, I pictured a housewife whose husband knocked her around a bit, maybe gave her a black eye or two when she'd had a few too many G&T's at the country club."

"Someone like me, you mean?"

"Yes, frankly. Someone exactly like you."

Kitty slammed her hand down on the back of Seth's recliner. "You ass! You thought it was me."

"I wasn't sure. It wouldn't have been the first time someone came looking for advice for 'a friend'." Aaron stared at his boots. "At first, I thought you were coming to me for a little validation."

Kitty rubbed her forehead. She could see how he could have thought that. She had pretty much thrown herself at him in the art room.

"But then, I got thinking after you left, and it didn't make sense that you were talking about yourself. There isn't a mark on you."

Bitsy's head popped up. She looked at Kitty wide-eyed. "My, my, Mrs. Haskell. And I thought Seth was the randy one."

"Shut up, Bitsy. You don't know what the hell you're talking about." Kitty looked at Aaron. "I still don't get it. What does it matter if it's Bitsy, instead of me?"

"I know Captain Evans." He glanced out the window and shuddered. "I'm sorry, Ms. Magnuson but there's something really off there. I used to see him down at the V.F.W. when I was still drinking."

"He wasn't like that when I married him. Korea changed him."

"Did he see any action in 'Nam?"

"Two tours. Mostly stateside."

Aaron sat in the recliner and patted Bitsy's hand. "I once saw him kick a dog to death for pissing on his tires. I can only imagine what it must have been like to live with him." He leaned forward and scrutinized Bitsy's face. "I'm not surprised you drink. It's amazing you've survived."

Kitty pushed Daisy off the couch and sat next to Bitsy. She hoped she felt supported rather than ganged up on. Kitty took Bitsy's other hand. "It's the money. That's what makes him stop, isn't it?"

Bitsy nodded. Kitty wanted to throw up. Bitsy was the cash cow that Chip hacked pieces off, yet didn't kill because she still gave milk. It all came down to money.

"He doesn't inherit when you die?"

"No, it would all go to my sister if I died."

"I'm surprised he didn't knock her off so you'd get her share."

"I've thought that too." Bitsy tugged the simple dress down over her thighs. "It wouldn't help him much, though. It all goes to Judy eventually."

"Does she know that?" Kitty shifted on the couch. She pictured Judy living in some bohemian flop house in California. "Does the guy she's living with know that?"

Aaron raised his palms. "Hold up. Who's Judy?"

"My daughter." Bitsy pushed a strand of hair out of her eyes. "She's dropped out of school and moved in with her boyfriend. I don't think she fully understands the extent of the Magnuson holdings. All she sees is my foundation work. I don't think she sees it as our money."

Kitty thought about Becky and Bobby and how difficult it had been to tell them that they were running out of money. Becky seemed to understand the gravity of their situation, but Bobby had yet to say much about it. "Kids don't think about money until there isn't any."

Aaron leaned back. "How much money are we talking about here?"

Bitsy picked up the coffee cup. "I'm not exactly sure. Thirty million, maybe forty."

Aaron blew out a quick breath. "Wow!"

Kitty looked across the coffee table at Aaron, and realized the danger she was putting him in by including him in Bitsy's secret. Chip wouldn't hesitate to kill him like that stray dog. "Look," she said, "I appreciate you coming over and all, and it's been great." Her chest muscles contracted as she recalled his kisses on her neck and trailing down her belly. "Really great. But you didn't sign up for this. You said it yourself. You thought I was nothing more than a silly little housewife who drank too much and wanted to blow off some steam with some young artist she met." She patted Bitsy's arm. "You can go. Bitsy and I will come up with a plan."

"No, you're not understanding me." Aaron leaned forward to look Bitsy in the eye. "I want to help. I don't care how scary Captain Evans is, there's no excuse for hitting a woman. And I know we don't really know each other, and until this afternoon I thought you were a bit of a snot, and I'm not sure exactly what I can do to help, but I'm in."

"Thank you, young man. You're sweet. And Kitty obviously likes you," she said with a smirk.

Kitty rolled her eyes and stood up. "Aaron, could I see you in the other room for a minute." As they walked out of the room, Bitsy lay down on the couch and waved at the dog to join her. In the parlor, Kitty turned to Aaron. "What's your angle here? Do you think she'll give you money if you help her?"

"Do you? Why are you doing this? You don't even seem to be very good friends."

"We aren't. I barely know her. She grew up across the street from my good friend, who I owe a huge favor to. Then Bitsy told me about what Chip did to her for all these years and I felt bad for her." Kitty fluffed the pillow on the rarely used side chair to avoid looking directly at Aaron. "Then she overheard something about my husband that she shouldn't have, and…that's not important." She squared her shoulders. "So can we trust you to keep this a secret?"

"Like I told Ms. Magnuson, I'm in. I love an underdog."

"Her or me?"

His shoulders slumped as he looked away. "I'm sorry. This is all a bit trippy. I was so excited to see you this morning, because I really like you. Then you laid this heavy trip on me about your drinking and your friend, who I totally didn't think was an actual person, so I wanted to be supportive and comfort you; but then you totally came on to me, so I went with it. I wasn't about to say no."

"So you thought I was just playing with you? Is that what you think of me?"

Aaron rocked back on his heels and looked at the carpet. "I have to admit, I did think you were just playing, but I was down with that. Hey, I'll take as much of you as I can get."

Kitty threw the pillow at him. "What's that supposed to mean?"

"I don't know. You're like no other woman I've ever met. As soon as I think I've got you figured out, you do something that completely weirds me out." He picked up the pillow and casually tossed it on the settee. "Every time we're together, I feel stoked. I like that feeling."

Kitty couldn't seem to breathe. *What is happening here? Things are way too complicated already. I should throw him out right this second.*

"Don't look so surprised. Did you really think I took three buses to return your shoes and check up on your imaginary friend?"

"She's not imaginary!"

"I can see that now." Aaron took a step toward her. "Come on, Kay. Be honest with me. Do you really want me to leave?"

"No, yes, I don't know." She sat down on the arm of the chair and tried to take a breath. "This feels wrong. I'm a married woman. A mother."

"Meaning? Is your husband coming back?"

"No."

"Do your children want you to be unhappy?"

"Not at all."

Aaron sat in the chair so he was behind her. "What do you want me to do here? I can stay and try to help you and Ms. Magnuson come up with some sort of plan to get her out of town, and we can act like nothing happened between us this morning. Or, I can stay and we can be together, which is my vote. Or, I can leave and pretend I don't know anything about any of this."

"Won't the people at the shelter wonder where you are?"

"I'm just the artist guy. They'll think I've wandered off looking for materials."

"I do need help keeping Bitsy safe."

He put his hand on the back of her shoulder. "And?"

"And, I don't know. I need to think."

"Fair enough," Aaron said. "I could use a little time to get my head around all this too." He stood up and walked back into the foyer. He looked around as if assessing the house for its ability to be defended. "Do you have a gun in the house?"

"I have one," Bitsy said from the family room. She rose from the couch and staggered into the foyer. "It's upstairs in my suitcase."

Kitty joined them in the foyer where Aaron steadied Bitsy with his arm. "How did you get one of Chip's guns?"

190

Bitsy lifted her chin to look at Kitty. "I just took it, Silly. He's really bad about locking the gun safe."

"Why didn't you shoot him?"

A wry smile crossed Bitsy's pale face as stood up to her full height. "Because, Kitty dear, despite everything he's done to me, I'm not the kind of woman who kills her husband."

Kitty hung onto the newel post as Aaron helped Bitsy up the stairs. She felt faint. Bitsy had heard her talking to Stacia earlier and, even pathetically broken, had managed to manipulate the situation. Kitty was impressed.

twenty-two

At the top of the stairs, Bitsy leaned against the wall. "I need to take this dress off. Do you two mind if I change into something a little more comfortable?"

"Sure," Aaron said. "Show me which room you're staying in."

Kitty shook herself out of her thoughts and climbed the stairs. "There's clean towels in the bathroom. I'll go see if Becky has anything comfy that might fit you." Aaron left Bitsy in the guest room to get organized and followed Kitty down the hallway with Bitsy's gun tucked in his waistband.

"So, this is your house. It doesn't suit you."

"How so?"

"Too vanilla. The walls are all white. Where's the color? Where's the artwork?"

"Seth didn't want me to hang any pictures. He said he didn't want me to put holes in the walls."

"There's this neat thing they have now. It's called caulking putty. Perhaps you've heard of it."

Kitty opened the door to Becky's bedroom and went to the dresser. "Give me a break and help me find Bitsy some sweatpants or something. She's all arms and legs and no body. It's like trying to put clothes on a spider."

"Oh wow, I just had a great idea for a sculpture." He went to Becky's desk and pulled a piece of paper from the stack of notebooks there. "I could make the woman's body out of rubber spiders, or no! Rubber rats. And the arms could be wire hangers." He sketched madly for a moment then scratched out part of his drawing. "Or no, spinning needles? Or, rubber tubing?" It was exhilarating to watch him think. Kitty liked being so close to that kind of raw passion. He drew a few more lines before folding up the paper and shoving it in his pocket. "I'll have to come back to that later. I'm beginning to mix my metaphors."

"Where would you even get that many rubber spiders?"

"People throw out a lot of stuff. You'd be surprised what I've found at the dump. Just last week, they found a human hand in one of the trucks. One of the guys at the shelter works there and was telling me all about it."

Kitty turned and separated two slats in the wood blinds to scan the cul-de-sac. Aaron moved to her side and nudged her with his elbow. "Hey, what gives? Your smile just went out like someone flipped a switch inside your head." He followed her gaze out the window. "What are you looking at?"

"You mentioned garbage trucks which made me think of my neighbor, Betty Oliphant, who I swear would go through my garbage cans if she could get away with it. It's impossible to keep a secret around here. I'm worried that she's going to see Bitsy and recognize her."

"Why would anyone recognize her?"

"You did." Kitty removed her fingers and straightened the blind. "Most of my neighbors would recognize Bitsy from church."

Aaron picked up one of Becky's swimming trophies and looked at the plaque on the base. "You all go to the same church?"

"Anyone who's anyone around here goes to Pinnacle Point Presbyterian."

"Sounds like a cult."

"More like a minimum security prison," Kitty said with a laugh. She disliked the religion preached at Pinnacle Point for being more about piousness than emulating Christ. Seth had considered church attendance as an opportunity to sell golf equipment over coffee and stale cookies.

Aaron replaced the trophy and picked up another one. "Wow, Rebecca's good."

"She's not good; she's excellent." Kitty took the trophy from his hand and replaced it on the shelf above Becky's desk. "By hook or by crook, she's going to leave here and have a life of her own." She ran her finger along the line of notebooks on Becky's desk. "She's not going to end up like me or Bitsy."

"I think Bitsy will be okay here." He sat on the bed and looked up at Kitty. "If we keep the blinds closed and she stays inside, no one will ever know she's here."

Kitty straightened the blind again, making sure there were no gaps. "Maybe, but you'd be surprised how sneaky these people are. Sometimes I swear that Betty Oliphant has binoculars trained on my house. I can't change my shoes lately without the whole neighborhood finding out about it."

"That sounds a bit paranoid."

"She might sound paranoid," Bitsy said from the hall. "But that doesn't mean they're not out to get her."

Kitty remembered why she had come into Becky's room in the first place and opened the bottom drawer of the dresser. At the back of the drawer, she found a pair of soft sweatpants that would serve Bitsy's needs. She held them out.

"I have an idea. Maybe we should change your appearance somehow, so if someone does catch a glimpse of you, they won't immediately recognize you."

Bitsy cocked her head. "What do you have in mind?"

"We could start with your hair. Change the color. Change the style."

"Why don't we dye it the same color you dye your hair? Then I could be some visiting cousin or something if someone sees me."

"I don't dye my hair," Kitty said indignantly. She'd thought she'd done a good job of matching her natural color when she'd started to turn grey.

"Then whose boxes of Miss Clairol are those under your sink?"

"You were snooping around my bathroom?"

Bitsy blushed and looked away. "I got bored while I was waiting in the closet earlier. You really should go see my girl. She could do a much better job on your hair."

"Seth would never allow that," Kitty replied as she refolded the things in Becky's drawer. She looked up and noticed both Aaron and Bitsy staring at her. She kicked the drawer shut. "I'll think about it. Maybe I'll become a brunette."

"No, a brighter red," Aaron said. He winked at her, but there was pity in his eyes.

She took Bitsy by the shoulders and turned her to face the mirror above Becky's dresser. "So what do you think? Should we change your hair?"

"What do you think? An updo?"

"Cut it short," Aaron said. "Like Mia Farrow's. People know you by your blonde bubble hairdo. If you dye it a different color and snip it close to the skull, people won't immediately recognize you."

Bitsy turned her head back and forth on her fragile neck. She smiled at Aaron in the mirror. "I like it. And I could a wear a wig if I needed to wear a disguise."

Kitty stood behind her and tried to imagine Bitsy without her signature hairstyle. "That would change your appearance a lot. With different clothes and hair, it won't be quite so obvious who you are."

"I could be your long lost sister here for a visit."

"I have a sister. You wouldn't like her."

"Do you have a pair of good scissors?" Aaron asked. "I'm pretty good at cutting hair. I used to cut my sisters' hair when we were kids, and they were squirmy little runts." Kitty liked the image. She couldn't imagine Seth ever doing anything so domestic. "You girls sort out the hair dye thing and give me a call when you're ready to cut. All this talk of nosy neighbors is making me paranoid too. I'll be downstairs figuring out a place for Bitsy to safely hide if Captain Evans gets wind that she's here."

Kitty took Bitsy into the master bathroom and had her strip down to her bra and panties. Without clothes, she could see how frail Bitsy was. Her left arm bowed away from her body more than her right and a patchwork of pink scars and slickly healed burns ran down her back. Kitty pulled a monogrammed towel from the linen closet and wrapped it around Bitsy's shoulders.

"Wait, you'll ruin the towel if the hair dye drips."

"I don't care. It was Seth's towel."

Kitty mixed the color and started combing it through Bitsy's hair. "What color is your hair naturally? Were you blonde as a child?"

"It was more of a yellow blonde." Bitsy pulled the towel tighter across her chest. "To tell you the truth, I was usually covered with so much horse hair and hay, it was hard to tell what my hair looked like most days."

"Stacia said you liked to ride." A drop of red dye dripped onto the fluffy white towel. It spread like a drop of blood. Kitty didn't bother trying to wipe it off. "When this is all over, do you think you'd like to get another horse?"

Bitsy caught Kitty's eye in the mirror. "Really? Can I?"

"Bitsy, you're a grown woman. You can do whatever you want, as long as you've got the money. And once we figure out how to get your hands on your money without Chip finding out, you'll have plenty. Buy a whole ranch if you want."

"I don't know about that. I'd be happy with a small house with a big barn. And maybe a ring and some pasture land."

"That seems reasonable." Kitty covered Bitsy's hair with the cap and set the timer. "So, about your money. What exactly are we talking about here? Do you have a trust? Stocks? What?"

"I know this." Bitsy's eyes lit up like a kid's when they are called on in class and realize they know the answer to a difficult question. "A few years back, I started paying attention to everything Chip made me sign. My grandfather set up a trust for me and my sister after my father died managed by Huston & Crawley. A Mr. Pike sends me a dividend check on the fifteenth of each month."

Kitty dabbed at a trail of hair dye weeping down the back of Bitsy's neck with the corner of the towel. "How much do you get every month?"

"Around five thousand dollars." Kitty stopped and caught Bitsy's eye in the mirror. "Is that a lot?" Bitsy asked.

Kitty quickly did the math in her head. Bitsy's dividend check was more than ten times what she was making and double what Seth had ever brought home. "More than enough to live on." Kitty sat down on the edge of the tub so she was eye-to-eye with Bitsy.

"Are the checks written out to you or to Chip?"

"Me, but Chip has me sign them over to him."

"Okay." Kitty adjusted the towel on Bitsy's shoulder. "How well do you know this Mr. Pike? Do you think he can be trusted?"

"I don't know, but I don't want Mr. Pike to know anything that Chip could manipulate out of him."

"Fine. You do need to at least contact him though and tell him to stop sending the checks to the house. Chip could probably forge your signature easily enough."

"He can. He learned how when he broke my wrist."

"When was that?"

"Three or four years ago." Bitsy held up her hand and showed Kitty how she couldn't fully rotate it. "I didn't have a cast or anything, so you wouldn't have known."

Kitty ran her fingers over Bitsy's wrist. She could feel lumps and bumps along the tiny bones. "You must have been in excruciating pain. How did you do anything?"

"I didn't." Bitsy looked away. "I don't think you fully understand what my life has been like. I don't do anything. I go to a few board meetings here and there and I played with Judy when she was little, but most of the time I just sit around and read."

"You must have read a lot of books."

Bitsy thrust out her chin. "Over six thousand now."

"You kept count?"

"My third grade teacher had us keep track of the books we read on index cards. I loved looking back over the cards at the end of the year, so I kept it up. Sometime in high school, I moved from index cards to journals, but the idea was the same. Every year, I get a new journal and write down what I'm reading and what I thought of the book."

"Where do you keep all those books?"

"I mostly take them out of the public library. I'm one of the largest donors to the Library Trustees and serve on their board, so they order whatever I want."

"I'm surprised that Chip let you go to the library at all," Kitty said. "You could have asked someone to help you."

"Dorrie was always with me."

"You could have left an SOS note in one of the books."

"And let the whole city know my business? I'd rather die!"

"Are you ashamed? Of what?"

As she looked away, Bitsy's face hardened into the patrician mask Kitty recognized from their previous encounters.

Kitty rose and ran the bowl of dye under the tap. As the dye mixed with the water, it reminded her of how Seth's blood had dissipated in the water as his body sank.

Holy crap! Where do I get off judging Bitsy? I'm no better than her. When Seth was sleeping with Marni last year, I was far more concerned about my neighbors finding out about the affair than what it was doing to our family. If I had been more honest about what was going on, maybe it wouldn't have escalated the way it did. I let my pride get the better of me, and for what? Everyone already knew Seth was a cheating bastard. I wasn't actually hiding it from anyone. I should have walked away like her.

Kitty looked at Bitsy's reflection in the mirror. With her hair slicked back and covered with dye, Kitty could see the scars along her hairline, above her eye, and near her nose. "I'm sorry, Bitsy. I understand how you'd want to keep your personal life quiet. The only thing you have to be embarrassed about is marrying the wrong guy."

"Oh, and you made such a great choice?"

"Not at all."

Aaron cleared his throat in the bedroom. "You two ready for me?"

"I'll be right there," Kitty called as she wound a fresh towel around Bitsy and set the timer. "Sit tight, I'll be back in a few minutes." She closed the bathroom door behind her and sat next to Aaron on the bed.

"If I'm going to stay and keep an eye on you and Bitsy, I need to crash somewhere. Can I bunk in Bobby's room?"

Kitty thought about how particular her son was about his things. When he was younger, he wouldn't let anyone touch his intricate Lego towers and he still got upset if anyone moved anything in his record collection. "Bobby wouldn't like that."

"The couch looks comfy," Aaron said with a hangdog look.

Kitty ran her head over the edge of the satin bedspread. She wanted to invite Aaron into her bed, but that felt too forward. She wasn't the Mrs. Robinson type. She leaned forward and gave him a quick kiss. "I can't make any promises, so start out on the couch and we'll see how the evening goes."

"Okay, no biggie."

The timer dinged in the bathroom and brought Kitty back to the task at hand. "Hold on while I rinse the color out of Bitsy's hair, then you can cut it. The scissors are near the sink."

When she returned to the bathroom, Bitsy was already standing in the shower stall. Kitty pulled the shower head down and adjusted the water temperature. Bitsy leaned over to let Kitty rinse the dye from her hair. "This process is much more pleasant at the salon."

Kitty laughed and flicked some water at her. "Feel free to leave me a tip if it makes you feel more comfortable." She gently ran her fingers through Bitsy's hair to make sure all the color was out. Her skull was a patchwork of scars and ridges. Kitty wondered what kind of story Bitsy told her hairdresser to explain away the scars and how much Chip paid her to keep her mouth shut. Kitty turned off the water and draped a fresh towel around Bitsy's head. As she helped her back to the vanity, Kitty thought about Renee, the housekeeper that had spitefully spread the Lookers' secrets around the neighborhood like a virus. The Lookers had all trusted Renee and each of them had thought they were only one she gossiped with over a glass of sweet tea when she should have been scrubbing toilets. Bitsy's hairdresser was probably no better. No matter how careful she was, secrets had a way of getting out.

Bitsy pulled a comb through her hair. "I hope I'm not being too forward, but what did you ever see in Seth? You're so talented and bright, I can't believe you didn't have other prospects."

"No one serious." Kitty paused and thought back to the days when she was first dating Seth. He had been so charming and had made her feel special. She now realized that he made every woman feel special. He was a natural salesman and he was the product. She couldn't really blame him for being that way; it was his nature. She was the fool that had fallen for the sales pitch.

"I was young, and a sucker for a nice smile. By the time I realized I wasn't the only girl he was smiling at, I had Becky and we were already living down here."

"You could have divorced him. You must have had plenty of evidence to make a case."

Kitty pointed to the scar running along Bitsy's hair line. "So did you. I guess we're both too damn proud."

Bitsy put the comb down on the vanity and stared at herself in the mirror. "I can't tell you how many times I planned out how to kill him. I just never had the courage to go through with it. How did you ever get the nerve?"

Kitty reeled back. "You've got me wrong. I didn't plan it; I just did it. It was over before I even realized what had happened." She smeared a drop of hair dye on the floor with her toe into the shape of a teardrop. "I'm sorry you overheard Stacia and me talking. But now that you're in on my secret, you need to keep it. I know you can do that." She looked at the back of Bitsy's head and thought how easy it would be to simply call Chip and let him eliminate Bitsy as an impediment to her plan.

She didn't want to do that. She liked Bitsy. There was a darkness deep inside her that spoke to Kitty. She put her hands on Bitsy's shoulders. "You need to understand something. I didn't intend to kill Seth. It just happened. But now that it has, I don't intend to get caught. Keep that in mind."

Bitsy met Kitty's eye in the mirror. A wicked smile spread across her face. "And that, Kitty darling, is why Stacia brought me here."

The phone beside Kitty's bed rang and broke the tension in the bathroom. "Hold on a sec, that might be my sister." She moved back into the bedroom and picked up the receiver. Aaron stood at her elbow. She tried to sound casual as she said hello.

"Hey, Mom," Becky said across the crackly line.

"Becky! How are you? Are you all right?"

"I'm okay. How's everything there?"

Aaron pointed to the phone inquiringly. Kitty put her hand over the receiver and mouthed "My daughter." He visibly relaxed and moved to the bathroom to check on Bitsy.

"Fine, sweetie. Just fine. How's your brother?"

"Good. He's still seeing that girl. They're adorable."

"Don't be patronizing to your brother, Rebecca," Kitty said. "How's the job. Are you still getting along with the other lifeguards?"

"They're nice enough. A little stupid." Kitty hoped Becky would be knocked down a few pegs when she got to Brown. She was very full of herself lately. "How are you doing? Any word from Dad?"

Kitty realized that she hadn't even bothered to tell the children what was going on with the investigation into their father's disappearance. She felt like the worst mother in the world. "Remember when we talked last time, they'd found your dad's car in a parking lot near a lake? So, Joe convinced the police to open a missing person's case. They've done all the required paperwork and have declared him officially missing, but I don't think his case is a big priority."

Oh," Becky said. She paused. "Hold on Mom, I need to put more coins in." There was a skip in the line before Becky's voice came back. "I only have a few quarters left, so I'll talk fast. I wanted to remind you that the camp is closing down for the two weeks around the Fourth of July this year. I guess they're using the land for some Revolutionary War reenactment thingie. Bobby and I'll be home sometime on the thirtieth."

"So soon?"

Aaron popped his head out of the bathroom with a pair of scissors in his hand. "What?"

"Mom? Did I just hear a man's voice? Is someone there with you?"

"Yes, my friend, Aaron." She pulled the mouthpiece away from her face and said, "Everything is fine. The kids are just coming home a few days sooner than I thought. Won't that be great?"

"Mom, what's going on?" Becky sounded worried.

"I'm here," Kitty said. "Everything's fine. I'm just surprised, and happy that you're coming home so soon. We'll just have to shuffle some people around a bit because I've got a couple of houseguests staying for a few days."

"Who?"

"My friend, Aaron." Becky harrumphed through the line and Kitty could have sworn she heard her grumble "friend, yeah right" under her breath. "Along with another friend who is having some trouble with her husband. Since you and Bobby are away, I said she could stay for a bit. Until she gets back on her feet."

"Why do you always have to talk in euphemisms, Mom? What do you mean by 'trouble'?"

Kitty scowled at the phone. "He beats her bloody. Is that exact enough for you?"

"Did you call the police? Report him for assault?"

"Unfortunately, the police aren't likely to help her very much. I'm not saying they don't care, but it's not illegal to beat your wife in North Carolina."

"Hold on, Mom." There was clicking sound followed by another skip in the line. "Okay, I'm back. It's 1976! Women are still legally considered chattel?"

"I'm afraid so, sweetie. That's why you need to be very careful about the man you marry."

"Or never get married to begin with. Or get a gun."

"No, sweetie. Violence against violence is never the answer." Kitty looked through the bathroom door where Aaron was sheering off long pieces of Bitsy's hair. "But that's why your generation of girls needs to get an education and never get yourselves into situations where you're dependent on a man, be it legally or financially."

"It's Molly Blevins, isn't it?"

"What? No! What would make you say that?"

"She has a terrible husband who she obviously hates."

"It's not Molly. Not that she would come to me for help anyway. It's someone else. Better you don't know who exactly." She looked again at Aaron gently combing through Bitsy's hair. Never mind Bitsy, how was she going to explain Aaron to Bobby and Becky? "There are some things it's best that you just not know about."

"Mom! Have you learned nothing over the last year or so? You are craptastic at hiding things from people. We're not stupid, Mom. We know stuff. Hell, everyone always knows stuff way before you ever do."

"Hey! Show a little respect. I am still your mother."

"Sorry, Mom. I'm just a little thrown. I don't understand why you're helping some woman when you, frankly, have plenty of problems of your own. And who is that guy?"

"He's an artist I met through work. You'd like him. I'll introduce you when you get home." Kitty picked up a pillow from the bed and fluffed it into shape before tossing it back on the bed. "I'll explain the situation with the woman we're helping when you get here. Once you hear what her husband has done to her, you'll want to help too."

Becky's voice cracked. "Dad never hit you, did he?"

"Oh no, sweetie! He would never do that. He's not that kind of a guy. Unfaithful, irresponsible, and immature; but not a bad guy."

"You don't think he's coming back, do you?"

Kitty pictured her daughter leaning against the wall in the snack shop. "No, Becky. I'm assuming he's gone for good. We need to move on with our lives."

A warning chime sounded on the line. "I've only got thirty seconds. I'll try to get some more coins and call back. If not, I'll talk to you about all this when I get home." Kitty sat down and reviewed their conversation in her head. Becky had taken all of her news in stride.

When had her little girl become an adult?

twenty-three

Stacia could see Weldon and her cousin Quentin sitting on their dock as she returned from her morning swim. She considered skirting the shoreline and getting out at Kitty's slip so Weldon wouldn't see that she'd been swimming without a spotter. He worried about careless ski boat drivers hitting a lone swimmer out in the water; that was why Stacia wore brightly colored swimsuits.

As she got closer, Quentin waved and foiled her plan. She picked up her pace to close the distance with a flourish. She liked to please an audience. At the dock, she pulled herself up in a fluid motion despite her fatigue. As their dance mistress had pounded into her and Von's heads, she never let them see her sweat. "Hey, boys!" She motioned to the beer bottles at their feet. "You bring one for me?"

Quentin produced a tall plastic cup from the cooler behind his chair. "I thought you'd prefer a glass of tea, Ladybug."

"You know me so well," she said as she peeled off her cap and googles. She took a big gulp of the sweet tea and leaned against the post at the corner of the dock. "So what brings you by? Were you showing a house?"

Quentin put his beer down. "I came by to see you about a rumor I heard about your pal, Kitty Haskell."

Stacia concentrated on not choking or showing too much surprise. The situation was at such a precarious point, she couldn't afford to pique her cousin's interest. "Oh? What did you hear?"

"Well, a little birdie told me Wachovia is going to serve her a foreclosure notice next week."

Weldon shook his head. "So you could swoop in and sweet talk

Kitty into listing the house with you before any other agents can get a hold of her? No one else has a fighting chance. You Tates have this city in the palm of your hand."

Quentin leaned down and tossed him another beer. "And aren't you glad to be a member of the family? These little tidbits of information help you get a leg up from time to time too."

"I know," Weldon said. He popped open the can and slurped the foam off the rim. "But I don't have to feel good about it." He turned to his wife. "You and Kitty are close; is she having money problems?"

Stacia played with an imaginary loose thread on the towel beside her. "Of course she is. Her husband walked out on her. She's broke, and it's not looking like Seth's going to resurface anytime soon." She heard the words that had just come out of her mouth and clumsily took another gulp of her tea to cover up her alarm. She had to be more careful.

"She called me a few weeks back and asked me about putting the house on the market," Quentin said. "I took it from our conversation that the house is only in Seth's name. I didn't say anything to my guy at the bank, because I want him to keep calling me with tips, but I don't know whether or not there's all that much I can do to help Ms. Kitty. Seth seems to have left her high and dry."

"I don't know if she needs too much of your kind of help," Weldon said. "I got a call from Liam Logan the other day. You made a pretty penny in commissions off the sale of their place on Serenity."

"Anything I can do to help," Quentin chuckled.

Stacia perked up at the mention of the Logans. She missed Deirdre and still regretted the way she had had to force her out of the Lookers when they'd run into trouble with the bank, but foreclosures reflected badly on Overlook. "Did Liam say anything about Deirdre and the kids? How are they settling in?"

"They seem to like Hudson and Deirdre likes being closer to her folks there in Massachusetts. We mostly talked about Liam's new job. This Digital Equipment outfit seems like a real up and comer. We may need to buy some stock."

"Really? Remind me later and I'll do some research."

"You two and your stock portfolio," Quentin said. "How can you make any money investing in these computer companies? They don't actually make anything. It's all bits and bytes of nothingness."

"You don't seem to have any trouble holding stock in the power company." Weldon looked over Stacia's head to the coal plant on the far side of the lake. "Electricity is nothing more than electrons moving through a wire."

"I don't understand that either," Quentin admitted amiably. "Land. Houses. Give me something concrete to buy and sell. That I understand." He popped open a second beer. "Back to Kitty Haskell. Why would Seth ever leave a fine woman like that? You don't think she'd be interested in some company, do you?"

Weldon drained his beer. "Give her a break."

"I think it's a bit soon for male companionship," Stacia said. "So, what was this banker saying about foreclosing on her house. How can they do that? She can't be more than a month or two behind on the mortgage."

Quentin lost his jolly tone. There was nothing frivolous about real estate. "Apparently, Seth used the house as collateral and someone's calling in a loan. That would make the bank move forward with a foreclosure. My contact didn't give me many details, just that I should be prepared to get it listed quickly. What's the inside like? Is Kitty a good housekeeper? Any pets?"

"They have a golden retriever, but Kitty has a service that comes in." Stacia paused. "Although, she may have let them go. I seem to remember hearing something about her doing that." She thought again about how Kitty's refrigerator had been so empty the day before. Stacia had assumed that, with the kids gone and Kitty working, she had neglected to go to the market. Now, she wondered if Kitty didn't have much food in the house because she didn't have the money to buy it.

★★★

That afternoon, Marcus and Weldon settled down to watch a baseball game. Stacia placed a tray of snacks on the coffee table. "I think I'll go for a quick jog. My hamstrings are a bit tight after my swim earlier." Weldon didn't say anything, but she thought he'd given her a disbelieving look. She didn't know how other people kept so many secrets from their husbands or wives. It had been less than forty-eight hours since she'd taken Bitsy to Kitty's house and the strain made her feel as though she had aged ten years.

She jogged down the raised walking trail to Kitty's house. Despite the heat, it felt good to stretch her muscles. She missed her daily runs with Kitty; they had been another casualty of Seth's murder. It was a murder, after all. She needed to start thinking of it in those terms. Whether or not Seth had deserved to die, the fact remained. Kitty had murdered her husband. It was a criminal offense and Stacia was an accomplice after the fact.

Poison ivy and wild grape vines encroached on the path leading up to Kitty's backyard. Stacia had to be careful not to get tangled in vines as she climbed the short slope up to the square of mown grass. As soon as she reached the steps up to the deck, the blinds in the family room snapped shut and a slim man appeared at the sliding glass door. Daisy stood alert at his side. Stacia rushed up the stairs to demand to know who the man was, until she noticed the pistol in his hand. She stopped and waited to see what he would do.

She didn't want to say anything or make any sudden wrong moves. Who was this man? Was Chip with him? Had Chip come back early? And where was Bitsy? Had Kitty safely gotten her out of the house? Where was Kitty?

Daisy let out a single welcoming bark and the man relaxed his grip on the gun. He laid a hand on the dog's side and gave her pat. "Kay? Do you know a pixie with a penchant for pink?"

Kitty quickly came to the door and slid it open. "Good heavens, Stacia! Come in, come in." She shoved the man aside and pulled Stacia inside. "Put that away. You probably scared her half to death." The man tucked the pistol in the waistband of his jeans with a practiced motion that Stacia found disconcerting.

"Who are you?"

"This is my friend, Aaron. He came by to help me with Bitsy--"

"He knows?" Stacia whispered. She looked at the couch where she had last seen Bitsy. It was empty.

"She's hiding, ma'am. As soon as we saw someone coming she went to a safe area."

"She's hiding behind the dryer," Kitty said as she walked toward the kitchen. "Bitsy! You can come out now. It's just Stacia." There was a small crash and a shuffling sound before Bitsy emerged from the laundry room.

Stacia didn't recognize her at first. She looked like a teenager in a t-shirt and shorts. She took in the apricot fringe around Bitsy's face. "What did you do to your hair?"

Bitsy ran her hand over the top of her head. "Do you like it? It was supposed to come out Kitty's color but it's still pretty light. Then Aaron cut it. He's very good with a pair of scissors. Look, you can barely see the bald spot."

"Well, I am an artist."

Stacia spun back to Kitty. "Why is he here? I can't believe you told someone else. This was already too complicated."

"Why are you here?" Kitty took Stacia's arm and led her back toward the door. "I told you. I'll take care of it."

"I don't particularly like the way you take care of things," Stacia whispered.

"Neither do I," Bitsy said as she poured herself a drink. Stacia started, then glared at Kitty.

"Don't give me that look," Kitty said. "She overheard us talking about it yesterday."

"Excuse me," Aaron said. "What are you talking about?"

"Nothing," Kitty said. "It's nothing, really." Bitsy winked at her from behind Aaron's back. She was having fun watching Kitty squirm. In that moment, it dawned on Kitty why she felt so comfortable with Bitsy. She was like Rose, annoying and snide, yet loyal to the core. She made a mental note to keep Bitsy and Rose apart. They could gang up on her and make her life miserable.

"Look, I can't stay long. Weldon thinks I'm out for a jog and will get worried if I'm not back soon." Stacia looked at Aaron and seemed to consider whether or not to continue. She took a deep breath and went on. "Anyway, I came over to give you a heads up about a rumor Quentin heard about you having trouble paying your mortgage."

"Who told him that?" Kitty saw Aaron roll his eyes and cross his arms.

"Never you mind. The point is, he heard it and told me." Stacia dropped her voice. "Evidently, the bank is planning on foreclosing."

Kitty sat down at the kitchen table. "That was fast."

"How far behind are you?" Aaron asked.

"Only a few months, but Seth took out a second mortgage and a couple of credit cards with huge credit limits that I never even knew about." She looked back at Stacia. "Would the police automatically contact the bank when someone is declared missing and presumed dead?"

"I don't know. Quentin's buddy told him because he knew that Quentin and I are cousins, and you and I are friends. I think they were hoping Quentin could help get you out of a bind before they have to take the house."

"It never hurts to be cozy with the Tate family if you need help with a land deal." Bitsy reached for the bottle of vodka on the counter, but Aaron got to it first.

"You've had enough for now," he said. "We need you to be alert enough to run in case you need to." He moved the bottle to a high shelf in the cabinet. "Let me get this straight. You're Stacia Tate, as in Lake Tate and the Tate Building and Tate Power and Electric?" He looked between Stacia and Bitsy as if piecing together what he had been told throughout the last twenty-four hours. He shook his head and put his hand on Kitty's shoulder. "You got me again, Kay. You told me that Bitsy and your friend grew up together. I should have figured out that her childhood friend would be someone like this. So how do you come in? Are you the heir to a railroad or something?"

"No, nothing like that. I'm broke. Broker than broke. Seth left me in debt up to my eyeballs. And I can't even sell this stupid house because it's in his name. And I can't inherit it because he's only presumed dead rather than officially dead."

"I could give you the money," Bitsy said from the kitchen.

"And how do we explain that?" Stacia asked. "Is she supposed to tell the bank that the money fell out of the sky? People would ask where the money came from, and then you'd be found. No, you can't give her the money."

"You could give her the money, Stacia."

"I already thought about that. I don't think Weldon would go for it after I refused to bail out the Logans last year."

"Have you heard from Deirdre?" Kitty asked.

"She's still not talking to me, but Weldon talked to Liam not too long ago. They seem to be fine." Stacia tried to swallow the lump that formed in her throat whenever she thought about Deirdre. Perhaps she should have been less concerned with how a foreclosure would affect Overlook's property values and helped Deirdre get out of their financial troubles. "I'll talk to Weldon again," she said with a sigh.

Bitsy walked around the counter and sat down across from Kitty. "Why can't I give her the money? Why can't we tell everyone she got a big life insurance check?" One corner of her mouth ticked up as she looked at Kitty. "You and I both know that the key to a secret is to imbed a little bit of the truth in a lie, then stick to it. People will believe anything if you act like they're stupid for questioning it."

Stacia recalled how haughty Bitsy had been about the time she fell down at the Magnuson Foundation Gala. One woman had whispered something about her being drunk and Bitsy had crushed her like a bug in front of the whole ballroom of partygoers. She was drunk, and anyone could have seen that if they had the courage to look carefully, Stacia among them.

"That could work, at least until I get back on my feet," Kitty replied. "We just need to have your banker send those checks somewhere where we can pick them up."

"We can't give him this address," Stacia said. "I don't want anything to lead back to an address in Overlook."

"Of course not." Kitty got up and started pacing. "We can have him send the checks to a PO box somewhere."

"Not here in Magnuson. Chip would sit and wait for her to check the mail."

"I could check it," Aaron said. "No one will be looking for me."

Bitsy quietly stared at the table for a moment. "I think I have an idea. I read a mystery a few years ago where the villain covered his tracks by having a package forwarded to different post offices. It took the detective a long time to catch him because the post office is a federal agency. It's a crime to tamper with the mail."

"What are you talking about?" Stacia asked.

"We need to get post office boxes all over the country and have the checks forwarded a few times before they get back to me. They could even get forwarded right here because no one can legally look in your mailbox."

"That seems too easy."

"Not really, someone would need to go and physically fill out the forms to open the PO box accounts."

"I see where you're going with this," Stacia said. "If the checks get forwarded to a PO box, say in California, Chip would go looking for you there, but the checks would never leave the back of the post office because it would get forwarded to the next place."

Bitsy nodded thoughtfully. "The trick is finding someone to open the different accounts."

"I have army buddies all over the country," Aaron chimed in. "I could have them go open PO boxes in their towns. I could tell them I'm setting up forwarding addresses for some of my guys who do migrant work." He turned to Bitsy. "I see what you're saying about a little bit of truth in the lie to make it seem plausible. I do have guys at the shelter that are migrants, and I talk about them all the time to my buddies."

Once they had decided how they were going to reroute Bitsy's dividend checks around the country then back to Magnuson, Bitsy's years of managing charitable organizations came into play. Within a few hours, she and Aaron had a plan for how and where the different PO boxes would be and who would open them. She also came up with a list of aliases to put on the accounts to further muddy their trail if Chip got the first address out of the banker. In the process, she realized that she could simply change the forwarding addresses whenever she decided to move on and settle down.

The one thing they struggled with was how to contact the banker with the first address without tipping him, or Chip, off to her whereabouts. She couldn't send him a letter postmarked from Magnuson. Kitty and Bitsy were brainstorming more and more convoluted plans when Stacia cut them short.

"Just call him."

"Phone calls can be traced."

"They only put a trace on a call if they're expecting a kidnapper or a terrorist to call. No one is tapping the phones expecting you to call." She got up to leave. "It's really not that complicated. You pick up the phone and ask the man to send all your correspondences to the first PO box in California. He works for you. You said it yourself. If you don't act like anything is out of the ordinary, they won't think anything is out of the ordinary. Just be your normal difficult self."

twenty-four

That Sunday, Stacia sat in her usual spot in the balcony of Pinnacle Point Presbyterian and watched the congregation file in. Weldon had wanted to skip the service that morning and spend time with Lana and Marcus, however, Stacia had insisted they attend. She hoped God would speak to her through a line in a hymn or a Bible passage, and tell her how to help Bitsy while still keeping her distance. Instead, he spoke to her by simply compelling her to be there to see Chip Evans walk down the aisle in his dress uniform and sit in the Magnuson family pew. He smiled and shook hands with the people around him as if he were a normal man going to church, rather than a monster capable of unspeakable cruelty. As if to make sure Stacia didn't miss His signal, a cloud momentarily blotted out the sun as Chip looked up and met Stacia's eye.

Stacia looked away and rubbed the scar on her knee. *Okay, I get it. He's a bad man. Why don't you go ahead and smite him down then? What am I supposed to do about it?* Instead of a deep movie announcer voice echoing through her head with a divine response, Von said, *You're in over your head.*

Stacia spent the rest of the service mutely going through the motions of faith. Her thoughts were on Kitty and Bitsy's plan and all the ways it could go terribly wrong. There were too many moving parts that could fail at any point in the process of getting Bitsy to safety. She was in over her head and could no longer see the shore in the distance.

As soon as the service ended, she headed for the choir balcony stairs in order to leave through a side door. She didn't want to run into Chip during the coffee hour. Now that she knew what he had done to

Bitsy over the last twenty years, she was afraid to be in the same room with him.

She paused in the small entryway intended for brides and latecomers to unobtrusively enter the sanctuary, when she realized that Weldon was not behind her. She suspected he had stopped to talk to someone as they filed out of their pews. She put her bag down on the small lectern where the church placed guest books before and after weddings and funerals to find her sunglasses and stopped dead when she heard Chip's voice coming down the passage. She slipped her sunglasses over her face and steeled herself to not react when she saw him.

"Stacia! Imagine running into you out here? Too hot today for coffee?" He smiled at her. She had always thought that smile reserved and a bit standoffish, maybe even shy. Now she recognized it as evil and false. "Are you on your own today?"

She took a step back and slid her hand along the lectern feeling for a pen in case she needed it to defend herself. "No, not at all." She tried to steady her voice. She sounded shaky. "Weldon was right behind me a second ago. And my brother and father are around here somewhere too."

Chip didn't react to the undercurrent of fear in her voice. He reached around her and placed his empty coffee cup on the lectern for someone else to clean up. "I'm on my own today."

"Oh?" Stacia looked up the stairs willing Weldon to come to her rescue.

"Bitsy's away for a few weeks." He almost sounded wistful. "I've been away on exercises for a few days so it was a good time for her and Judy to take a little trip."

Does he know that Judy is gone too? Does he think they're together somewhere? Is that good, or even worse than thinking that Bitsy has left on her own? This is too much.

Stacia felt a drop of sweat roll down the center of her back. She was glad she had managed to put her sunglasses on because she was sure her eyes would have given her away. She was not nearly as good as Kitty or Bitsy at lying. "Oh? Where did they go?"

"A resort up in Michigan. It's supposed to be wonderful there in July. All lakes and camp fires."

"I didn't realize Bitsy liked that kind of thing."

"Oh sure, she loves the mountains, as long as she has a soft bed and people to wait on her hand and foot. I'm sure she's getting spa treatments and lounging beside a lake today."

"No hiking?"

"Not my Bitsy," he said with a derisive smirk. "She might break a nail."

Stacia forced herself to laugh along with Chip. She felt a heaviness fill her frame. How many times had she betrayed the Bitsy she had known as a girl by laughing at Chip's disparaging remarks about her? When she saw Bitsy at church functions and charity events, she had been so standoffish and stiff, that Stacia had been taken in when Chip had poked fun at her. He came across as a regular guy married to a socialite.

"Oh no, heaven forbid she break a nail or twist an ankle."

Chip brushed an imaginary piece of lint from the sleeve of his uniform. "She's been pretty accident prone lately. She's getting pretty old. Maybe her eyes are going bad."

A cold finger of revulsion traced Stacia's spine. She pressed her lips together and nodded dumbly. She didn't trust herself to say anything.

Thankfully, Weldon came down the stairs behind her. "We should go," he said as he put his large palm on her shoulder. Stacia immediately felt safe with her husband there. "We have that thing this afternoon."

She shouldered her bag. "Yes, let's go."

"Good to see you, buddy," Chip said. "How's the construction business treating you? Swinging that hammer much?"

"Going well," Weldon replied. "Lots of changes going on. Keeping my ear to the ground."

Chip glanced back toward the passage as if seeing someone he'd rather be talking to. "Good talking to you, Stacia. We'll all have to get together real soon."

He disappeared back into the church. "What the hell were you and Chip talking about?" asked Weldon. "You looked like someone was holding a gun at your back and forcing you to talk to him."

"Not far from it." Seeing Chip had made the danger of what she and Kitty were doing real. Stacia put her hand into Weldon's much larger hand. "I have something I need to tell you."

She told him the whole story on the drive home. "Let me get this straight." Weldon rubbed his hand across his scalp. "You went over there thinking Bitsy wanted to talk about that editorial, which we will come back to later Missy, and when you got there, Bitsy told you that Chip beats her?" Stacia nodded. "Are you absolutely sure this couldn't be some kind of trick?"

"You need to go over to Kitty's and see Bitsy without her makeup on. There are scars all over her face. Her arms have lumps in them from where he broke her bones and they didn't heal right."

Weldon pulled into their driveway and turned to face her. "Are you sure that she's not playing you? She knows how much you love to help people."

"She's not that good an actress."

"If all this is actually true, then Chip is crazier than I thought he was. He's liable to do anything. What if he finds her and comes at her with a gun? I don't want you doing anything heroic and getting hurt or killed."

"I understand."

"Can't Kitty handle it on her own? And who is this Aaron guy?"

"He's some artist that Kitty knows. I think he was in the service judging how comfortable he seemed with a pistol."

"Then let him deal with Chip. You stay out of this." Stacia started to get out of the car, but Weldon reached out and stopped her. "I'm serious. You call and check up on them all you want, but I don't want you going over there. And I don't want Marcus going over there, or Lana. Stay out of it."

twenty-five

Becky had called from the pay phone outside the restaurant where they stopped for lunch, so Bitsy and Aaron were safely hidden in the laundry room when Coach Campbell dropped her and Bobby off. Kitty met them in the driveway and didn't invite the Campbells to linger. Once inside, Becky dropped her bag at the base of the stairs. "Where is she?"

"She's hiding until the coast is clear. We didn't want the Campbells or any of the neighbors to see her." Bobby sat on the stairs looking interested, but not confused. Becky had apparently shared what she knew with her brother.

"So who is it? Mrs. Morton? Mrs. Foster?"

"Mrs. Magnuson-Evans," Kitty said in a half-whisper.

"Bitsy? You don't even like her."

"I didn't really know her. And that has nothing to do with it. She needed help. I helped her. I can't just kick her out on the street now."

"Why here?"

"It's complicated." Kitty paused and thought about how much the children really needed to know. "Frankly, the less you two know, the better."

Becky rolled her eyes. "You should print that on a t-shirt."

Kitty turned her back on her daughter and walked to the laundry room door. "Okay, you two, come on out." Aaron emerged with Bitsy close behind him. "It's okay, Bitsy. It's just the kids."

Bobby stood next to his mother. "Hey, Ms. Bitsy. I'm sorry to hear about your troubles. I hope my mom can help you out." Kitty put her arm around him. It made her proud to see him being so kind to Bitsy.

She'd done something right along the way.

Bobby looked up at Aaron skeptically. "Hey."

"Hey," Aaron replied. "I'm Aaron."

"Is that a real gun?"

"Yup."

"You know how to use it?"

"I was in Vietnam, so yeah, I know how to use it."

"You friends with my mom?"

"You could say that, but I'm mostly here to defend Ms. Bitsy from her husband."

"Who's defending us from you?" Becky asked from the hall. Aaron suppressed a smile as he winked at Kitty.

Bitsy leaned on the side of the refrigerator. She looked like she needed a drink. "Bobby," Kitty said. "Grab your bag and help me take Bitsy upstairs. I think she could use a nap."

Once Bitsy was settled in the guest room with a few ounces of vodka and a book, and Bobby was in his room unpacking, Kitty started back downstairs. She paused on the landing when she heard raised voices in the kitchen.

"So what's your deal?" Becky asked. "How do you even know my mom?"

"We met. We got talking about art. We became friends. What more can I say?"

"You know she's married, right?"

"Yeah, I know. I also know your dad walked out on her." It sounded like someone was moving around the room opening and closing cabinets. "And I gather he wasn't a crazy good husband."

"She doesn't have any money."

"Is that what you're so hostile about? You think I'm after her money?"

"Well, yeah! Why else would you be into her? It's not like she's young and pretty." Kitty's stomach dropped. After all that she had done recently to protect Becky's future, how could she think so little of her? She crept down a few more stairs to peek at Becky and Aaron glaring at each other across the kitchen.

"Watch it, you little snot. Your mother is one of the coolest people I've met in a long time. She's kind. She's smart. She's spontaneous."

"Are we talking about the same woman?" Becky pulled a Coke from the refrigerator. "There is nothing spontaneous about my mom. She thinks if you ignore something, it will just go away. And, she is mondo uptight."

"You're right, that's not the woman I know. The woman I know's been dealt a raw deal and is rolling with it."

Becky poured her Coke into a glass and turned back to Aaron. "How old are you?"

"Old enough to not need your permission to be with your mom."

"Eww! I don't want to think about my mom like that!"

Their argument was interrupted by the doorbell. Bobby came running down the stairs. "There's some lady at the door." In all the hubbub, no one had noticed the small blue Chevette pull into the driveway. Like a well-rehearsed team, everyone took their places. Aaron bolted up the stairs to get Bitsy into their hiding place in Kitty's closet, and Kitty went to the dining room to make sure Chip wasn't with the woman. She nodded to Bobby to open the door.

"Wow!" Bobby exclaimed. Before Kitty could stop her, Becky sprinted into the foyer. There was a shuffling of feet, the sound of breaking glass, then both children yelled, "Mom!"

Shelly Sullivan and Becky stared slack-jawed at each other while Bobby stared at Steven in Shelly's arms. Kitty kicked aside the remnants of the drinking glass as she pulled Shelly inside and slammed the door shut. Becky seemed to snap out of her shock and started peppering Shelly with questions.

"Who the hell are you? And why do you look like my mom? We don't have any cousins, do we?"

Kitty nudged Becky's shoulder to slow her down. "Sweetie, this is Shelly Sullivan and her baby, Steven."

"Dang!" Bobby said. He moved into the parlor and started pacing in circles while muttering under his breath.

"What? Bub, what's the matter?" Becky looked at him gesturing wildly at the furniture. "Am I missing something, other than that this chick looks like she could be our long lost sister?"

"She's not family." Bobby spit out the words like teeth after a fight. Kitty couldn't remember the last time Bobby had sounded so incensed off the baseball field.

"Shelly is a friend of your father's," Kitty said. Shelly shifted Steven in her arms so that he was looking over her shoulder. He was only wearing a diaper. Kitty thought he seemed to have gotten bigger, although he still looked thin. Shelly looked quite a bit thinner than she had when Kitty had last seen her. Her simple wrap skirt hung off her hips rather than her waist and there were dark circles under her eyes, as well as a sprinkling of acne across her chin. The term that popped into Kitty's mind was haggard.

Becky took another look at Shelly as if noting the light auburn hair, the blue eyes, the slim build in a different light. "Oh! You've got to be shitting me. This is Shelly? As in I've-fallen-in-love-again Shelly?"

"Bingo!"

"You're like my age!" Becky took a step toward Shelly as if to strike her. "Where the hell is my dad?"

Shelly backed away. "I don't know!" She raised her hands to fend Becky off and let go of Steven. With reflexes only found in seasoned mothers, Kitty instinctively stepped forward and caught the baby. She gracefully moved him out of the fray and stood back. Shelly seemed to register that she had dropped her child seconds after he would have hit the floor and froze.

"What do you mean, you don't know? Hasn't he been with you all this time?"

"Wait a minute," Kitty said. "Back up! You two knew about Shelly? Why didn't you say anything to me?"

Becky put her hand up to silence Shelly and turned to her mother. "You knew about Shelly? We didn't know you knew about her at all." The children's lackluster reaction to their father's disappearance made much more sense to Kitty now. It wasn't so much that they didn't care that their father was gone; they thought they knew where he was. With Shelly.

Becky turned back to Shelly. "So? Where is he?"

Kitty stepped between the two young women. "He hasn't been with her. Shelly and I met a few weeks ago, after the police found his car by that lake. He ran out on her too, Becky."

Shelly craned her neck to look around Kitty. "Becky? You're Becky?"

"I told you he was older than you thought he was," Kitty said. "You

220

can't be more than a few years older than Rebecca here."

Shelly's face turned a shade of green as she looked at her lover's children. "I thought you were lying when you said she was old enough to go to college."

"Why would I lie? I'm the injured party in this scenario. You're just the mistress."

"Why hasn't he come back?" Shelly said, like a child complaining after dropping her ice cream cone on the pavement.

"He's not coming back, Shelly. He's just not."

Bobby walked over to his mother. "Is this little guy our brother?"

"Half-brother," Kitty said. "Although, he looks just like you at this age."

"Cause his mother is a cheap knock-off of the original." Kitty felt a bit vindicated by her children's cold reception of their father's mistress.

Steven squirmed in her arms and latched on to her bicep with his little mouth. She gently pulled him off and readjusted him in her arms. "When was the last time this child was fed?"

"I don't know." Shelly looked at the bag slung over her shoulder. "A few hours ago. It took us forever to get here. I had to keep stopping to change his diaper, and he wouldn't stop crying."

"He's not crying now," Kitty said as she looked down at the smiling baby. "Was the sun in his eyes?"

"How am I supposed to know? He doesn't talk."

"He can't talk, you idiot," Becky said. Bobby put his finger out for Steven to grasp and tickled his little bare feet.

"Why are you here?" Kitty asked. "Do you want something? Because I don't have anything to give you and I haven't heard from Seth."

Shelly burst into tears. "I can't do this. He cries all the time. I lost my job. The credit cards don't work anymore. I can't pay my rent." She wiped at her nose with the back of her hand. "I didn't know where else to go."

"So you came here?" Becky asked. "What do you expect my mother to do, you skank?"

"Becky! Language," Kitty said, covering the baby's ears.

Shelly's body slumped. "You're such a good mother. You take him."

Kitty stared at Shelly, dumbfounded. "Pardon me?"

Shelly looked away. "You take him. He's Seth's baby. You're Seth's wife. These are Seth's children. He should be with family."

"What?"

"Just for a few days." Shelly handed Becky Steven's diaper bag.

Kitty was appalled. At no point, no matter how tired or frantic she had been, would she ever have given her child to another woman, even for a few hours. She was a mother, first and foremost.

"Just a few days. Just until I catch up on some sleep."

Kitty looked down at Steven resting his little head against her chest. His ears had the same little twist in them that Becky's had. She couldn't send him away with this young woman. She was too unstable. Kitty would never forgive herself if something awful happened to her children's sibling.

What the hell. I've murdered my husband, harbored a battered woman from her violent husband, and had a fling with a younger man. What's watching my husband's illegitimate child for a few days compared to all that?

She nodded to Becky to take the bag. "Just for the holiday weekend."

"Mom! Don't do this," Becky yelled at her. She tipped her head toward the stairs. "What about, you know."

"It'll be fine, Becky. We can take care of a baby for a few days." She opened the front door and nodded to Shelly. "You get some sleep now. Come get him on Tuesday."

As soon as Shelly walked out the door, Aaron came running down the stairs. "What the hell! Who was that? And why are you holding a baby?"

"Yeah, Mom. What the hell?"

"Everyone calm down." Kitty walked into the parlor and watched Shelly pause and look back at the house before getting in her little blue car.

Aaron followed her into the room. "Your sister?" he asked.

"Seth's mistress." Kitty jiggled Steven in her arms until he laughed. "And this little bundle is their love child."

"He left you for her?"

Becky rolled her eyes and made a gagging sound as she stormed off toward the kitchen. "What are you going to feed the brat? It's not like you can nurse him."

Kitty handed the baby to Aaron and followed her. "Hey! What

exactly is your problem, young lady? Are you mad that I went to see Shelly?"

"You weren't supposed to know about her." Tears streamed down Becky's face. "This isn't the way things were supposed to go."

"You're mad because I know about your father's mistress? Really? Aren't you the girl that's always giving me grief about keeping my head in the sand when it comes to your father?" The pitch of Kitty's voice was rising with each word and she was feeling the familiar tingle in her chest that heralded a lapse in judgement. "Well, I'm not pretending anymore! How about you? How long were you and your brother going to wait before you told me that you thought your father was holed up with her? Until I was selling my jewelry to put food on the table? Until we were living on the street because your father stopped paying the mortgage and the bank took the house?" Becky gaped at her and backed away from her. "What? What needed to happen in your eighteen-year-old brain before you deemed me worthy of knowing about Shelly?"

Becky put her hands up. "This isn't the way it was supposed to go down. There wasn't supposed to be a baby. You were never supposed to meet her."

Bitsy drifted down the stairs and stood between them. She shot Kitty a shaming look before she put her arm protectively around Becky like a mother hen protecting her chick. "Explain it to us, hon. What did your dad say would happen?"

"He called me the day before I got the big envelope from Brown," Becky said. "He said he'd met someone and was going to ask Mom for a divorce, and did Bobby and I want to stay in Magnuson and live with him or go with Mom."

"He asked you that?"

Bitsy glared at Kitty. "Go on, Hon. What else did he say?"

Betsy wiped her face with the sleeve of her t-shirt. "Not much, really, now that I think of it. He kept blathering on about how Mom didn't need him anymore, and that she was getting all independent, and how that made him feel emasculated." She looked up at her mother. "I remember that. He used the word emasculated. He never uses words like that. He must have read it in a magazine or something. Yeah, he definitely said emasculated." She stood up straighter as she recalled the rest of their conversation. "I remember he said that he wasn't on a business trip and would be home soon to talk to Mom about a divorce, but then he never showed up. Bobby and I just assumed he chickened out and was still with what's-her-face."

"So you thought he ran away to play with that woman?" Bitsy asked. "And that he'd be back?"

"Of course I thought he'd be back. He wasn't going to actually leave Mom. That woman was just another one of his toys, like a new set of clubs or a new car."

"But he didn't come back," Kitty said. "How long were we supposed to wait?"

"I kinda thought maybe after the summer? I didn't want him to stop me from leaving for school. I thought he'd just show up eventually and act like nothing had ever happened." She looked pleadingly at her mother. "You know Dad. He'd flash you one of his smiles and you'd forgive him. You always do, and then you'd make him a pineapple upside-down-cake."

Becky's words were like darts in her chest. She couldn't move to pull them out because they were true. For all of Becky's life, Kitty had done exactly that - she would forgive Seth and bake a cake. She was ashamed that her daughter would expect no more from her.

"That's not the woman I know," Aaron said from the doorway. He held Steven in his arms with ease, something Seth had never mastered. "The Kay I know is a woman of action. She's creative and decisive. She took in Bitsy here at great risk to herself. When she needed advice, she wasn't too proud to come to me and ask for it. She hasn't been hiding from the truth at all." He moved further into the room so he was beside Kitty. "When your father abandoned her, with no money by the way, she didn't fall apart. When she found out that he had also abandoned that Shelly and her baby, she showed a little compassion and helped her out. She didn't need to do that. She could have just as easily slammed the door in her face. But, no. She adjusted her stride and moved on."

Kitty was touched by Aaron's words. He had no idea how wrong he was, yet she was still touched that he was saying those things about her. She liked the woman he was describing.

"You barely know her," Becky said dismissively.

"Okay. But you don't either. Have you ever bothered to get off your spoiled-ass high horse and actually talk to her? Or have you been too busy acting like she's your servant?"

"I, ummm, I, what?"

"I think what he is saying, hon, is that you're being too hard on your mama," Bitsy said. "You don't know everything that's happened over the years. You only see what they show you. Your mama is very good at coming across as the happy homemaker, but she hasn't always been happy. If you were really looking, you would have seen that."

Becky turned and looked at Bitsy's scarred face and seemed to be reconsidering everything she had thought she knew to be true for the past eighteen years. She shook her head and looked back to Kitty. "What are we going to do? He's not coming back, is he?"

Kitty stepped forward and hugged her daughter. "No, sweetie. He's not."

★★★

The next morning, Kitty rested while Steven napped. It had been fourteen years since she'd had a baby in the house; her mothering muscles were stiff yet the muscle memory was there. Still, she was tired. The last time she had managed midnight feedings and 2:00 AM diaper changes, she'd been in her twenties. In her forties, she needed more sleep, but was also far more calm and experienced. She knew Steven would be fine if it took her a few minutes to get down the hall in the middle of the night. She reveled in the sensation that anyone wanted her attention that much.

She also had help. Bitsy doted over Steven, and Bobby was a natural with the baby. Only Becky kept her distance from the boy. She stayed in her room brooding while Bobby and Aaron pulled the old crib out of the crawl space and found the boxes of baby clothes and paraphernalia. Kitty thought she would give Becky some space to think things over. It was hard to be eighteen and realize you didn't have all the answers.

Kitty was pleased to find her fastidiousness in putting up Bobby's baby clothes had paid off. His little blue jumpsuits and sleepers were in excellent condition and fit Steven perfectly. While Kitty napped, Bitsy and Bobby did loads of laundry to freshen up the blankets and stuffed animals that had grown musty in the garage.

The phone rang through the house. Half asleep, Kitty heard Bobby

225

running across the kitchen to answer it on the first ring. She heard some muffled voices then footsteps on the stairs. Bitsy knocked gently on her door before sticking her head in to say that Stacia was on the line. Kitty sat up slowly and picked up the extension. A soft click signaled Bobby hanging up in the kitchen.

"Hi, Stacia," Kitty said quietly. "What's up?"

"I'm not going to beat around the bush. I told Weldon."

"Why?"

"Chip is back in town." Kitty felt a chill run down her spine, but made an effort not to show her concern on her face. There was no need to alarm Bitsy any more than necessary.

"And how did you find that out?"

"Is she right there?"

"Yes."

"Okay, just listen to me then." Stacia sounded stressed. "I talked to him briefly at church…and he is telling people that Bitsy and Judy are away on vacation for a few weeks…so I think that means that he might know that Judy is gone too. He probably thinks that they're together, which might work in our favor because he'll be looking for the both of them, rather than Bitsy by herself."

"Mmmhmm."

"He was so cold. He scared me, and Weldon picked up on it."

Kitty looked at Bitsy and smiled as if Stacia was saying unimportant things. "I understand."

"Anyway, Weldon knows and he's forbidden me to have anything to do with the plan. I can call and check up on her, but I won't be coming over any time soon."

"That's okay, I totally understand. Don't worry about us. I hope you feel better."

At that point, Steven let out a wail. Bitsy responded like a mother and sprinted down the hall. "It's okay," she called. "He's wet, that's all."

"What was that sound?" Stacia asked. "It sounded like a baby crying."

"That was Steven." Kitty cleared her throat. "I don't think I ever told you about Seth's mistress, Shelly."

"No, why?"

"Well, she had a baby."

"How is he there?"

"Shelly came looking for Seth and begged me to watch him for a bit."

"Kitty! What about Bitsy? Did she see Bitsy?"

"Not at all. She and Aaron were hiding upstairs the whole time. She had no idea there was anyone but the kids and I here."

"Becky and Bobby are home? Christ, Kitty! What are you doing over there?"

"It's okay. I've got everything under control. And I had to help her. She's got a terrible case of the baby blues. I was afraid she might do something to the baby." Kitty heard Stacia grumble something under her breath. "Oh, come on. If you had seen that pigsty of an apartment, you would have agreed to help her out too."

"No I wouldn't—"

"Yes, you would. You'd help a total stranger if they were in need. Look at the way you've helped Bitsy. And Debbie, and Eileen, and me. You wouldn't have turned your back on a mother and baby in a million years."

twenty-six

itty's maternal radar woke her and propelled her downstairs before Steven had a chance to work up a full-on cry in the night. The baby had fallen asleep on Aaron's chest that evening and it hadn't made sense to risk waking him by moving him to the crib. Aaron was content to sleep in the recliner, rather than the couch. He and Kitty agreed she should let Becky and Bobby get to know Aaron before she invited him into her bed. Their motley group had enough to worry about without inciting any further indignation in Becky.

"Thank goodness," Aaron said as Kitty came into the kitchen. "I have no clue how much to feed this munchkin, but I didn't want to wake anyone."

Kitty opened the refrigerator and retrieved a bottle. "You keep him happy and I'll warm this up."

Aaron danced the baby around the kitchen while Kitty put a pan of water on to simmer. "Will he drink that whole thing?"

"Uh huh." Kitty rubbed her eyes while she did the mental math. At the rate Steven was going through bottles, they would run out of formula before the Fourth. "Someone is going to have to buy more formula." She opened the refrigerator again and took stock of its contents. "And milk, and bread, and chicken maybe. We're quickly going through the groceries Stacia bought." Kitty closed the door and yawned. "We can't ask her to go anymore because Stacia told Weldon about Bitsy, and now he won't let her come over here."

"Who's Weldon?"

Kitty adjusted the heat under the pan and put the bottle in. "Her husband. If you still go to the VFW, you might know him. He's on some advisory board down there."

Aaron continued swaying from foot to foot to keep Steven happy. "Hmmm, Weldon...advisory board. You can't mean Weldon Curran. The construction guy?"

"Yeah." Kitty swirled the bottle in the pan. "He and his brother built all the houses around here."

"Tall black guy? Shaved head?" Kitty nodded and tested the formula against the inside of her wrist. "He's married to the pixie princess?"

Kitty chuckled at Aaron's description of Stacia. "Do you know each other?"

"Not really. The Korea guys tend to keep to themselves, but I know who he is."

"Well, he doesn't want Stacia involved with the whole Bitsy thing anymore, and I don't blame him. The less people coming in and out of the house, the better." Kitty tested the formula again and turned off the heat. "This is ready. You want to feed him, or should I?"

Aaron took the bottle and leaned against the counter. The baby started slurping down the formula as soon as he could get his mouth around the rubber nipple. Aaron smiled as he looked down at Steven. "I need to go back to the shelter for a bit. I could pick-up a few things on my way back."

"You're leaving?"

"I need to put the finishing touches on St. Francis and move him out to the garden. It shouldn't take more than a few hours. Plus, I need to get my tools and some clean clothes if I'm going to keep hunkering down here with y'all."

"Who will protect us if Chip shows up?"

"It's only three bus trips each way. I'll go in the morning and be back by nightfall."

"That's too long. Take the car."

"I can't do that. Becky will think I'm stealing it."

"That's probably true." Kitty rubbed her eyes again. "I'd feel safer with you and your military experience here. I'd drive you, but I won't leave the children here alone with Bitsy."

"Could Becky give me a ride? She can drive, right?"

"We'd have to ask her, but I don't see why she couldn't drop you off at An Open Hand while she picks up a few groceries. You can leave after breakfast and be back in time for lunch." Kitty gazed across the kitchen at Aaron holding Steven so naturally. It made her chest ache to think how he'd been a better father to Steven in the last day than Seth would have been in a lifetime.

★★★

Kitty hadn't realized how much Aaron's presence in the house made Bitsy feel safe. As soon as he and Becky pulled out of the driveway, Bitsy began pacing with the pistol in her hand. She would start in Becky's room and peer through a slit in the blinds for a few minutes, then move to Kitty's bedroom to check that no one was approaching the house from the lake. Kitty tried to distract her with cups of tea and the promise of a new book, but Bitsy was too agitated to sit for more than a few minutes. Kitty eventually gave up and sat with Bobby in his room while Bitsy stalked up and down the hallway.

Bobby and Kitty were in an intense conversation about whether or not he should clean out his sock drawer when they heard Bitsy let out a sharp cry in Kitty's bedroom. They both bolted down the hall, but Bitsy was nowhere to be seen. Kitty saw a movement in the trees between the yard and the walking trail and snatched up the pistol from where Bitsy had dropped it in front of the window. She didn't think about what she was doing; she simply reacted by heaving the window open and training the gun on the path. The adrenaline pumping through her veins made her hearing dull and her vision narrow to the point that if Bobby hadn't tackled her from behind, she might have killed Molly Blevins as she walked into the back yard.

"Give me that!" Bobby yanked the gun out of his mother's hand. "The last thing we need right now is you mowing down our neighbors." He put his hand on his chest and blew out a deep breath. "Now go downstairs and deal with Mrs. Blevins. I'll keep Steven and Bitsy quiet."

Kitty staggered toward the hall as the enormity of what had almost just happened hit her. She would have killed Molly Blevins for walking into her backyard without even thinking about it. Is that what her life was like now? Her stomach churned as she made her way downstairs and out the sliding glass door to intercept Molly in the yard.

"Hey," she called from the doorway. "Out for a walk?"

Molly stopped in the middle of the yard and held her dog at her side on a shortened leash. Her eyes scanned the flower beds nervously.

"You're garden looks good."

"I haven't weeded in weeks." Kitty leaned on the railing to hide the fact that her hands were shaking. "What do you want, Molly?"

"I haven't seen you in weeks and they tell me you have a huge pile of boxes waiting for you at the Arts Center. You okay?"

"I'm great. Everything's just peachy around here." Kitty ran her hand over her hair and tried to appear casual even though her heart was racing and and her legs felt like rubber as the adrenaline dissipated from her system. "Did you come by to check up on me or gawk at the woman whose husband abandoned her?"

"I, umm, look I'm sorry if I offended you that day in the conference room—"

No, you're not!" Kitty gripped the railing and grit her teeth to keep from saying more. It wasn't the time to have it out with Molly about how hurt she'd been by her attitude. She had bigger problems than a failed friendship. "Look Molly, I really don't want to talk to you about Seth's disappearance, and I haven't been at the Arts Council for a while because I've busy taking care of things here. Okay?"

Molly took a step back as if Kitty had struck her. "I really sorry—"

"Save it, Molly." Kitty tilted her chin in the air and moved back to the sliding glass door. "I'm really not interested anymore." She went inside and stood at the door until Molly turned and walked back down the path toward the lake. Only then did she collapse into a kitchen chair and put her head in the hands. The emotions and sensations running through her body overwhelmed her for a moment. She was appalled that she had nearly shot Molly, yet it had felt terrific to tell her off. Still, she needed to pull herself together and stop flying off the handle like that. She had too many people depending on her.

Bobby and Steven crept down the stairs. "Is she gone?"

"Yup." Kitty stood up walked into the kitchen where she splashed water on her face. "I don't think she'll be back either."

"I heard you guys talking. What did she say about Dad?"

"It's not important, honey." Kitty wiped her face off with a paper towel and dabbed the damp towel against the back of her neck. It really wasn't important, she realized. In the past, Molly and the Lookers opinions of her would have meant everything to her, but now that Seth was dead and she had Bitsy and Steven to take care of, she simply didn't care anymore.

"Where's Bitsy?"

"I'm here," Bitsy said from the stairs. "I thought I could defend myself as long as I had the gun, but I ran like a scared rabbit as soon as I saw that dog through the trees." She looked sheepishly at Kitty. "By the way, you're going to need to throw out that hamper in your closet."

"Oh, Bitsy. Really?"

Bobby tapped the pistol tucked in his back pocket. "And I think I will be keeping the gun until Aaron gets back. I don't trust either one of you with it anymore."

★★★

Three hours later, Becky pushed the garage door up and roared inside. She knocked over Bobby's bike as she shoved the car door open and stormed into the house. Aaron slid the heavy door closed and quietly brought the groceries in. Kitty took a bag from his arms. "Where have you two been all morning? Bitsy's been frantic." She and Bobby had agreed to not tell Aaron about Molly's visit and how Kitty had nearly shot her from the upstairs window.

Aaron went back out to the garage and returned with a duffle bag. "We ran into a hassle at the shelter."

Kitty put the milk and meats in the refrigerator. "How so?"

"Well, it took me a while to grab a few things and draft a few of the guys to help me move St. Francis outside." Aaron handed Kitty a bottle of orange juice. "Everything would have been cool if Becky had chilled in the car like we agreed."

"She went inside? By herself?"

"Some of the guys found her wandering around the first floor and—"

Becky rushed out of the powder room and shoved Aaron into the refrigerator door. "Don't go laying it on me. All I did was go looking for you. You're the one that blew it up."

"Okay, take a chill pill." He pushed her away. "I did. I totally overreacted."

"Will someone tell me what's going on?"

"He told those bums that I was his girlfriend!"

"It was the first thing that popped into my mind, so shoot me!"

"Don't tempt me, bonehead. Like I would ever go out with you."

Aaron turned to Kitty. "I came in from the garden to find her in the gymnasium surrounded by a bunch of the guys." He wiped the back of his hand across his forehead. "They were circling her like a pack of hyenas. There are reasons why women aren't allowed inside the building."

"Really, Rebecca. You need to be more careful." Kitty exchanged glances with Aaron. "Those men could have…You should be thanking him, not yelling at him." She turned back to the groceries. "Did you get plenty of formula?"

"Yeah," Becky grumbled. "The checkout girl gave me a dirty look when I gave her the money. So first, the idiot at the Food Lion thinks I'm a teenaged mother, then a bunch of bums think I'm hanging out with this stooge."

"You've had a busy day, haven't you? Pass the frozen peas."

Becky handed her mother the peas and stomped up the stairs. She slammed her bedroom door, which was promptly followed by Steven waking from his nap.

Kitty turned to Aaron. "You couldn't come up with a better way to get the men away from her?"

"I know I screwed up. I saw them closing in and I started to say that she was my girlfriend's daughter, but thought better of it mid-sentence and it came out as her being with me. I'm sorry, I'm not as good at lying as y'all."

Kitty raised her eyebrows at him and shoved the peas in the freezer. He sighed and pulled a box of cereal from the bag on the counter. "Anything happen while I was gone?"

"Not much. My sister called a while ago. She's accepted the nursing job up in Rhode Island. My brother-in-law is paying to have movers come down and pack up all her things some time next week."

"Why isn't she coming herself?"

Kitty thought about Rose and how disappointed she'd been with her for getting involved with Aaron. It was probably best they not see each other. Some things can not be unsaid. "She wants to stay and watch the tall ships parade through Narragansett Bay before they go down to New York on the Fourth."

twenty-seven

nlike most neighborhood Fourth of July picnics, where the men hover around grills and the women fuss over their potato salads, the Overlook Bicentennial celebration was an all-day affair that started with midday cocktails around the pool and ended with a flotilla at dusk. The party committee had gone above and beyond their usual flag bunting and greased watermelon games to transform the Overlook Swim & Tennis Club into a 1976 extravaganza. Flags sprouted from each of the fence posts. Red, white, and blue streamers snaked through the wrought iron fencing. Each table around the pool had arrangements of sparklers stuck in pails of sand. There were hours of planned activities for the children, so the parents could stand in the hot sun and drown themselves in Seabreeze cocktails.

Kitty donned her only blue sun dress and slipped her feet into a pair of white slides. A bright red ribbon held her hair back from her face. It was getting long enough to wear in a ponytail; she'd cancelled her last two salon appointments. Aaron didn't think she should attend the party; however, Bitsy and the kids agreed that tongues would wag if Kitty didn't at least make an appearance at the pool. She would skip the sunset flotilla. No one would fault her for that; she no longer had a boat. Stacia, on the other hand, would be the grand marshal, as usual.

The welcome table at the club was manned by a perky young woman Kitty didn't recognize. She must have been new to Overlook. There were more and more new faces every year. Kitty wondered which Looker this young gal was replacing. Kitty smiled blandly at the woman as she checked off her name from the master list. It felt odd to see Seth's name there under hers with an empty box next to it. As she moved to walk into the pool area, she caught the woman behind the table glance down at her name, then quickly look up to get a better look at Kitty. The woman may have been new, but she'd heard about her and Seth. Kitty made a good cautionary tale of how not to deal with a cheating husband.

A swarm of Lookers hovered around the bar. Kitty walked the other way. Since she'd stopped drinking, she found the Lookers tedious. She wondered how she'd ever found those women fun.

Kitty spotted Rachel Robertson's husband, Dave or Doug or Don, talking to her insurance agent, Hal Eflund. Hal and Seth had been golf and tennis buddies, as well as business acquaintances. Kitty had left at least ten messages with Hal's secretary in the last week. She needed to talk to him about Seth's life insurance. Now that Golf Systems had sent her the last check covering Seth's accrued vacation and sick time, Kitty couldn't ignore the shrinking balance in their checking account. Even after selling the Volvo, she would run out of money again soon. She walked over to the two men with a big smile plastered on her face. "Hey Hal," she sighed. "You get my messages?"

"Kitty Cat," Hal said with a smile that didn't extend to his eyes. "I've been meaning to call you all week."

"I bet," she replied.

Hal gestured with his beer bottle to the man standing next to him. "You know Drew Robertson, right?"

Kitty dabbed a drop of beer from her arm with a pool towel hanging over the nearest chair. "Of course, Rachel and I have been in PTA together for years." Drew smiled appreciatively at Kitty. She wondered if she should have worn a less revealing sundress to the party. Now that she no longer had a husband to speak of, the men of Overlook would be looking at her differently. Aaron's face flashed through her mind. She wished he was there to protect her.

Kitty leaned in to Hal. "Did you figure out what I need to do to get Seth's life insurance?"

Hal signaled for the three of them to sit down at one of the round tables along the fence. "Seth had a ton of life insurance. He bought it all from me ten years or so ago, but the company won't pay out on the policy until he's officially declared dead."

"That could take anywhere from a few months to seven years,"

Drew Robertson said. Kitty remembered that Drew was a lawyer.

"I find this all very confusing," Kitty said. She pulled her shoulders back. If these two were going to keep staring at her cleavage, she might as well play it up for all she could. "I never even knew he had life insurance, until I found the paperwork in his office a few weeks ago."

"He had a policy on himself and, until recently, a policy on you."

"What do you mean?" Drew asked. "He cancelled the policy on Kitty?" Kitty saw him write something down on the napkin under his beer bottle.

"Sure," Hal replied. "Once their eldest turned eighteen, he didn't need to insure Kitty."

Drew's ears turned pink and Hall was suddenly fascinated with the label on his beer bottle.

It slowly dawned on Kitty what Hal was implying. Kitty had become superfluous once Becky was an adult. It was no longer necessary to insure against the financial burden of their mother's death. Canceling that life insurance policy made it abundantly clear how Seth felt about her.

Kitty turned to watch the teenagers primping and preening for each other on the other side of the pool. Their youth and promise left a bitter taste in her mouth. She tapped a cigarette out of her enameled case, a gift from Seth after one of his 'extended layovers' a few years back. "Did he have any other policies? On anyone other than himself?" She was afraid Hal was going to say Seth had a policy out on Shelly.

He shook his head. "Nope, just the one on himself and the typical house and car insurances."

Drew lit her cigarette for her with his dented Zippo lighter. "What about health insurance, Kitty? Is your coverage through his work?"

She felt her dress sticking to the skin under her arms. "I don't know. I hadn't thought about our health insurance." That was one more thing she would have to take care of on her own. She doubted she could afford it. "What other things should I be thinking about, Drew?"

"You'll need to close out all your joint credit card accounts and reopen new ones in your own name. Now remember, as a woman they will give you a much lower credit limit."

"I have a job," Kitty said. "And I have never been late on a bill."

"Seth has never been late on a bill," Drew corrected her. "All the financial stuff was probably linked to Seth's social. You wouldn't have much of a credit rating of your own."

Kitty stood up and made a show of looking for someone, even though she knew exactly where everyone was. "I guess I need to take care of all that right away, huh?"

"On the bright side," Drew said, "banks are much more accommodating to widows than divorcees." That word sounded like an expletive in his mouth.

She excused herself and made a beeline for the drinks table. The pitchers of punch were tempting, but she had gotten this far without falling off the wagon again; she could get through a few more minutes of the party without alcohol. She helped herself to a glass of cranberry juice from the cooler under the table, and stepped away from the boisterous Fourth of July partygoers to sit on the low wall at the edge of the ridge. She balanced her cup beside her and made sure her center of balance leaned toward the pool side of the wall. If she lost her balance and tumbled over the wall, it would be a long hard slide down the riprap retaining wall to the water.

On the other side of the pool, Weldon and Stacia stood with her cousin, Quentin Tate. Weldon looked like a giant next to the two Tate cousins. Although not as tiny as Stacia, no one would consider Quentin a tall man. Quentin was gesturing wildly and tugging at the lapels of his red sport coat in a way that made Stacia giggle. It was the first time Kitty had heard Stacia laugh since Seth died. Quentin finished his story and wiped his brow with a red, white, and blue striped handkerchief as the three of them turned to survey the crowd. Weldon's broad smile disappeared when he noticed Kitty. He said something to Quentin and steered Stacia away to a table. Quentin walked around the pool toward the drinks table. He poured some punch in a tall red cup and stepped over to Kitty. "Hey, Kitty," he said. "How are you this fine Fourth?"

Kitty didn't know Quentin Tate well enough to know whether he was flirting with her or just being a gentleman. The Tates all had an innate Southern charm that made her wonder if they were genetically predisposed to being smoothly manipulative, or if the elder Tates actively taught their children how to rule their little fiefdoms.

"A little warm, but altogether fine," Kitty replied.

Quentin took a sip from the cup in his hand and made a face.

"Yowza! Ladybug didn't make the Seabreezes this year. She would never put this much alcohol in the pitcher. This is cranberry tinted vodka."

"Goodness, people will be tumbling into the pool soon." Kitty lifted her glass of cranberry juice in a toast. "I'm glad I'm sticking with juice today."

"Wise choice," Quentin said as he poured the contents of his cup over the wall. "Where did you find juice? All I saw over there were Cokes and pitchers of Seabreeze."

Kitty stood up and moved toward the table. "Come on, I'll show you the secret ingredient stash." Quentin stayed right at her elbow. She could smell his citrus-tinged cologne. He smelled clean and masculine at the same time. Kitty again became acutely aware of the plunging neckline of her halter-style dress. Since she had been working more and running less over the last few months, she had gained a few pounds, all in the chest.

"I'm glad I ran into you," Quentin said. "I've been thinking about our conversation a few weeks back. Are you still thinking about putting your house on the market?" He poured himself a glass of juice and led Kitty to a quiet section of the wall before laying out exactly what she could and could not do with a house she had no legal rights to. It wasn't good news. She had all the financial responsibilities of home ownership and none of the rights.

★★★

As the sun started to drop in the sky, the Overlook families boarded their boats and made their way out to the center of the lake. The Lookers tied up, one to the next, in a big circle with the other families in concentric circles around them. The younger children splashed around under their parents' not-so-watchful eyes inside the circle and the teenagers formed a raft of inner tubes off to one side. Everyone had brought enough sandwiches and beer to feed their family, and a bit more to share. It was a pleasant way to watch the sun set behind the coal plant before the fireworks display.

Kitty watched the clump of boats grow from a simple circle to a flower from the safety of her bedroom. Becky was spending the evening with Lana Curran and Bobby had gone to the party with the family that bought Deirdre Logan's house. Kitty went by after the picnic to meet the mother and sent a batch of whoopie pies with Bobby. It felt wrong to see the heavy oak furniture the family had shipped from Michigan in her former friend's house. Deirdre had favored French provincial in the formal rooms and had a penchant for wicker in the rooms that looked out on the lake. Kitty had left quickly without registering the new woman's name.

As the sun set, Aaron played with the baby on the bed and Kitty and Bitsy watched the flotilla form out in the lake. They didn't light any candles or torches so they couldn't be seen in the window by anyone passing on the walking trails or out on the lake. Bitsy looked through a pair of binoculars she had found in Bobby's room. "Do they do this every year?"

"It's amazing no one has ever drowned, the way they're all drinking out there. Even the guys who are supposed to be watching the little ones are blotto."

"Wasn't that you and Seth?"

"Seth was out there every year setting off the fireworks. It's amazing he never blew his hand off."

"Really, Kitty. You talk about Seth like he was a monster. He was just a man. Men cheat. Men lie. Your life was pretty good." She took one of Kitty's lemon cookies from the tin under her arm. "You have a good job doing something you seem to like. You have two great kids. You're healthy. What have you really got to complain about?"

Kitty turned and glanced around the master bedroom. She lived in a beautiful home in a sought-after neighborhood. Other people would sacrifice to have the life that Kitty didn't want. Had never wanted. Up to that point, she had been living a life that Seth had chosen. That was another reason she felt such a kinship with Bitsy. Granted, Chip had treated Bitsy with violence whereas Seth had had only barbs of deceit, but they had both been patronized by a man. Neither one of them were independent women.

"You know, we have something in common. We're both at a similar spot in life, aren't we?"

"How so? Are you saying that Seth knocked you around? Did he lock you up?"

"No, nothing like that. Or, at least not in the way you mean. But he did knock me around in a different way. He stole my independence."

"Get a grip, Kitty. He didn't lock you up in a glass prison. He married you." Bitsy took another bite of cookie and let it melt in her mouth. "These are really good, by the way."

Kitty watched Aaron play with Steven on the bed. "I want more than a comfortable life in suburbia." She thought about how Aaron made her feel when they were alone, and when they talked about his work. "I want excitement. Passion. I had such big dreams when I was younger. Didn't you?"

"Not really," Bitsy said. "All I really ever wanted to do was be with my horse."

"Stacia said you won all sorts of ribbons when you were younger. Why did you stop riding?"

"Chip made me sell my horse when I got pregnant with Judy." Bitsy bit her lip. "That was one of the worst days of my life. Worse than any of the beatings. I loved Sparta." She wiped a tear from her eyelash and looked at Kitty with a watery smile. "I guess I should have seen it all coming then. I loved that horse more than anything. We could have boarded it nearby. It was just an act of cruelty to make me get rid of him."

"Did he give you a reason for selling the horse?"

"It was my punishment for getting pregnant."

"Ummm…isn't Judy…?"

"She's Chip's, but he never wanted children. He didn't like it when I got fat."

"You were pregnant."

"He saw it as fat. As weak. As my fault."

"It takes two to tango."

"You know what he said to me when abortion became legal? He said it would have saved him thousands of dollars over the last nineteen years if I had aborted Judy."

"I hate to ask this, but does he treat her the same way he treats you?"

"No, thank God. She's very good at not making him angry. And if she does, I'm the one that pays for it. Not her."

"Does she know?"

"I tried to keep it from her, but children are very observant. It didn't take her long to see what was happening around her. The first time we

241

left, it was her idea. When Chip found out, he forced her to watch as he broke my leg and then made her lie to the emergency room doctors about me falling down the stairs. After that, I always left alone and never told her my plans."

"Where is she, really?"

"She's out in California."

"Chip thinks she's still in school in Tennessee?"

"We moved her into the dorms last fall and she's been writing her father long letters about how much fun she's having and had her roommate mail them from the school, so Chip thought she was there all year. He'll figure it out soon enough. Judy had to withdraw eventually, so there won't be a tuition bill for this fall's semester."

"So where is she living?"

"Berkeley. She's working as a waitress and living with some musician. She doesn't tell me much. She seems happy. She helped me screw up the courage to ask Stacia for help."

"Do you need to tell her where you are?"

"No!" Bitsy choked on a cookie. "She can't know anything. If Chip ever finds her in California, she needs to not know anything."

"But she's your daughter, you can't just never speak to her again."

The idea of being separated from Becky or Bobby like that terrified Kitty.

"Not forever. We agreed to not contact each other until we feel it's safe and then I'll find her, not the other way around. We have a code we'll use. I saw it in a Hitchcock movie."

"What would you have done if Stacia had said no?"

"I knew Stacia would say yes. And Chip would never expect me to call her. He thinks we hate each other."

"I think most people think you hate each other."

"We were rivals for so long that it must appear that way. I know Stacia, though. I knew her mother and father. I saw how she took care of her mother when she was sick. And then, there was the accident."

"When Weldon's sister died?"

"Did you know that she crawled almost a mile with a shattered leg and a broken pelvis to get help for those girls? She wouldn't let the ambulance take her to the hospital until they went for the other girls first. The newspaper said that they couldn't take her until she had

242

passed out from the pain."

Kitty pressed her nose against the glass. "Stacia is a good person in a crisis."

twenty-eight

Kitty dropped a soiled diaper in the garbage can and wrapped a fresh one around Steven's little body. "Wasn't that easy?" She tickled his belly until he giggled. She was beginning to see a real personality in his little face. He was much more pensive than either Becky or Bobby. She slipped a clean kimono-style shirt under his back and snapped it over his chest before handing the baby to Bobby who was watching the midday news for the sports scores. "Watch Steven for a minute while I warm up a bottle." Bobby took the baby and settled him on his lap. "I can hear Aaron banging around in the garage. Where's everyone else?"

"Bitsy's in the parlor reading, of course, and Becky's at the pool with Lana."

Kitty put a pan of water on the stove and went out to the garage to see what Aaron was doing. He appeared to have disassembled the toolkit and had spread it across the floor of the garage. He looked up at her. "Are these all the tools you have?"

"There's a screwdriver in the junk drawer."

Aaron gave her a crooked smile and shook his head. "I was thinking more along the lines of a blow torch or an air compressor."

"I don't think we have anything like that. If it required anything more than a screwdriver or wrench, Seth would call someone. He didn't like to get his hands dirty."

Aaron moved to the small workbench and picked up a long sharp hook with a wooden handle. "Then why did he have this instrument of torture?"

"That's mine. See the rack above the bench? Those are my tools for restringing my tennis racquets."

He crossed the garage and pulled her toward him. "You restring your own tennis racquets? What, the pro shop doesn't pull the cat gut tight enough for you?"

She giggled and swatted him away. "No, they don't. I have a powerful backhand that requires a different tension than most people. Now, stop clanging around out here and come inside. We'll have some lunch as soon as I feed Steven."

They returned to the kitchen arm in arm. "Mom! Come quick," said Bobby. "Look at the TV! They're showing it again."

A television reporter standing on the side of a highway. He was reporting on the multiple highway fatalities that occurred during the holiday. The report went to footage of mangled cars festooned with flags and streamers, then went to a small blue Chevette that appeared to have driven full-speed into an underpass.

"Wow, that color must be more popular than I thought," Aaron said as he sat down next to Bobby and Steven. "Doesn't Steven's mom drive a car in the same garish blue?"

"That's what I thought too when they did the teaser at the top of the hour."

Kitty sat down on the recliner. A cold lump was forming in her stomach as she listened to the reporter talk about teenagers driving too fast. The footage returned to the underpass and zoomed in on the compact blue car. "In a bizarre accident that seems unrelated to the holiday revelry, a woman lost control of her vehicle in the early hours of the morning and drove into the I-40 overpass south of High Point. The woman, who was killed on impact, did not appear to have been drinking, but may have been under the influence of drugs. The driver's name has yet to be released due to the inability to locate a next of kin."

Aaron looked down at the baby sitting quietly on Bobby's lap. "That's because he's hiding out here in Magnuson."

"Good thing she left you with us," Bobby whispered in Steven's ear.

"That poor girl." Kitty was stunned. She didn't need to wait for an autopsy report to know that the accident was anything but a suicide.

★★★

They spent the rest of the afternoon in silence. Aaron stared out the parlor window with the pistol on his hip. Bitsy read upstairs, while Bobby napped beside Steven's crib. Kitty was afraid to say anything about Shelly in case she appeared to be relieved at the young woman's death. She was profoundly sad that Shelly had felt so desperate and regretted her role in contributing to that desperation. On the other hand, as Rose would say, Shelly no longer presented a loose end in Seth's death. If the police ever did suspect foul-play in Seth's disappearance, Shelly's suicide would make her a suspect.

Kitty spent time peeling vegetables and thought about how Steven was now an orphan. He wasn't even sitting up on his own yet. It broke her heart to think of him alone in the world. At five o'clock, she slid a chicken in the oven and sat down to watch the evening news. She wanted to see the story about the traffic accidents again in hopes there would be new information.

Instead of the highway, a reporter stood on the Lake Tate dam with the coal plant looming over his shoulder. The report went to footage of police boats circling the area near the dam. "Early this morning, Rory Willet and his brother were fishing off their dock in the new Fox Chase neighborhood and caught more than minnows." The footage changed to a policeman holding up an evidence bag containing the sweatshirt Kitty had been wearing the night she killed Seth.

Kitty gasped and let out a short yelp. Aaron came running. "Last night Lake Tate was filled with boats celebrating the Bicentennial," the reporter continued. "Police are concerned that one of the partygoers fell overboard. Judging from the size of the article of clothing found in the water, police are canvassing residents in the Fox Chase neighborhood for information on any missing children. Residents should notify the authorities if they know of any missing boats from the area."

Kitty felt like her chest was going to explode. Their plan had fallen apart. They'd found the sweatshirt she's wrapped around Seth's bloody face. It was just a matter of time before they dragged the lake.

Aaron looked at the television. "Is that this lake?" Kitty nodded dumbly. As Aaron watched the rest of the story, she clenched her jaw to keep from screaming.

Think, Kitty. Think! What would Rose do at this point?

Okay, they found the sweatshirt, but no one has any way of knowing it was mine. The blood would have rinsed out by now. It's just a shirt. Anyone could have lost it. They're looking for a kid who was partying way down near the dam. They're not even looking in the middle of the lake.

Think, think. You can make this work.

The phone rang in the kitchen, giving her an excuse to leave the room. "Did you see the news?" Stacia said. She sounded frantic.

"I just saw it," Kitty whispered.

"What are we going to do?"

"I'm not sure." She lowered her voice. "They're not even sure anything's happened at this point. I have at least a few days to figure something out. They're not looking in the right part of the lake. Whatever happens, you don't need to worry. I've got your back." With that Kitty hung up the phone and rushed into the powder room to vomit.

★★★

That night, Bobby knocked on Kitty's bedroom door. She pulled on a robe before tip-toeing to the door and opening it a crack. "What's up, sweetie?"

"You feeling better, Mom?"

She stepped out into the hall and closed the bedroom door behind her. "I'm okay. I think I was more upset about Shelly than I realized."

"I can't sleep."

"It's all right, I'm sad about Shelly too."

"That's just it. I'm not sad. I'm kind of happy that Shelly's dead. I love Steven and didn't want her to come back to get him. I'm not sad, and I'm sad that I'm not sad. Just like I'm not sad that Dad's gone." He hung his head. "I'm actually kind of glad he's gone too. He was really pissing me off lately."

"Oh, honey. Don't say that. I know you two don't always get along, but your Dad loves you very much."

"Save it, Mom. You know that's not true, or he wouldn't have just left us like that." Bobby signaled for her to follow him back down the hall to his bedroom. Once inside his room, he sat on the bed. "Anyway, like I said, I couldn't sleep. And, I was thinking about how Bitsy got to a point where she couldn't take it anymore, so she left; and Dad got to a point that he didn't want to take responsibility for the things he'd done, and left; and Shelly couldn't take being a mother anymore, and, depending how you look at it, left." He looked at his mother. "Why don't we just leave?"

Kitty sat on the small chair in front of Bobby's desk. "What do you mean, leave?"

"Let's blow this popsicle stand. I heard you and Aaron talking about the bank kicking us out of the house."

"But that wouldn't happen right away. Don't worry. I'm sure I can work something out."

"I'm not worried, Mom. I want to leave. Walk away. Make a run for it. Go on the lam."

Kitty rubbed her eyes and looked at her son. He was no longer a little boy that she could shield from the realities of life. Seth had seen to that when he'd brought Bobby into his confidence about his various women. She needed to do the same and stop talking to him as though he was a small child.

"Okay. What's your plan?"

Bobby smiled and pulled a piece of paper off his nightstand. "Well, here's the deal. Becky is leaving in a few weeks, right? So, she starts telling everyone at the pool that she was chosen to do this special thing at Brown where she has to be there early. No one understands anything about her going to Brown other than it's a fancy-schmancy school up north, so they won't think that's weird."

Kitty saw the kernel of truth in what Bobby was saying and nodded. "We could say we were helping Rose move."

"Yeah, we can pack up a U-Haul with all of Becky's stuff and throw in some of our stuff too. Then, we all get in the car and simply drive away. No one will think twice about it."

"What about Steven? Bitsy?"

"Steven will come with us."

"That would be kidnapping. He's not my child."

"One, I don't think anyone is looking for him. Two, you'd take much better care of him than the foster care people. And, three, he's family. Steven is mine and Becky's half-brother and you are legally his father's wife. If we ever got arrested for kidnapping, I think we would have a case for custody anyway."

"Since when did you become a lawyer?"

"I watch a lot of Perry Mason."

She leaned forward and rested her elbows on her knees. "You've obviously thought this through. What else have you got there?"

Bobby looked down at the piece of paper in his lap. "I was stuck for a while because I couldn't figure out how we were going to fit you, me, Becky, Bitsy, Steven, and Daisy—"

"Daisy? Oh right, we'd need to take her with us too, wouldn't we?"

"But then I had an idea. What do you think of this? We give Aaron some money so he can buy us one of those VW buses—"

"Is Aaron part of this plan too?"

"I thought you'd want him to come with us."

"Do you want him to come with us?"

"Sure, I like Aaron. He can hang with us for a while. If it doesn't work out between you guys, that's okay too."

"So much for propriety."

"Mom, I think we should keep him around at least until we know Ms. Bitsy is safe from her husband. Do you know how to shoot a gun? And I heard him talking to Bitsy the other day. He plans to get her to stop drinking. I think it's worth bringing him with us just for that."

"Good points, honey."

"Anyway, so I take Daisy for a walk and meet Aaron with the bus somewhere. Then, you and Becky can hide Bitsy and Steven in the back seat of the car and drive off with the U-Haul."

"That is a good idea," Kitty said. "We are going to need another car. That way, we could leave the Bug with Becky in Providence and no one could trace Bitsy and me by using our license plates." Kitty and Bobby spent the next hour going over his plan and running different scenarios for how to avoid detection while driving Becky to school, and where to go from there.

Kitty encouraged Bobby to get some sleep so they could present the plan to Bitsy and Becky in the morning, and rushed down the stairs. She nudged Aaron awake. If she thought too much about what she was doing, she would talk herself out of it. She dispensed with any pleasantries and blurted out, "Are you up for an adventure?"

"What kind of adventure?" Aaron rolled over on the couch with a grin. "Never mind, I'm up for it. Let me scoot over."

She felt her skin flush under her robe. "Not that kind of adventure, although it's nice to know you're so game." She sat on the edge of the couch and crossed her legs. She didn't dare get too physically close to Aaron, or she'd get distracted. "Bobby has come up with a plan that just might solve most of our problems."

"In the middle of the night?" Aaron sat up on the couch and propped a pillow behind his back.

"You know how Becky's leaving for school in a few weeks?" Kitty brushed her hair off her cheek. "What if we pack up her things and take her now?"

"Okay, why?"

"The idea is to leave as if we are going away for a few days to help Becky move in, and just never come back. Kind of like Seth did." Kitty had to keep reminding herself that Aaron didn't know that Seth was in fact dead and never coming back. "We could head west. Find a small ranch where Bitsy can quietly read and raise horses."

Kitty thought what it might be like to live in a farmhouse far from nosey neighbors. "Maybe I could open a bake shop or something. Or find a museum where I could be a docent. I don't know."

"What about the baby? Have they found his family?"

"We're his family." A rush of maternal love infused her heart as she thought of Steven's little hands holding on to her fingers. "Like Bobby just pointed out to me, he's my husband's child and my children's half-brother, so I'm closest thing Steven has to family." Her heart pounded in her chest as she looked at Aaron. "I think I could pull off acting like I'm his mother. Would you ever consider acting like you're his father?"

Aaron launched himself across the couch and knocked her against the arm of the couch in an embrace. "Do you mean it? You want me to come with you? What about your kids?"

"It was Bobby's idea to have you come. I think he likes having you around."

"Wow! That's trippy. I like hanging out with him too." Aaron pulled back from their embrace. "Becky's going to hate this idea."

"She doesn't get a say. She can stay with her aunt until school starts."

"She's still going to hate it."

"That's just tough. It's my decision." Kitty started to squirm out of his arms. "I understand if you're not interested. It's a big commitment."

"You're the one that's risking stuff by up and leaving town. I'm just an artist that moves from project to project. I've got nothing to keep me in Magnuson. Bitsy was my meal ticket for the last two years, and that's over now." He gripped her shoulders with his strong hands and looked her in the eye. "And I am very interested in being a father." He lowered his face to hers and kissed her. Her body felt as though it was melting beneath her. She'd read about a kiss making you feel weak. Now she understood what that meant. She was overcome by Aaron's continued desire to stand beside her, rather than dominate their relationship. He was kind, affectionate, and strong. She felt that things would work out all right if he continued to stay with her. She pulled away and twisted in Aaron's arms.

"I'm sorry," Aaron said. "I thought—"

"No, I'm sorry. It's not you." She pressed her forehead against his chest. "It's just that...I keep laying all this stuff on you and you just take it."

"You're pretty great too. So? What gives?"

"I was just thinking that even though it's been crisis after crisis lately and I am in serious trouble, on so many different levels, I'm happy. I'm excited to get out of this place and help Bitsy start over. I can't wait to see who little Steven ends up being, and I am so proud of who my kids are turning out to be. I'm really impressed at the great plan Bobby has cooked up. It even allows us to take Daisy with us."

"Of course it would," Aaron said with a smile. "He loves that dog."

Kitty smiled and tightened the belt of her robe. "Am I wrong to be excited? Is it wrong to want to forge my own path with you, and Bitsy, and Bobby, as a team? It's just that I've wasted so much time letting someone else tell me what to do. Is it too late to start making my own decisions? The last twenty years have left me feeling like a shriveled up piece of fruit."

Aaron ran his hand over her hip. "You're not a shriveled up piece of fruit. You're like a peach in July, soft and bursting with juices."

Kitty burst out laughing. "That was so cheesy!"

"I guess it was." Aaron wiped his hair back from his face. "You were getting pretty deep there and it sounded so romantic in my head."

"It was. And, you are so sweet to try to make me feel good. I wasn't laughing at you, really. I'm just a bit emotional right now. It's a big move to pile us all in a U-Haul and run away."

"You're telling me." He sat up. "So are we really doing this? Are we really thinking about skipping town with two kids, a baby, and a broken, alcoholic heiress?"

"Don't forget the dog."

twenty-nine

itty made Becky's favorite breakfast, banana pancakes, and waited for everyone to have eaten before she cleared her throat and said, "So, I think we need to have a family meeting." Bitsy rose to leave the room, but Kitty stopped her with a quick tap on the arm. "Stay. By hook or by crook, you are part of this family now. We feel responsible for you and little Steven and want you to be all right."

Becky refilled her coffee cup from the pot in the center of the table. "What do you want to say, Mom? Are you hiding another disaster in the pantry or something, because I have stuff to do today."

"Settle down, young lady. You're not going anywhere until we've talked this out."

Becky put her hands up in surrender. "Geez, now who's being all touchy?"

"Bobby and I were talking and we think we've come up with a way to solve our financial problems and get Bitsy out of town."

Bitsy's face lit up. "Really?" Kitty noticed that all the bruises around her eyes had faded and some color had returned to her cheeks.

"I think so, but the plan depends on Becky for it to work." Kitty looked over at Bobby who nodded for her to go on. "What do you think about leaving for school a few weeks early?"

Becky looked back and forth between her brother and mother with narrowed eyes. "How many weeks early?"

"Six," Bobby said.

"That's like...like now."

"We were thinking more like Friday, actually," Kitty said.

Becky looked around the table. Bitsy was looking down at her trembling hands and blinking furiously. Aaron gazed back at her over Steven's lolling on his shoulder and raised his eyebrows.

"Why doesn't he look surprised by this?"

"I asked Aaron to help us with a few things," Kitty said.

"So I'm the only one that wasn't in on the plan already?"

"I hadn't talked to Bitsy about it either."

Bitsy looked up at that point. "I'm in! Whatever you and Aaron came up with has got to be better than us sitting around in this house waiting for Chip to find me."

The indignant look on Becky's face faded. She sat back in her chair. "So, why do I have to leave for school early?"

Over the next hour or so, they ironed out exactly how they were going to pack up Becky's things as if she were leaving for college like any other college freshman and drive to Rhode Island. After the initial shock, Becky agreed with Bobby that she wouldn't miss living in Overlook. She was eager to move on with the next phase of her life and didn't feel a need to come back. Once she understood that she could stay with her Aunt Rose until it was time to move into the dorms, Becky agreed to go along with the plan.

Once everyone knew what they needed to do to make the plan a success, Kitty took Becky into the study and gave her the instructions for how to withdraw the money her grandfather had put aside for her education and gave her the contact information for the law firm that managed the trust. "My dad would have been so proud of you," she said. "He was so excited when you were born, he set up this trust for your education."

"What about Bobby?"

"Him too. And any children Rose would have had."

Becky flipped through the file in front of her. "But Rose doesn't have any children."

"We were still in our twenties when he died. I'm sure he thought Rose would eventually get married and have a house full of kids."

"I can't believe you want me to stay with Aunt Rose for the next few weeks."

"She's going to need help moving into a new apartment." Kitty winked at Becky. "And if she gets too nutso, you could always go stay with your Uncle Joe."

"Yeah right, he'd probably make me become a nun."

Kitty opened the drawers of the desk and picked out the few important documents they would need. She slid Becky's birth certificate, social security card, and passport into a large envelope and placed it next to the folder of financial information.

Becky looked at the envelope with tears in her eyes. "This is it, isn't it? You and Bobby are running off to who knows where, and Dad is theoretically dead, and I have to go stay with Rose."

"Only for a few weeks. Then, you can start your fabulous life at Brown. And Bobby and I won't be gone forever. Once the dust settles, I'll be in touch." Kitty hugged her daughter for several long minutes. The next time they saw each other, Becky would be a grown woman with a life of her own. She hoped she had done a sufficient job raising her to be a good woman. "I love you so much, sweetie. I want you to remember that no matter what happens for here on out, everything I've done since the day you were born, was for you. You and your brother have always been my first priority."

"I'm beginning to understand that now, Mom. I'm sorry I've been such a tool lately." Becky stepped back from their hug. "It's just that I really thought Dad would be back. I wasn't thinking about what you'd be feeling at all." She sighed and picked up the things on the desk. "I really do hope you and Ms. Bitsy can find a place where she can be happy. Just be careful of that Aaron. You don't really need a man around, you know."

★★★

Packing up their lives was relatively easy once they'd all agreed to go. Bitsy wanted to head for Wyoming after dropping Becky off in Rhode Island and look for a horse farm. Bitsy had three weeks before her next check would be sent, so they were confident she could reconfigure her train of forwarding addresses so they would meet the August check in Jackson. From there, they planned to find a place to settle down far from prying eyes.

That afternoon, Bobby and Kitty helped Becky pack everything she would need for college while Bitsy and Aaron drove to Durham and collected Bitsy's monthly check from the post office there. Bitsy chose to forward the envelope around the country and back to the nearby city because the large Main Street post office would have people coming in and out all day. No one would notice a plainly dressed man coming in to check his mail. From there, they went to the bank and cashed the check. Bitsy wore a dark wig and had Aaron stay at her side with the pistol tucked in the waistband of his jeans. She was worried that the teller would question her or alert the manager, but they gave her the money without batting an eye. As they walked back to the car, she turned to Aaron. "This is going to work, isn't it?"

"Kitty has a good plan. It'll work."

They returned with a beat-up red VW bus which Aaron parked it on a side street a few blocks away from Overlook so Kitty could shuttle the few things she and Bobby would take with them to the bus over the next day or so. If any of her neighbors noticed Kitty going in and out so much, they would assume she was running out to pick up last minute items for Becky. Bitsy drove the Bug back to the house along with a small U-Haul trailer for Becky's things. She had taken off the wig before she drove through Overlook and wore one of Kitty's blouses. Unless they looked closely, the neighbors would assume it was Kitty driving the small car.

Once inside, Bitsy retrieved her one suitcase and eased it down the stairs to add it to the growing pile of things for Kitty to transfer into the bus. She looked out the window at the lake. "When should we call Stacia and say goodbye?"

Kitty pulled the heavy suitcase out to the garage. "Never."

Bitsy stopped in the middle of the kitchen. "We have to call Stacia."

Kitty turned and looked back at Bitsy. "No, she can't know what we're doing. She can find out we're gone with everyone else."

"But we've been in this together all along. Don't you trust her anymore?"

Kitty thought about all the things that Stacia had done for her. Stacia didn't ask to see Kitty kill her husband, yet she'd helped Kitty hide the crime. She didn't invite Bitsy to share Chip's abuse with her, yet she'd sprung into action when she saw someone in need. Stacia had sat with Debbie and held her hand until the end. She had kept Von's memory alive decades after her death. Stacia was a true friend that would sacrifice her own well-being to help a woman in need. That was why Kitty and Bitsy couldn't share their plans with her.

She had earned some ignorance.

"I trust her implicitly, but we owe her too much to burden her with our problems anymore. Let her biggest problem be who's going to be PTA president this year."

"But she'll be angry that we didn't tell her."

"Better angry, than dead." Kitty slammed the trunk shut. "If Chip ever catches on that I helped you, Stacia can't know anything that could implicate her." Bitsy frowned, but she seemed to agree.

After several trips to the bus, Kitty returned to the house and packed one suitcase of clothes for herself. She didn't want anything else from her life in Magnuson. A new life would need new things. She did pack every piece of jewelry she owned and their unused silver service. She had been saving it for "best." Now she would probably pawn it somewhere along the way. She didn't care. She never had liked the ornate silver pattern. Her mother had picked it out. At twenty-two, it was easier to go along with her mother's decision than make a fuss. At forty-eight, she found sterling silver flatware a waste of good metal.

Becky walked into the dining room as Kitty nestled the polished flatware chest in a bed of crumpled newspaper. "Where's Bobby? I need help carrying a heavy box down the stairs."

"He's upstairs watching Steven. Ask Aaron to help you."

Becky rolled her eyes. "You're taking the silver?"

"I'm only taking these things because they're valuable. I don't necessarily want them." Kitty looked around the dining room. "Is there anything you want to take for a keepsake?"

Becky walked over to the china cabinet and removed a statue of a swan. "I've always liked this. It's small enough that I can keep it no matter how many times I move."

Kitty paused a moment to think, then opened a drawer in the foyer table. She pulled out a stack of photo albums. "You take your baby album and I'll take these." She handed one to Becky and put the others in the box with the silver. "I can't leave these behind."

Steven yowled from the second floor. "I take it playtime is over," Kitty said. "I'll go relieve Bobby and ask him to help you with that box." She climbed the stairs and left Becky to look through the house for anything else she wanted to take with her.

After changing Steven's diaper, Kitty settled down with the baby to feed him a bottle. They were both nodding off when Becky came into the bedroom with a wide smile on her face. "I wanted to take one of Dad's monogrammed golf balls so I was fishing around in his old golf bags and..." Becky tossed a wad of cash on the bed. "Look what I found in the shoe pocket of the plaid bag."

Kitty shifted the baby and picked up the money. The roll was as big as a can of soup. "How much do you think is here?"

Becky took the baby and put him on the bed. "Go ahead, count it."

Kitty removed the elastic band around the bills and counted the pile of hundred dollar bills. "Oh my goodness, this is almost four thousand dollars."

"That will hold you and Bobby over for a while."

Kitty peeled off ten bills and tossed them on the bedside table. "You take some and keep it as your emergency fund and I'll keep some in case Bobby and I run into trouble." She rerolled the rest of the bills and pushed them in her pocket. "And let's keep this between you and me. The others don't need to know about this."

Becky shook her head. "I don't know what to say, Mom. How did my prissy mother become such a bad-ass?"

"It took me a long time, but being married to your father taught me to recognize what's really important in life - my children." She pulled her wedding and engagement rings off her finger, tightly rolled the ten hundred dollar bills, and slipped her rings over the money. She dropped the bundle in Becky's hand. "Put those to good use."

★★★

In a late afternoon thunder storm, Bobby and Daisy walked out of Azalea Lane for the last time. As they made their way up to the entrance of Overlook, Bobby waved to Betty Oliphant and Blaire Morton as they drove by, then turned into the side street where the rest of the group waited. Becky and Kitty sat in Becky's car attached to the U-Haul. They waved to him as he pulled the door open and climbed into the VW bus. Aaron tossed Bobby a towel. "Any problems?"

"No, I took Daisy for a walk just like I've taken her for a walk a million times before." Bitsy looked up from where she sat on the floor with a book. The baby slept on a pillow at her side. "What have you two been doing while you were waiting for me?"

"We've been listening to the news. They had to suspend the search of Lake Tate because of the storm, but they think they might have found more of the missing kid's clothes."

258

epilogue

4th of July, 1977

Stacia picked up a drink from the refreshments table and scanned the pool area for prospective clients. Summer was the best time to buy or sell a house in Overlook, and she wanted to pick up every commission she could. In the six months since she'd started working with her cousin Quentin, she had already become his top-selling agent. Her biggest, and most satisfying, sale was Bitsy's house. Without Bitsy, Chip had no real income. When he'd spoken to Stacia about listing the house, he'd said that he'd taken an assignment overseas and Bitsy had gone ahead to set-up house. Weldon had heard through the VFW grapevine that Chip had officially retired from the Army in order to get his pension and moved to Florida. Stacia didn't care where he went as long as it was out of Magnuson. The commission on the house had been wonderful, but the real reward was the look on Chip's face when he met the buyer, a female professor of African-American Studies. She couldn't wait to tell Weldon how Chip had sputtered through the closing and run out of the room as soon as it was over.

She spotted the couple who had bought the Haskell's house come in and grabbed a tray of drinks. They seemed nice enough. He was a banker and she had been a teacher before she started her brood. They were from somewhere up north. Stacia didn't bother to remember where. She smiled a brief hello to the husband and spoke to the wife. "Can I offer you a Seabreeze?" The wife took a cup from the tray in Stacia's hand and took a big sip. "Careful there, they can sneak up on you."

The woman looked horrified as she glanced down at the cup in her hand. "Is there alcohol in the punch? There are children here."

"There are cokes over there for the kids," Stacia said. She looked at the woman's conservative blue slacks and simple blouse. A bit plain and her hair was dull, but she would do. "The party is put on by the Homeowners Association. You might want to get involved. I was on it for years before I started selling real estate. Of course, I don't have time for things like that anymore."

"I'll have to talk to Betty across the street about that. She's been so helpful since we moved in."

A thin smile pulled at the edges of Stacia's lips as she took a sip from her drink. She could only imagine the things Betty Oliphant had filled the woman's head with. "So, how do you like living in Overlook so far?"

"It's lovely. We didn't expect a foreclosure to be in such good shape."

"Kitty kept a nice home. You know her husband died and she had to move on?"

"Where did she go that she left everything behind? Her clothes, her dishes, even a beautiful velvet couch."

"That is a lovely couch," Stacia agreed.

"Honey," the husband said. "Did you remember to bring that envelope?"

"Oh yes," the woman said with a start. She handed her cup to her husband and fished around in her pocketbook for a padded envelope. "This came in the mail a week or so ago. I almost tossed it out with the junk mail." She handed the envelope to Stacia. It was addressed to Stacia Tate Curran, Overlook Homeowners Assoc., c/o Current Resident, 4 Azalea Lane. There was no return address.

Stacia felt her mouth go dry when she recognized Kitty's handwriting. She tucked the envelope under arm and said, "Thanks. I'm sure it's nothing." She took a sip from her drink and looked over the woman's shoulder as if seeing someone she needed to talk to. "Well, enjoy the afternoon and don't forget they do fireworks out on the lake later."

She stepped away to put the tray of drinks down on a nearby table and ran her nail under the flap of the envelope. Inside was a postcard showing a horse wearing pink sunglasses. She plastered a smile on her face to cover any signs of shock. Her friend had been gone for almost a year, and this was the first she had heard anything. She flipped the card over and read the few lines.

We are safe and happy.
I am working in a bake shop.
She is volunteering at a library.
Her horse had a foal.
The baby is running us ragged.

At least Bitsy got herself a horse. Stacia was still angry that Kitty and Bitsy had left without saying a word, however, she was relieved that they were gone. Although nothing had ever come of the sweatshirt found in the lake and Chip had left Magnuson, their leaving had convinced her to listen to the voice in her head and lay down the burden of being responsible for the well-being of those around her. She was taking Weldon's advice, and concentrating on their little family, instead of the whole city. Still, she missed her friend.

She jumped when the new residents at 4 Azalea Lane tapped her on the shoulder. "One more thing," the husband said when she turned around. "We have a boat slip out back. Did the Haskell's have a boat?"

Acknowledgments

No author writes alone. A small crowd of people supported me while I wrote this novel.

Thank you to the WIP critique group: Samantha Bryant, Elizabeth Carroll, R. Leandra, K. Lynn, Jason E. Feingold, Sarah Sugg, and Dawn Taylor for their patience and excellent questions. Thank you to my intrepid beta-readers: Rhonda Gilmour, Luccia Gray, Noelle Granger, and Don Cram. Your comments were a huge help.

I'd also like to thank my editor, Alison Williams, for her guidance and sharp eyes.

Finally, I'd like to thank my husband, Ted, for supporting me in all things.

Elizabeth Hein writes women's fiction with a bit of an edge. Her novels explore the role of friendship in the lives of adult women and themes of identity. Elizabeth grew up in Massachusetts within an extended family of storytellers. Her childhood was filled with excellent food and people loudly talking over each other. After college, she and her husband embarked on the adventure of parenting their two beautiful daughters. Motherhood led Elizabeth to start a small business, home school one of her daughters for several years, and learn more about competitive swimming than she ever knew possible. She and her husband now live in Durham, North Carolina.

Praise for
How To Climb The Eiffel Tower

"Fans of Jennifer Weiner, Sarah Pekkanen, and Amy Hatvany will devour *How to Climb the Eiffel Tower*. This book is for every woman, young or old." Judith Collins, Goodreads Top Reviewer & Blogger

"A vibrant story about grace and friendship in our most vulnerable moments." –Deborah Hining, author of *A Sinner in Paradise* (Foreword Reviews IndieFab Book of the Year Bronze Medal Winner)

"An empowering, redemptive novel filled with wisdom and kindness." –Summer Kinard, author of *Can't Buy Me Love*

"This book has become one of my all-time favourites..." Daniela, Only Books and Horses

Also By Elizabeth Hein

OVERLOOK

HOW TO CLIMB THE EIFFEL TOWER